SOPHIE JONAS-HILL

BROKEN PONIES

SOPHIE JONAS-HILL

BROKEN PONIES

BOOK 2 OF THE CROOKED LITTLE SISTERS SERIES

Urbane
PUBLICATIONS

urbanepublications.com

First published in Great Britain in 2018
by Urbane Publications Ltd
Suite 3, Brown Europe House, 33/34 Gleaming Wood Drive,
Chatham, Kent ME5 8RZ
Copyright © Sophie Jonas Hill, 2018

A CIP catalogue record for this book is available
from the British Library.

ISBN 978-1-911583-70-7
MOBI 978-1-911583-71-4

Design and Typeset by Michelle Morgan

Cover by The Author Design Studio

Printed and bound by 4edge Limited, UK

URBANE
urbanepublications.com

CHAPTER ONE

THE SAVANNAH HEIGHTS CASINO did its best. Above the two gaming levels, there were six floors of reasonably priced hotel rooms, which were reasonably clean and reasonably anonymous, a woefully under-used pool deck and a 'skyline' bar. This translated to a room that ran the whole length of the building, offering a panoramic sweep of the city, though the view was mostly the back of everything else, as if The Savannah Heights was a short kid come late to the school photograph.

At 3.30 a.m. above the background hum and trill of slots, the click of chips and the dull, subterranean thump of the generators, an angry noise began to rise from table four. I'd seen the guy playing there when I'd come onto the floor after my break and was pretty sure he'd been there long before that, though guys like him were pretty hard to distinguish from one another, or indeed the fixtures and fittings. This one had the same hard, chiseled expression as the faux, carved wooden Tiki heads dotted about the place, until of course he lost, which he just had – big time.

Like Mormons us security operatives are supposed to travel in pairs, but Olaf was still in the bathroom, which meant I alone was the sole representative of Savannah Heights law. With no time to wait for Olaf to wash up, I strode toward table four, nodding to its operative Barbara to let her know I'd seen what was happening.

'You goddamn' bitch–' Tiki man, pot-bellied and crackling with anger, jabbed his finger at her face. 'I said stick, and you goddamn went an' hit me. What the hell you go and do a thing like that for? You deaf, well as stupid?'

Somewhere off to his right one of the slots chose that moment to pay out and play the opening chords of 'Sweet Home Alabama'. It didn't improve anyone's mood.

'Sir –' I began, 'Sir, is there a problem?'

Tiki man struck the table top, sending cards, chips, beer an' all skittering to the floor as Barbara, trapped in the table's central well, arms jammed across her chest, let out a yelp of protest.

'You heard that then, you stupid bitch!'

The lucky few still awake at this hour turned to get a good look, necks craning out of plaid shirts and sports collars.

'Sir!' I tried again. My hand on his shoulder, I was dimly aware of Olaf hurrying through the archipelago of tables while doing up his flies. Then Tiki man swung round to face me. He was wearing a blue shirt crowded with images of pigs dressed in grass skirts and flower garlands – really, I thought, hula pigs? Now, did you buy that, or was it a gift? I mean, seriously, did you actually look at that and think - hey, now that's the one for me?

'Sir, you're gonna have to calm down here ...'

One of our boss Jose's theories was that you need women on staff because men are more reluctant to hit them. As Tiki man threw a punch at me, I made a mental note to question this at our next team meeting.

'Oh no you didn't,' I heard myself say. His blow connected with my left arm; I deflected it but was hit instead by a waft of aftershave and stale sweat. Tiki man didn't get the hint. Backed into a chair he rounded on me quicker than I'd expected. He didn't swear either; most start calling you names and threatening legal action, proving

BROKEN PONIES

they're more bark than bite. Tiki man said nothing, just went for me, hard and mean.

Time snagged on the bright lights and chatter of voices. The world stuttered to a halt, that god-awful shirt traced blue and pink on the back of my eyes, spreading out like an ink blot. I saw things both as if I were him and as if I watched him; Tiki man, still angry, still in that shirt, but in another place, his knuckles bloodied and broken, standing over someone else, someone smaller, someone weaker - someone Tiki man thought don't got no right to sass mouth him that way. I was somewhere else for a moment, looking through Tikki Man's haunted, piggy eyes.

Oh no, I thought, oh no you didn't!

'Oh yes he did,' Margarita said.

Reality snapped back fast enough to flinch me away from Tiki man's fist. I caught his punch with both hands letting the force of his blow carry him off balance. He was face down on the table before he'd time to catch his breath, arm all twisted up behind his back. That should have been it; I should have been calling him 'Sir' and warning him that the authorities had been called, only the hot-black, heartbeat moment twisted inside me and wouldn't let him go.

There was the dull thud of impact, then the ricochet as its force crunched back through me. I lost Tiki man and the casino and everything as memory swelled up, molasses dark and rich, bringing the taste of river water, blood and the itch of fire. When Olaf's arms closed around me, it took everything I had not to slam my fist into his face.

'Rita!' he yelled from the edge of the void. 'Rita, what the fuck?' I made myself go limp, gasping for air as if I were breaking the surface again. Around me the casino hissed with exclamations, all those yellow white faces tutting and sniggering at the show.

Barbara was jabbering that Tiki man '...deserved everything he got comin' to him. Hell, I'd have slapped him myself, if I hadn't been stuck inside this goddamn doughnut!'

'Rita?' Olaf, hands on my shoulders, steered me away as two other security guys darted in behind us, one to pick up Tiki man, now mewling like a stuck kitten, and one to try and calm Barbara.

'It's always me what gets shit like this, all the goddamn time. Hell, only the other week some bitch sprayed me with her Christian Dior. I hate that crap too, had to get my wig dry cleaned and who's gonna pay for that?'

'Rita?' I slid my gaze back to Olaf. Margarita jubilant, her smile on my lips. I pulled from his grasp. 'What the hell was that?' he demanded, but I was already walking away.

I strode into the locker room and kicked door number seven. The boom it made did nothing to stop the roar echoing around my head. I threw myself down onto the bench and jammed my head into my hands.

'Don't act like you didn't enjoy it,' Margarita said. 'You were lovin' it, just the same as me.'

'Shut up,' I told her. 'You're gonna get us both fired.'

'Oh hush now,' she laughed. 'You think they'd can your ass over a piece of shit like that? I know what he did, I could smell it on him and so could you.'

'No I couldn't,' I said, but I was lying.

'Oh really?' she said. 'You keep on tellin' yourself that.'

'Rita?' It was Jose, who really didn't seem to have a home to go to. I glanced sideways at him and saw he'd crossed his arms across his chest in the same way Barbara had at Tiki man. Which probably meant he wanted to give me a goddamn slap as well.

'Aren't you supposed to provide single sex locker rooms?' I said.

'What the fuck?' he replied, his forehead creased in furious lines.

'I know,' I said, sitting back, hands held out in front of me. 'I crossed the line.'

'Crossed it?' Jose's eyebrows pitched a tent. 'You gone an' pissed all over the fuckin' line, that's what you done.'

'He went for me,' I said. 'Check the tape.' I got up and opened my locker, already knowing my shift was over.

'Tape?' Jose sniffed. 'What tape would that be?' Half way through yanking my rucksack out I stopped to look at him. He shrugged. 'We don't got no camera covering that table tonight, and you don't know any different.' He pointed at me. 'Never again, you understand? Whatever shit you got going on here–' he tapped the side of his head, 'don't bring it to work, alright?'

'He means me,' Margarita sniggered.

'You want this job, you don't want this job, all the same to me,' he said. I got my bag free and pulled off my uniform jacket to hang in its place. 'But you don't go making work for me. That piece of shit you put down's not gonna make no trouble, but the next time?'

'There won't be one,' I lied.

'Smart,' he said, flicking his hand toward my locker. 'You're done. Go home, don't come in tomorrow–' he raised his finger before I could protest. 'Don't come in tomorrow, don't come in till Thursday. Go sleep, go get fucked, whatever, but don't bring your shit again. Jesus, what? You get your hair done and it rots your brain or something?'

'I thought you liked me blonde,' I said and yanked my sweat top free of my bag. He watched me pull it on, the hand that had been pointing at me now gripping the back of his neck, where the hair was longer and bushier than it had any right to be.

'Where the hell you learn shit like that anyway?' he asked. I shouldered my bag.

'I was home schooled,' I said.

CHAPTER TWO

I SHOULD HAVE gone home like Jose said, but I didn't. I was two nights in of four on, and the last thing I would be able to do was sleep. Especially since I'd just rabbit punched Tiki man in the kidneys, and adrenaline was still crackling through me like summer lightening.

'You can't go to bed now,' Margarita told me. 'Hell, you won't sleep for hours yet. Can't we go play somewhere?'

'No,' I told her. As I couldn't think of any other way of shutting her up, I headed to the gym on the twelfth floor. Half hour on the punch bag, and no matter how hard I hit it, I couldn't knock the shit out of my head. I slammed my fist into it with a great yell of anger, caught it as it swung back at me, and became dimly aware of someone watching me.

He was tall, dark and, well, handsome. Looking at me as if he knew he shouldn't, but really wanted to. Like I said, I already knew I wasn't going to sleep for hours.

We had sex in his hotel room, as if both of us had a point to prove to somebody else who wasn't there. In the cold light of the morning after, while he sat on the edge of the bed and bent down to retrieve his shorts, I pulled the bed sheet over myself and surveyed the ruins. There was a glass ashtray on the bedside table, but when he got out his cigarettes and lit up, he flicked his ash into the wire wastepaper basket instead. When I glanced over, I saw a flash of gold against the glass.

'D'you want one?' he asked.

'No, thanks,' I said. Watching him smoke didn't make me feel anything, other than he was showing off.

'Oh, you don't mind if I ...?' I shook my head. He flicked his ash again. 'So ... you wanna hang?' It was light outside already, the sky raked with high white clouds burning pink at the edges. You could see all the way to the desert, to the mountains drawn as if with smudged fingers against the glass horizon. 'My flight's tomorrow evening.' He was looking over his shoulder at me, his dark fringe falling over one eye, skin pulled into sharp creases by the twist of his neck.

'Can I get a shower?'

'Sure, no problem,' he grinned. 'Just let me use the john?'

Trying not to listen to the sound of him urinating, I glanced about the room. His suitcase was on the desk under the window. He'd not bothered to unpack, but then Savannah Heights wasn't a place where you bothered to unpack. There was a chair drawn up to the desk, a laptop on its seat with a charger cable snaking into the shadows. The cell phone attached to it buzzed and the screen lit up. I saw a rectangle of iridescent blue and the picture on it fade as the caller rang off, before the bathroom door opened.

'All yours.' He'd put on the hotel bath robe. 'I booked, like, an extra day here after the convention.' He dragged his hand through his hair then scratched the side of his face. 'I had some lame idea it might be fun. Me time, shit like that.'

'How's that working out for you?' I asked. He grinned.

'I was gonna have some ... do you mind if I ... do you want some coke?'

He was cutting it out when I finished my shower. He smiled at me as I picked up my sweat pants and t-shirt. I was glad when he looked back to the table; his watching me dress felt more intimate than the sex. More personal.

'I don't, like, do this a lot but ...' he shrugged. He twirled the razor expertly in his fingers, tapped it on the surface of the coffee table. The dollar bill he teased from his wallet curled up as it came free, rolling itself into a loose tube just as if it knew what was required of it. He coughed into his fist.

'I'm obsessed with narrative,' he was saying, as if I'd asked. 'It's what really drives me, you know?' Oh yeah, he was a writer or something. 'It's all about an immersive experience. Gaming is the way forward for storytelling–' that was it, he wrote computer games. He had told me, I just hadn't really been listening. I'd never considered it a job grown-ups did, not men pushing forty as I realized he probably was. 'So, hey, you must have one hell of a story.'

'What makes you say that?' I asked.

'Well–' he put down the blade and picked up the rolled note. 'It's pretty out there, female security guard. I mean, not like it was once, sure, because I mean, we got women practically in the front line an' all, but even so, that's, like, quite ... out there?' He lowered his head, sniffed.

'My story? You don't want to know,' I said.

'Yeah I do.' He sat back against the bed, blinking, pinching his nostrils. 'Go on, start with the basics. How long you been in Vegas?'

I narrowed my eyes at him. 'How long you been married?' He stopped, nose between thumb and forefinger. He was of course. I could imagine her packing for him, even after the argument, him telling her it was just a work thing, that just because it was in Vegas, didn't mean he was going to do anything stupid.

'Ahh,' he said and let go of his nose. 'How did you ...?' He scratched the side of his face again, grating against the stubble on his cheek. 'Fucking obvious, I suppose.'

 **BROKEN PONIES**

'Look, it's none of my business,' I said. 'What stays in Vegas and all that.'

He rolled his tongue over his teeth again, grimacing to himself. 'Okay, so ... how d'you know?'

'The ashtray.' He looked over at the bedside table, though the ashtray was now on the coffee table. 'You didn't use it. I'm guessing you're not meant to be smoking either.' He reached for the lighter, emblazoned with the hotel logo, and clicked the flame. Well, he hadn't brought that with him, now had he?

'You worked that out too?'

'Sure. Leaving your ring in the ashtray, it's something you do out of habit. I guess when you're home, you put it in a dish by your bed. Couldn't put your smoke out on it, now could you?'

He took another cigarette defiantly, lit it and clattered the lighter onto the table. He leant back, working his mouth into a grimace.

'That it?'

I met his gaze and smirked. 'Well,' – here was an immersive narrative he was going to love – 'your suitcase is navy blue, which is masculine enough, but you've got gold heart-shaped tags on the zips. I expect it came as part of a whole matching set, you know, vanity case and wash bag? Like the one in the bathroom. And there's your phone, of course. You got a call. You'd left it on silent, so you didn't hear it ring. She's pretty, the girl on your screen saver, but she's not an actress or a character from one of your games. Too real, so I guessed that's her. You got no kids though, or it would have been them. Wives get bumped for babies.'

'Fuck,' he said. He flicked his ash into the ashtray. He'd probably slipped his ring into the drawer of the bedside table when I was in the shower, hoping I hadn't seen it; out of sight, out of mind. Wherever it was, it had left a line against his skin, which I'd seen as I'd watched his nimble fingers at work.

'I'm sure you love her,' I said, and I meant it. This wasn't something he did all the time; it was opportunity, and not just for casual sex. He was lonely and hanging out was not a service provided by girls on flyers for forty bucks an hour. 'You're just going through a bad patch.' He looked as if he were going to argue, then his expression relaxed into acquiescence.

'She cheated on me,' he said. He reached for the lighter, picked it up, tapped it on the table, dropped it.

'I'm sorry,' I said as I stood up and fetched my jacket. 'But you'll forgive me if I don't stick around. I've had enough of other people's revenge scenarios to last me a lifetime.' He didn't watch me leave.

'Well, he wasn't really our type, was he?' Margarita asked inside my head. 'Nothing at all like Red, now was he?'

CHAPTER THREE

BETHANY, MY COUNSELLOR, looked at her notes. 'Can you tell me about this man, you call him ... Red?'

I stood against the long window in the room where we met. I always sat there, as if I needed to be sure there was a way out, to notice my exits. The wind, coming right off the desert, stirred the black grass planted in pots in the courtyard, even though it was hemmed in on all sides by the buildings of the retreat. When it was strong, and the grass blew almost flat, it looked like the flicks of a pen on paper, handwriting angled with the same slope.

'Red's his nickname, I suppose.' *Those who know me, call me Red.* 'He's Rooster, Rooster Levine.'

'And he married your sister?' Bethany prompted, aware we only had an hour together.

'My older sister, Lisa. She was ... after what happened, when we were younger, our parents sent her away, one school after another. She'd get herself expelled, run away. She got pregnant, got sent away to deal with that–'

'She had a termination?'

I nodded, aware of her pencil scratching over her notebook, imagined the word, 'termination' underlined. 'When she was twenty-two, she broke off all contact with the family, everyone but me.'

'You said she emailed you?'

'She went to Vegas, tried to be an actress, was a waitress. Then she met Red in a bar. He …' I shrugged, waved my hand, 'he saved her, took her back to his house.' I saw it, pictured it, as if it were slowly pulled into focus through a lens; a white death's-head skull of a place, picked clean by time. 'Carillon.'

I was quiet until she said, 'And then?'

I exhaled. 'He was a solider, US army. From what I know, from what I found out, he went overseas, maybe Bosnia and Eritrea when he was younger, though his career's kind of … obscure. I know he was in Iraq one, then Iraq two. He was on leave when he met Lisa, they married, then he went back out there.' And she was all alone, my big sister, a princess in her castle. 'She was bored, restless. She messed around on him.'

'She had an affair?' Bethany asked.

'Yes, with this guy she met, this guy called Paris.'

'And when her husband came back, he found out?' she asked, but she was jumping ahead.

'No, not then. When he came back, he was in some kind of shit, and it all went to hell back home.' When Bethany asked me what had happened to him, I said I wasn't sure. 'I looked into it, tried to find out. After she was gone, after she stopped emailing me, after I'd been told by the police there was nothing they could do, I started to investigate him. I don't know if what I found out is the truth–' because how could I tell her what I found out came in a vision, a dream, a moment when the space between memory and reality had dissolved and I'd found myself looking through Red's eyes, at another place, another time – 'but I think someone he knew, someone he cared about, a solider, got kidnapped. He … tried to get information from a captive, what they call enhanced interrogation techniques–' I could see her reflection, saw she raised her eyebrow at that, 'but it went too far, the prisoner died. The soldier was

 **BROKEN PONIES**

beheaded, video went out on the internet. Fallout was Red was sent home, not in official disgrace but might as well have been. Lisa wrote me how he came back, how his father was furious, and how he ... I don't know, what do you call it? Post-traumatic stress?'

'And ... you think this contributed to his change in behavior towards your sister?'

'I did.'

'You aren't sure?'

'I was then, totally sure, totally sure he'd killed her, out of his mind with what had happened in Iraq. And when nobody would listen to me and no one would do anything, I did.'

'You created Margarita?'

'I made her strong.'

'Which was real sweet of you,' Margarita said.

'Is she with you now?' Bethany asked.

'No,' I said, not meeting her eyes in the reflection. I told Bethany how I moved out, how I created an online persona for Margarita, all so that I could be my own alibi.

'I joined these survivor groups, you know, support groups? To be close to people like Lisa, people who'd suffered like she had with our father.'

'Suffered like you had,' Bethany said. I ignored her.

'There was this girl I met online, Mary-Mary. It was her, you know, her screen name. She made friends with Margarita, we talked a lot – they talked a lot. I kind of told her what I was doing, no names you know, but it was good to have someone to talk to you.' She nodded. It was how she made her living, after all. 'When the time came, when I was ready, Rita flew to Mexico and I became Margarita. Work was real sorry to see me go but there you are, people never like to get in the way of you doing good. I told them I was working at an orphanage for a year, that sort of deal.'

'What were you really doing?'

And this was the part where I really couldn't look at her. 'I found Paris. He was a grifter, a con artist, and when he didn't know where Lisa was I asked him ... I convinced him to let me stay with him, work cons too.' Though I don't say how I pretended to fall in love with him, and thought he'd fallen in love with me because after all, I was paying.

'Paris and I ran a con, the big one. Paris, he got into a poker game with Red and his father, then lost to them big time. He arranged another game, you know, to give me the chance to win it all back, but a smaller game, just him and them. I dressed up like some white-trash hooker' – this annoyed her, I could see, more so than the crime I was confessing to, seeing as I was being so judgmental and all – 'and Paris staked me in the game. He won, I was mad as hell about it, so I shot him.' I looked round at her. 'I mean, it was a fake, all part of the con?' She nodded, just so I knew she didn't think I was confessing to murder. 'Pappa Levine, Red's Daddy – he was up for election so wasn't about to get caught in a backroom with a hooker and her dead pimp. In all the confusion, I switched the money bags, and they ran off with a sackload of hooker flyers.' Even then, months afterwards, I couldn't help smiling at the memory.

'Red came after us, of course. I wanted him too, I'd prepared for it. I'd rented a crazy old shack out in a nature reserve, and I'd got it ready, meaning to ditch Paris and lure Red there, make him confess what he'd done to Lisa, only ...'

'Only?' Bethany leant forwards despite her professional manner.

'I made a mistake. I thought Paris loved me, thought I was using him. Like an idiot I felt sorry for him when I should have ditched him at a gas station like I'd planned–'

'I'd have done it,' Margarita told me.

 **BROKEN PONIES**

'But I didn't, and when he found out what I was doing, we fought. We were driving, and we crashed and ... I hit my head. When I woke, I'd found my way to the shack, only ...' and then I didn't tell her. I just said how I confronted Red, and how no matter what, he denied killing Lisa. I didn't tell her how I lost my mind, my memory of who I was, and how I found it again. I didn't tell her about when I had Red tied to a chair with a gun to his head, and how good it felt.

'You remember it, don't you?' Margarita asked me, her voice sly and low. 'I know I do, the way he felt under us, the way he begged us to do it, to kill him, the way he wanted us to.'

'Shut up,' I told her. Then I told Bethany how I let him go, but even as I told her, the memory of Red's body under mine, the scent of him, his gaze, itched under my skin.

'He didn't kill her,' Bethany said.

'No. She wasn't dead. She was Mary-Mary.'

'She was the person you met online?' And she had been, Lisa, all along. Working with Paris, when she'd vanished from Red's house, Carillon, with as much jewelry as she could manage.

Bethany knew this of course, because Lisa was staying at the refuge too. She'd already had sessions with her alone, sessions with us together; it was part of the deal I'd paid for, with money Paris and I'd conned out of Red.

When Lisa and I are in a session together, Bethany always asks me if I want to ask Lisa a question. It's because Lisa always talks and I listen, most of the time, and so as the facilitator, Bethany has to prod me into talking, to stop it being a monologue.

'Rita?' I wasn't listening; I was watching the window again. 'Rita?' Bethany smiled at me. 'Lisa asked a question about this persona you created, this ... Margarita?'

I dragged myself back to the room, to the three of us sitting on institutionally comfortable chairs with institutionally appropriate paintings on the wall. Inner peace through interior decorating. 'That was nothing.'

'What?' Margarita said. 'You sayin' I meant nothing to you? God damn girl, I thought we had something.'

'It was just cover,' I said. Ignoring Margarita, I imagined Bethany presenting me, suitably anonymized, at a conference of her peers, their laptops clicking as they took notes. 'I don't think I ever became Margarita–' I paused, waiting for her to chip in. 'Maybe sometimes, when it was really hard, when I was frightened …' I glanced at Lisa. She looked away from me, bit the side of her finger. 'It was like Lisa when we were little. She looked out for me and when I got hurt–'

'Don't,' Lisa said. She picked her feet up off the floor and drew her knees to her chest, wrapping her arms about them.

'Lisa looked after me when we were kids, and Margarita did once Lisa was gone,' I finished.

Lisa was crying. Not big tears, small ones that oozed from her eyes and traced wet lines down her cheeks. Her nose didn't run, her cheeks didn't go blotchy - she was beautiful when she cried, like the heroine in a period film.

'I knew you'd be alright, because you're so clever,' Lisa said. 'You were always the clever one. They always said so, didn't they? Mom and Dad?'

The arm chair's legs squealed against the floor as I got up in a rush and strode away to the far side of the room.

'Rita,' Bethany said. 'That's a very strong reaction, do you want to–'

'So, you let me believe you were dead because you thought I was clever? Because Mom and Dad thought I was clever, you thought I'd be okay with what you did?' I yelled. 'I wasn't so goddamn clever, cos I didn't guess what was going on, that you were lying to

me all the time I was getting ready to kill for you?' Lisa clutched at the neckline of her shirt.

'Do we need to have a timeout here ...?' Bethany said, clipboard gripped in her hands.

'That was all your idea!' Lisa snapped. 'You were already halfway there when I started speakin' to you, you'd already decided–'

'Speaking to me!' I rounded on the counsellor. 'She says that like she just picked up the phone like a normal person, oh no!'

'Don't try and get her on side,' Lisa folded her arms. 'That's just what you always used to do, always trying to be everybody's favorite.'

'I did what, when now?'

'I really think we need a moment to reflect–'

'She pretended to be an abuse survivor and–' then I jammed my hand to my mouth, trying to snatch back the words.

'I am an abuse survivor,' Lisa snapped.

'Well, I didn't mean–'

'I am an abuse survivor,' she said again, her face pale. 'I took it and I took it and I took it from Dad. Every time he wanted it, I gave it to him, then Mom sent me away.'

'Lisa, I'm sorry, but that doesn't mean you had the right to–'

'What does it mean?' she said.

We were quiet for a while, both of us watching the garden, how fine lines had been raked into the gravel, how the black grasses were stirred by the wind, and the fountain sparkled over the wet stones.

'It didn't mean you could lie to me like that,' I said.

'You think I don't know that?' she said. 'It was terrible, it was the worst thing I've ever done. But it wasn't the worst thing that ever happened to me, and ...' She was silent again, mouth open, waiting for the word to drop, and I waited, and Bethany waited. It started to rain.

'I remember school,' Lisa said. 'The one I got sent to. One time, when it had all gotten so bad I thought I was gonna burst or somethin', I went to the call box. It was night, we weren't supposed to be out, but I knew how. I used to get out all the time.' She'd told me before, how she'd snuck out to sleep with the gardener, or go down to the road and try and hitch a ride to buy liquor.

'I got all my pin money, everything I had left, and I pushed it all into the slot. The lights in the phone booth were on and the bugs – they were crazy big out there - all these bugs were crashing into the glass over an' over. Mom answered, and I just said I wanna come home, Mom, I wanna come home. She just cried, said I couldn't. Said it wasn't ... safe yet. So, I kept on ringing her back, over an' over, till she just held the line in silence and I sat there on the floor, with all them dead bugs falling down on me and listened to home.' Dead bugs, bodies fizzing and twitching then lying still at Lisa's feet, legs all curled up and crispy.

'And how did that make you feel?' Bethany asked. Lisa didn't answer until she'd glanced at me from under her lashes.

'It felt good, in a way,' she said, 'because I knew she was thinking about me.' Her fingers picked at the piping on the oatmeal-colored chair. 'Because as long as I had quarters to feed the phone she couldn't hang up on me. I had her, you know?'

'You were in control of someone, when you'd previously been feeling powerless?' Bethany said. I thought of the bugs, the impact of their bodies on the glass of the call box, their feather-light fall to earth at Lisa's feet; and Mom, unable to hang up on her after all.

When we were alone again, Bethany and I, weeks after Lisa had discharged herself, she asked if I'd forgiven Lisa. I said, yes. Then she'd asked if I'd forgiven Red.

 **BROKEN PONIES**

'You have to forgive them both,' she said, 'if you've any chance of forgiving yourself.'

'I'm still working on that,' I said. It was my turn to be curled up in the chair, chin resting on my knees. 'I'm looking for ... a way to do it.'

'What are you doing?' she asked.

'You remember the story, the thing that happened in Iraq, about the solider who died?' She nodded. 'There's nothing official about it, no record of who it was. All the others, everyone else who's been killed like that, there's shit loads about them. Heroes, martyrs, right? Not this one. So, I'm trying to find out who it was, if I can.'

'Why?' Bethany's forehead creased into a frown, under her compassionate bangs.

'Something to do, I guess,' I said. 'Hell, everyone needs a hobby, and I'm not the knitting type.'

'Why are you really doing this?'

'Because I don't know the truth, all right?' I snap, twisting round to look at her. 'Because I don't trust my judgement ... because I need to know if Red told me the truth about what happened to him in Iraq, because if I know that, then I might understand what happened between him and Lisa. Because ...' I got to my feet, dragged my hand through my newly blonde hair. ' If I knew he really did kill a man trying to save a captured solider, then I'll know ... I'll know ...'

'What will you know?'

'That maybe he did act all crazy with Lisa, I mean, enough to make her scared, enough to do what she did, to try and make me kill him.'

'And that would make you feel better about what she did, if you felt he somehow deserved it?'

I let my hand fall to my side. 'No. But perhaps it would stop me thinking about him all the time. If he was mad then he wasn't bad, I guess.'

Bethany put down her notes and stood up. She came and put her hand on my shoulder. 'Are you scared of him, Rita? Scared he might find you?'

I let her hand stay for a moment, before I moved enough so that she had to let go of me.

'No. I'm scared because I want him to find me. I live like I do not because I think he's looking for me, but because I need to stop myself looking for him. Because he's all I can think about and trying to find out what happened gives me a way of distracting myself.'

'Will you come back next week?' Bethany asked.

'Thanks,' I said, 'you've been great, but ... I kind of need to go it alone for a while.'

'Aw, you're never alone, doll. You'll always have me,' Margarita told me.

BROKEN PONIES

CHAPTER FOUR

THE DAY AFTER the Tiki guy and the married man, I was back on the hunt again, taking the bus because it was more anonymous than driving a car. Old habits dying hard, and all.

'Why don't we walk all the way from Vegas?' Margarita asked. 'I'm bored, come on. Hell, I'm so full of energy I could burst - we could half-jog it?' I ignored her. 'Wait,' she said, taking a different tack. 'Is this place on your list?'

'It's somewhere to get something to eat,' I tried, but she was wise to that.

'Bullshit, this one of your places, ain't it? What is it this time?'

'Nothing ... just a memorial. Someone online said the owner here lost his son out there, that's all.'

'We're goin' grave robbing, are we?'

'We're going to have breakfast.'

I'd found out about it during my weekly internet session in a games store coffee shop. Under the cover of flashing lights and geek noise, I'd bought an Americano and an hour on a terminal on which to break my vow of non-involvement. I had rules; no emails, no Facebook, just picking over the scraps of my previous investigations, looking for shadows and whispers and distraction. I'd located three deaths in Iraq around the right time so far; this was the second of them. There'd been a memorial built, an unofficial thing in the hot baked heart of Nowhere Nevada and, seeing as I'd got unexpected leave, I thought I'd give it a go.

The diner came into sight after only twenty minutes or so of walking, which was long enough for sweat to have collected between my shoulder blades, and for my dreams of ham and eggs to morph into vanilla ice-cream and mango juice. The place was on the other side of the road, a long, low building of corrugated tin with a shallow pitched roof, all painted up in a bright kaleidoscope of colors. Black, abstract outlines, reminiscent of both cubism and Native American art mapped the surface, and had been filled with glorious sweeps of colors, red and turquoise and ochre and rust. More color spilled onto the line of rocks that delineated the road side, emerald and fuchsia and blue, vibrant against the dry orange dust and the outcrops of prickly pears. The three gas pumps under the tin roof were still in corporate colors, but what else there was had been swirled in purple, pink and mauve. Behind the diner and the pumps was a second, larger building, dressed in Joseph's coat colors, just the same. No cars were pulled up alongside the diner or the gas station, though I got the sense that someone was home.

There was a small cairn of rocks built on the opposite side of the road to the diner, dwarfed by a shack. Built from cast-off chipboard, packing cases and whatever detritus the wind must have blown its way, there was something appealing about its structure; a desert caddisfly drawn to the diner as if to an exotic flower. A front awning hung over the entrance, fashioned from woven plastic grocery bags and held up by washing poles. Where it joined the shack's roof, a row of plastic dolls' heads pouted and blinked at me, their color half-bleached to nothing, their eyes an eerie, dead white. The same harsh sunlight that had bleached the dolls flashed off CDs hung at the door, suspended in rows to catch the wind, and up-ended beer bottles were thrust into the earth to form a glassy picket fence. There was a neatness to it all, an order to its chaos; lids from take-out coffee cups nailed up as flowers, Coke cans stamped flat and made into tiles, a mosaic of spent lottery tickets, scratch cards and calling cards, overlapped and jigsawed together on its walls, a greater thing than the sum of its parts.

A man came out so suddenly I got the impression I'd conjured him, standing under the cover of the awning to shade his eyes with his hand. He wore nothing but blue combat trousers, knees worn though, pockets eviscerated.

'Where you goin'?' he asked. He spoke with no obvious accent, his tone firm, as if he were the keeper of the memorial and it was his business to know. When I didn't answer, he stepped out from under his awning, barefoot, but walking as if he wasn't. 'Where you goin'? You a long way from home.' He twitched his head as if a fly were bothering him, looking a foot to the left of where I was.

'I was going to get breakfast,' I said, seeing no point in lying. There was a tattoo on the right side of his chest, a winged heart with a dagger thrust through it. Under it was a series of numbers, too many for it to be a date, and on the other side was a black cat drawn as if it were hissing at an unseen enemy, back arched. A scroll under it read 'Lucky to die' and his name, or someone's name – Johnny.

'You, hey, you – you don't look like you eat much,' he said. 'You need to get some weight on you. She ought'a feed you up, the other one.'

'Thanks,' I said. He bit his lip, looking as if there was something he wanted to say, then shook his head. 'Do you want me to ... can I get you something? Something to eat or drink, maybe?' I asked.

He touched his hand to his ear as if he were finding it hard to hear, squinted, then frowned. 'I don't want nothin' like that. Hell, I don't need no charity.' He shook his head again and took a step closer. 'I look after myself, I don't need no charity – what the hell she sayin' that for? Sayin' I some idiot what needs a hand out?' I got the scent of him then; unwashed skin and hair and fermented sweat all slicked into human lanolin. He reached for me, brow creased into a frown, angry lines scissoring either side of his nose.

'Back off, solider!' I snapped. 'Front and center!' and he jerked to a standstill, as if I'd flipped his off switch. I glanced over at the diner, wondering if I needed to make a break for it, but Johnny, if he was Johnny, was now subdued, all the animation in his face spent. From that angle, with his head turned to reveal his profile and shoulders slumped, there was a familiarity to him, something in his petulant, adolescent air, like the boys I remembered from high school. Maybe it was just that they all look like Johnny after a while, men on street corners and in storm drains, like their faces were a uniform they'd been issued.

'Why goin' call me that?' Johnny said, though not as if he was expecting me to answer. 'Why she goin' call me that?' He frowned at something to the left of me, then mooched back into the shadow of the awning.

I made to cross the road but had to wait for a car to pass and saw a woman had come out of the diner and was standing in the doorway, at the top of a short flight of steps. There was a dog lying to the left of the steps in the shade cast by the building, head up and ears pricked, watching me too. I had the urge to say goodbye to Johnny, despite his shouting and inability to meet my gaze; this was his land, after all, and I was the trespasser.

'Well, goodbye,' I said to the beer bottles and the scratched-up CDs strung on orange twine, and the plastic dolls' heads in a row. Then Johnny came back out, ducking under his awning, his long, brown arms swinging by his sides. I took a step onto the road, but he stopped and held something out to me in his fist.

'It's for her,' he said to my left. 'This is for her.' I put out my hand, palm held flat, praying it wasn't going to be a dead mouse or a handful of toenail clippings. In a quick, fluid movement he put an object into my hand and closed my fingers around it, before I'd a chance to wonder why I let him touch me. Then he was gone, shouldering his way back into his home as if he'd been caught out, a prisoner passing contraband. I turned away and broke into a gentle run toward the diner, aware of the thing gripped in my fist.

The woman at the diner stood motionless, watching me as I approached. The dog was a grey and white husky type, only three generations away from a wolf. It stood as I approached, but the woman clicked her tongue at it and it dropped back onto all fours, bowing its head and yawning in complaint despite its obedience. The woman was tall and thin, dressed in grey slacks and a loose grey sweater vest, an apron tied at her waist. Her face seemed carved by wind and sun, her high cheek bones overlaid with dusky lined skin that recorded where she'd smiled and frowned in kidskin folds. Her hair was slicked back and tied in a great plait that swung over her shoulder, coming to rest against her thigh. Even more notable was its color, a rope of steel grey above her shoulder, a brilliant cardinal red below.

'He won't hurt you none' – which I took to mean the dog, until she said – 'Johnny.' The dog looked at me as intently, the markings on its face where grey met white giving it a permanent frown, as if it were contemplating some great evil.

'Oh, he was fine,' I said. 'I mean he didn't say nothin', not really.'

'He said something?' she said. There was a cigarette between her fingers. She reached into the pocket of her apron, took out a lighter and cupped its flame before she looked at me. 'Johnny spoke to you?' She lit up and tucked the lighter away again.

'Sure, I guess?' What he'd given me was still in my hand, something smooth, hard, about the same size as the lighter the woman dropped back into her pocket. I was desperate to look and see what it was, convinced it would turn out to be a bone or a knot of human hair tightly bound in saran wrap, but wanted to do so unobserved.

'So,' the woman said, finding her smile as she looked down at me, 'you got the place to yourself, season as it is. What can I get you?'

'What's good?'

'Nothin' in this world.' She grinned, inhaling the words with the smoke. Something about watching her smoke made me want to, or rather, it made me want to join her and have her light my cigarette for me, so we might sit together, like women must have done when to smoke was to be defiant, before we knew better. 'If it were me, darlin', I'd have the pancakes with syrup and bacon. Followed by a fruit platter. We buy them locally, fresh as we can. We got coffee, but I'd recommend the peppermint tea in this heat. I can ice up a pitcher for you?'

'That,' I said, 'sounds amazing.'

'Come on in then.'

She brought the cigarette with her, its smoke trailing elegantly in her wake, despite her limp and the stiffness in her left shoulder. She ground it out on an ashtray by the counter after she'd shown me to my seat. It seemed crazy assertive to see someone smoking inside like that, as if she were marking her territory against the world. The dog came too, its flank brushing my leg in its haste to stay with her. She clicked her tongue again and it threw itself down alongside the counter, muzzle on paws, eyebrows swiveling as it watched expectantly.

'You don't mind dogs, do you?' the woman asked, now it was too late if I did. 'This one's a stray. I took her in last fall when some kids been cruel to her.'

'She's lovely,' I said and dropped onto my knees to offer her my hand, the one not holding Johnny's gift. She looked to her mistress, then raised her head and deigned to sniff my knuckles, nostrils quivering. Then she moaned, muttering her jaws before she lay down – I'd been dismissed, so please, could I stop bothering her?

'They called her a devil, on account of her markings. Folks can be awful cruel when they got time on their hands. I call her Betty.'

The place was full of paintings, their frames like windows on past events. The largest was above the counter, a rough, raw landscape under an ominous sky of blue and purple. It was signed 'J.R Well' with a flourish in one corner. The woman looked up and saw me staring at it.

'My husband left it to me,' she said. "Bout the time he left me all together. I quite like it though, seein' as it came with this place attached.'

'It's ... it's very ... powerful,' I said.

'Powerful's what we got round here,' she said. 'It's subtle we don't got so much.'

'Hey, erm, can I use the bathroom?'

'Just to the left of you, darlin'.' I left my rucksack on the back of the chair and went to find it.

Soon as I clicked the door behind me, I looked at what Johnny had given me. It was a blue-grey stone, about the size of a songbird's egg but more cylindrical in form. Its surface was intricately carved with figures and marks that could have been some form of writing, all worked into its slick surface with a practiced hand. A hole ran through it as if it was meant to be hung on a cord, and there were flat, decorated terminals at either end. The light from the electric bulb that snapped on as the door closed, caught on a fine trace of gold that lingered on the terminals. Was it possible he'd made this?

Somehow, I didn't think so. I slipped it back into my jeans pocket, then took a leak.

The smallest room was an even bigger art gallery. There were pastels, pencil drawings, watercolor and oil paintings, the terracotta and blue of outside reflected and refracted through a hundred pairs of eyes. Photographs also, wetter and flatter than the paintings; people smiling at the camera, squinting into the sun. One caught my eye as I washed my hands, because it alone was not an image of rocks and sky and sun black shadow.

It was a girl, dressed as Red Riding Hood; a young, Asian woman, tiny and perfect as a china Geisha, with luscious eyes and mouth, pouting from under a red silk hood. She seemed lost in a forest of trees built from coffee mugs and takeout boxes, their leaves printed scraps of magazines and pizza menus. It was a junk-built wilderness in which little Red wandered with her basket of goodies, red apples writhing with maggots. Many of the pictures were scrawled with messages – from Gene and Laura, 'thanks for a wonderful stay'; from Marcie and Joe, 'here's to the next decade' – but Little Red was signed with just a name, Alison, and three long stroke kisses. Kisses someone had meant, once upon a time.

'I've met the wolf,' I told her. 'She's called Betty.'

Back in the main room of the diner, there was air conditioning enough to chill the fabric of my t-shirt and make sitting at the window overlooking the road an incomparable delight to being outside. The day was already rocketing up the thermometer, and I was glad this place wasn't any further from the bus stop.

'Oh hell, we'd have made it,' Margarita said. 'You know I'm always here for you, doll.'

'Yes,' I said. 'That's the problem.'

The air became delicious with the hiss of batter in the pan, and the warmth of coffee and the spit of bacon teased from under the grill,

all of which took me back to the thought of Red Levine and him cooking me breakfast in the shack, before either of us had known what we were about. *I do like to see a lady enjoy her ham and eggs.*

Stop it.

From my window, I could see Johnny's shack as I sipped the ice tea the woman brought me. He'd emerged again to erect a seat in the shade of the awning and watch away downhill with his back to me. The woman came up before I had a chance to study him any further.

'Like I said, he don't mean no harm,' she said, as she placed a plate of pancakes and bacon in front of me, followed by the fruit platter. She didn't ask but sat down opposite me, for which I was glad. You get tired of eating alone. She had coffee herself, in what looked to be a handmade mug, bulbous in form and painted with swirls and splashes of color. She took another cigarette and lit it without asking my permission, though I found I didn't mind. There was something different in its smoke, something I recognized as marijuana. She saw my expression and grinned.

'Cheaper than health insurance,' she said. 'My name's Martha, Martha Case.'

'Rita,' I said, my fork halfway to my mouth, and got the odd sensation I was lying about that.

'So, you met Johnny.' She smiled. 'He's a little like the dog, I guess. Another stray.' I stared out of the window at him again, sitting on his fold up chair. 'He won't come any closer, if that's what you're thinking.'

'Oh, no, I'm not worried, I mean–'

'I wouldn't mind if he did, of course, but he won't. Won't cross the road, just stays where he can keep watch on us.' The skin at the side of her eyes softened as a smile touched her lips, then it was gone. 'He's local, well, was once. Grew up here, just like my son,' she said. 'He went ... five, six years ago now. Maybe more. Joined up, just because we asked him not to. They do that, so many kids, no matter what you say to them. Get sold the idea that it's nothing but one big adventure, computer games brought to life. No one ever tells them nothing 'bout what war's like, what it does to people.' She said it as if she knew what war did, that she'd seen it before.

'Do you mean Johnny?' I asked. The slice of pancake was cool when I put it in my mouth and swallowed.

'My son,' she said. 'I meant my son.' I drank my iced tea and felt the press of the stone object in my pocket.

Martha watched Johnny through the window. 'He wrote, sometimes, my boy. He and my husband fought something terrible over his going, then stopped speaking to each other, even when it came time for him to leave. When he wrote, it was if he'd never had a father. Wouldn't speak to him, wouldn't mention him in his letters. Then he stopped writing altogether, and my husband left too. Eventually, a man came from the army, after I got the telegram an' all.' She said it dully, in such a matter-of-fact voice that it was a second before I realized what she meant.

'Oh, shit ... I mean–' I felt my cheeks flush – the memorial outside was for her son. 'I mean, I'm so sorry, really.'

'Nothin' you got to be sorry about,' she said, in a way that made my skin prickle with déjà vu. I wondered if I should ask her what had happened, but I couldn't find the words without sounding ghoulish. Just how did your son die, Martha? Was he blown apart or shot or something? He wasn't executed was he, his death fuzzy and dark on the internet? I was just wondering, that's all.

'I'm still really sorry to hear that,' I muttered to my plate.

'Gonna have to cross her off the list then,' Margarita said. 'Go bothering some other poor soul.' I ignored her and focused on Martha's face.

'Most of a year went by, then he turned up.' She nodded toward Johnny in his shack, put down her cigarette and took hold of her plait in both hands, sitting back and running the rope of hair through her fingers. Grey to red, grey to red.

'He was just there one day, standing on the far side of the road. I went to speak with him, but he wouldn't let me get close.' There was a twitch in her cheek as she said it, a nerve fluttering under the crushed coffee silk of her skin. Of course she'd let him stay, tried to help him, was helping him even now. Of course she would, a mother who'd lost a son like that.

Martha smiled, deepening the creases at the side of her mouth. She picked up her cigarette and put it to her lips.

'I like to think my boy did well out there. Hell, I've got it on good authority!' she exhaled the words with her smoke, turning her head to the side.

'Did you speak to them, I mean, do they tell you about what he did? God, I'm making it sound like a school report or something!' Or was I still digging in the dirt of her grief for clues, something that might uncover a link to Red?

Martha smiled. 'Oh, well ...' She glanced down at her hands. 'I don't rightly know what they do in all such cases, but I had a visit from ... well, his commanding officer, I suppose. Not that long ago, as it happens Took it upon himself to find me, said he'd been thinking of it for a while. I'm rather ... off the grid.'

'What did he say?'

'Not much.' A smile flickered over her face. 'He were just stopping by, paying his respects. He ... left an envelope with five thousand dollars in it. I never knew they did that, the government. Paid in cash.' Her smile cooled. 'This whole place has always been something for waifs and strays, you can make your own mind up as to which I am.'

I tried to picture the moment Johnny turned up on the far side of the road, him just standing there, his shadow a black line in the dirt behind him, hands limp by his side. Martha took a moment to focus on me again.

'Why, you're an easy person to talk to. Or maybe I'm in the mood for talking and you drew the short straw.'

'Not at all,' I said. 'It's great to talk to you. I'm ... I'm on my own quite a lot these days.'

'Now why's that?' Martha said. 'What about you, Rita?' She leaned back from the table. 'Who you thinking of?'

'No one,' I said.

Martha picked up her cigarettes and held them out to me. 'Pretty girl like you, come all the way out here on the bus, how come you travellin' alone?'

'Oh, I'm never alone,' I said. I took one and let her light it for me. It tasted of high school and holidays; summer in the park with the boys I shouldn't have been hanging out with and wasted afternoons and earnest conversation. I breathed deeply.

'It's ... it's complicated.'

'Yeah,' Margarita said. 'The whole you and Red tryin' to kill each other thing. I guess you could say it was complicated.'

'Oh, it always is,' Martha said. 'If it means anything at all, I'm not sure as how I believe in the one that people always go on about. But there can be the one you ain't done with yet.' She reached for her coffee.

'When he first turned up, what did he say, Johnny?' I asked, wanting to steer the conversation away from me.

'Nothin'. I looked at him, then came right back inside and got on with my day. What he say to you?'

'Oh, he just asked where I was going, I think?'

'Where you was goin'?'

'Yes, and I asked if he wanted something, you know, a drink or something. He got mad at me, but soon as I said back off soldier he did, I mean –' She narrowed her eyes, her gaze sharpening.

'Why d'you call him that?'

'Well–' I felt my skin itch under inspection. 'There's the memorial, I suppose, I was thinking about it. And his tattoos, I saw them. I guessed they were military by the serial number.'

She nodded, her expression relaxing. 'You're observant,' she said.

The building shuddered as a truck passed, so long and large it blocked out the light for a good few seconds. When it finally cleared, Johnny had moved and was standing to the side of his shack, hands on hips, staring into the sun.

'Did he build all that by himself?' I nodded toward the shack.

'Sure did. Seems good with his hands. He won't take nothin' directly from me, but if I leave things out by the colored rocks at night, they're gone by the morning. I run a guest house now, mostly for artists.' She looked to the rear of the dinner, where the windows showed us the long, low building at the back. 'It's basic but it's cheap and clean, that's what they like. The light's good here too, so they tell me. I've always found it so.'

I felt the stone in my pocket against my thigh, then put my hand over it. I liked the feel of it, liked that it was so solid and so unexpected, like finding treasure.

'He gave me something,' I said. 'Johnny, I mean - well, I thought he did. What he said was ...' It snagged in my pocket and I looked down as I wiggled it free. 'I mean, what he said was that it was for her, so I'm guessing he really meant you, so–'

Martha reached across and touched my arm. 'No,' she said. 'He didn't mean for you to give it to me.'

'But he said it was for her?'

'If he wanted me to have it, he'd have left it on the stones like always. Johnny don't speak to people.'

'But he talked to me,' I said. 'He said …' Martha tilted her chin up, her face impassive. 'He said this is for her …' Martha let go of my arm and folded her hands in her lap. I looked down at my plate, my knife and fork together, the hands of a clock at midnight.

'Then you're special, aren't you, Rita?' Martha said.

CHAPTER FIVE

I DIDN'T SLEEP WELL in the months after I came to Vegas. Lying in bed, all I seemed to do was bob over the surface, aware of the inside of my eyelids and the sheets above me. If I ever dipped below, it was always into dreams, oily thick and opaque, that were reluctant to let me go. Sometimes, it was wiser just to float.

I lived in a three-room apartment about a twenty-minute jog from The Savannah Heights, which I chose because it was the most anonymous apartment block I could find. That, and they didn't care about references if they got paid cash. After I'd checked Lisa into the clinic, which preferred to be called a refuge, I had enough to pay for three months' rent, eat, and join the nearest gym, where I met Olaf and his partner Ralph and through them, got the job working security at The Heights. Ralph was a fireman, which meant he worked shifts much in the way Olaf did, and the both of them spent most of their down time working out and swimming, much as I did. They were the nearest I got to friends there. Once or twice a month I'd even go round for dinner.

Ralph said I reminded him of the boys who came to Vegas from bible belt towns after they'd discovered they were gay, the ones who could never quite enjoy themselves, no matter how hard they tried.

'You can kind of always see them looking over their shoulders, and as much as they go wild and what have you, something keeps telling them that it just ain't quite for them.'

'I'm not sure how to take that,' I told him.

'Don't mind me,' he said and grinned. 'I'm just a nosy old queen, you can tell me to fuck off if you like.' But I hadn't. I liked him, and the way he'd seen through everything I was in an instant and yet still didn't mind me coming round.

I lived with no internet, no laptop and a pay-as-you-go cell phone with three numbers; the office, Lisa's cell and Olaf's. The Heights was not adverse to paying me in cash, once I'd shown them a social security number and passport they were happy to go along with; I kept it in a wall safe in the apartment. No credit card, no bank account, no store card, no loyalty card, seeing as I wasn't sure just where my loyalties lay anymore.

'You're such a liar,' Margarita told me as I drove back from the refuge. 'Goin' on like nasty ole' Lisa was all behind everything. Sure, she was there, but so was Paris, why d'you always forget about him? Like just because you slept with him, somehow he ain't to blame too?'

'Of course he's to blame, even worse.' I pushed the car up to seventy only to remind myself that it wasn't mine, and Olaf would be really pissed if I wrote it off. 'But I didn't really love him, did I?'

'Lisa says how it were all his idea anyway, says she was scared a' him, just as much as she were scared of Red. She said how she tried to stop you, but hell, you were havin' too much fun. Now ain't that the real truth?'

'Stop it,' I said, staring out into the darkness as it swallowed the road ahead and spat it out behind.

'Oh, I got you there,' she said, her voice dripping with steel and honey. 'You never had to do none of them things, not if you didn't want to. But you was having too much fun bein' me, or me bein' you, or whatever the hell this is. I'm you, sugar, I'm the real heart of you and you just can't stand it, can you?'

'One day,' I said. 'One day I'm gonna take you to a therapist and have you beaten the hell out of me, bitch!'

'Keep goin',' she said from the dark of the car, from the night outside the window, from all the way back to when we were children. 'You keep tellin' yourself that. But, just how much of you would there be left, if you ever did?'

One of the times I couldn't sleep, which was most of the time, I went out for a run. I put my headphones on and set out, the air at two in the morning the kindest Las Vegas in July had to offer. After a couple of miles, I was soaked, weaving though streets that were never empty night or day. People stared after me the way they do when they're on holiday and you aren't, as if you're all part of the safari they've come to see. I bought a bottle of water from one of the kids who sell them on overpasses and subways, and headed away from the Strip, meaning to do another couple of miles before I went back home, showered and tried again with the whole sleep thing.

Instead, I found I was standing outside the window of a tattoo parlor, its name a neon scribble. Thinking 'why not?', I went in.

The woman inside was about my age, looking up from the book she was reading as if I'd stepped into her library in violation of a 'do not disturb sign.'

'Can I help you?' she asked. 'You after a walk in, or you just wanna make a date?'

'I'm not sure,' I said. There were cupids at play about her neck, and the backs of her hands and fingers were spidered in lace as if she were wearing antique gloves.

'Well, you let me know when you made you' mind up.' She went back to her book. She had thick, curly red hair cut like a flapper girl, and a book of designs in plastic covers in front of her. I turned the first few over, then my gaze settled on one. It was a mermaid, drawn as if mermaids were something from the turn of the last century, in elegant Art Nouveau swirls and curlicues of blue and green.

'How much is this?'

'That?' She looked over her glasses. 'For your first? That's gonna hurt, you know?'

'I know,' I said.

I had a TV, but most of the time it was off. I had a portable radio which I tuned between local stations, moving on whenever the music got too much to bear.

When Lisa had lived like this, when she ran away from home and emailed me from coffee shops, I'd felt the pain of her loneliness seeping through her words, no matter how bright she'd sounded, until she'd given in and stopped pretending anymore. She'd gone to acting classes and auditioned for parts in plays and films when she saw them, and worked as a character waitress, and tried yoga, and to make friends. I hadn't done any of those things, though I figured that Ralph and Olaf were probably closer to the real thing than Lisa had managed while she was here, and probably a lot better than I deserved. Oh, and of course she'd met and married Red and gone away to his big, white house, which I hadn't done either. Not quite.

I liked it, living as I did. I liked the simplicity of the rooms, the floor and walls I painted white, the white bed linen I bought from an end of season sale, the white yoga pants I wore without the bother of doing the yoga. During the rest of the year, while Lisa was at the refuge, then discharged herself and met a man called Bob Breslau, of all things, and moved into a low, long flat-roofed house with him and his two sons, I lived in my white box and pretended I wasn't thinking about Red.

Lisa called at the start of December, when even in Vegas there was a certain chill in the air, Christmas lights creeping out from their hiding places. We talked as if we really were just two sisters, who lived far enough apart to make the drive to see each other significant, yet close enough to feel we were still family. After she'd gone through her litany of what Bob Breslau's sons had been up to, while I sorted my laundry and only half-listened, nodding from time to time even though she couldn't see me, she said 'So ...' and I recognized the tone in her voice and stopped, a half-folded t-shirt in hand. 'I was wondering if you wanted to come over, on the weekend?'

'This weekend?' I glanced at the calendar and saw that my block of four days off smugly coincided with it. 'I'll have to check my shift ...' but I couldn't quite bring myself to actually lie about it. 'Sure ... I guess?'

'Cool,' she said. 'It's been ages since you were over, you know? It's just one thing after another some days, and time goes on, and then it's been weeks since I've seen you.'

'Yes,' I said.

'And you never came for Thanksgiving, and you could have. It was really cute; it was just us and Bob's folks, but it was ... real, you know?'

'Sounds it,' I said.

'Besides, Bob's got a thing he wants to take the boys to on Saturday, and we can have a proper catch up, you know? Some girl time, just you and me. So, you will come, come early?'

'Sure,' I said. She said goodbye and hung up, and I wondered why I was faintly annoyed at her, apart from the whole being manipulated into killing Red for her thing. I shook my head; it was nothing, probably just the onset of Christmas, which had never been all it might have at our house.

'Do you hate me?' Lisa said once at the refuge. 'You got every right to.' She was curled up in the chair again, her arms wrapped around her knees. 'I know it's gonna sound stupid, I know you won't believe me, but through all of it, I kept tellin' myself that we'd be alright, you and me, and we'd just go off somewhere, just like we promised when we were kids.'

Like when we were kids. Like when we hid under the bed together, and she kept me safe.

'No,' I said, 'I don't hate you.'

CHAPTER SIX

DRIVING TO SEE LISA, I had the impression the freeway had been laid just for the two of us, a hot, grey lifeline that stopped us from drifting too far apart. Nothing makes me feel more American with a capital 'A', than driving with the windows down. The sky above seemed bigger than anything had any right to be, a great upside-down sea I was sure I could dive right into, if only I could let go of the earth.

I pulled off the freeway and slipped down a narrow side road that wound its way through a little valley of red-gold rock and cactus, where the tide mark of some prehistoric river was still visible, a chalky white seam running through it all. I headed to a gas station which had a reassuringly clean washroom, German standard, as my German grandmother would have said, where I put on make-up and did something with my hair.

It bothered me how much I looked like our mother, how my mouth became hers when I painted it with brownish-pink lipstick. Lisa's mouth was the same as Mom's too, our own chalk seam that ran through us both when we smiled. I hadn't seen Mom for nearly two years and she'd no idea where either of us were. I put the lipstick on the side of the German standard washbasin, pursed my lips at my reflection, and saw Mom at her dressing table.

I must have been eight or so, younger perhaps. It was summer; the light was strong behind her, she was almost in shadow. She was wearing a slip, something delicate with a frill at the hem. She was smoking, flicking the ash into a cut glass ashtray. Even then, I knew this was unusual, something other mothers didn't do.

I had Mr Pooter in my hand, rescued from my refuge under the bed. I'd pressed my face against him and the floor and not listened and, when it was over, I'd slipped out and scuttled across to her room with all the bravery Mr Pooter and his little blue jacket had given me. I'd gone to tell her, and ask her to stop it, stop what he was doing to Lisa, but there she'd been, smoking, watching the smoke curl in a grey tendril between mouth and nose, staring at herself. She looked at me, slowly, the smoke obscuring her expression as she breathed out, tears rolling over her cheeks.

'Mamma's got a headache, darling,' she said.

Bob's place was on a long, wide street of flat houses. They all had verandas out front and square pillars holding up grey porches. Bob and Lisa lived at 1131, Mayflower Avenue or something, but I knew it by the convergence of the recycling bins and the post box, which looked like a fat, blue frog.

'Rita! It's so good to see you!' Lisa was dressed in something matching and blue, with an appliqué of the state across the front. Her skin had turned an ominous shade of cedar brown since I'd last seen her, her nails sharpened into peach-colored talons.

'Hi,' I said. When she embraced me, one of those talons grazed my hand.

'Oh, look,' she said, 'I still ain't used to them. What d'you think?' She wiggled her fingers.

'Sharp,' I said.

'Your hair looks cute,' she said. 'When you get that done?'

'Oh, not long,' I said. 'It goes so fair in the sun anyway, so I

thought fuck it, why not? I had it pink once before, when I was on my last year of high school. I might do it again.'

'Really?' Lisa shrugged. 'Well, if any one could pull it off, I suppose.' Her hair wasn't as blonde as I remembered it from last time, more of a honey color she'd let grow and cut in bangs.

Bob was in the shed out back, fetching out a wooden sign that read 'Santa, stop here.' A slew of Christmas lights, fiberglass snowmen and reindeer had already formed a drift across their back yard. He waved, his bearded face breaking into a broad grin.

'Hey Rita! How's the drive?'

'Okay ...'

'We're just havin' ourselves a clear out, seein' as the weather's turned.' It was seventy-one degrees under a high, bright sky polished clean of clouds. His two boys, Brandon and Caleb, stared at me from behind the Christmas decorations. Neither of them spoke.

'Bob's takin the boys to get some new stuff,' Lisa said. 'We want to make a good show this year, you know?'

Christmas back when we were children had meant iron grey skies, sidewalks inches deep in leaden snow and ice, and steam billowing from subway gratings, caught in the air like thistledown. It had meant fights and fallings out, and school plays and carols and drinks parties, from which we were first excluded, then included, then bored by. It had never meant life-sized snowmen with the manic grin of the condemned praying for a reprieve.

'These old fellas' seen better days,' Bob said, smacking one on its shoulder. 'Ain't we all?'

Once they'd gone, Lisa made us coffee, and asked a lot of questions she answered herself. She cleaned up as she talked, taking things out only to put them away again, washing our mugs, wiping the surface before she put them down.

'Shall we have these in the lounge area, or are you okay at the breakfast nook? No, we'll sit down, because the seats are so much more cosy there aren't they? I mean, we're gonna get a new suite in the sales. I saw one I wanted, just got to see how much they're gonna mark it down by so I can decide. It's blue, do you like blue? I can't remember? Dark blue, you know, that sort of color that looks nearly black but not really black – Prussian, is that what they call it? Gosh, where is Prussia, is it Russia?'

'I think it's Germany now,' I said, sitting on the arm chair and wondering if it sensed its end was nigh.

'You think they'd change the name then,' Lisa said as she joined me. 'German blue, or something. I like the sound of that.' German standard, I thought.

She was finally quiet while she drank. When she put down her coffee mug, she moved a spare coaster to her side of the table, like someone playing their first card.

'So ...' she began, winding a strand of her not-quite-so-blonde hair about her finger. 'I think Bob's going to propose.'

'What ...?'

She smirked at me, her ankles wrapped together as if trying to cross her legs twice in excitement. 'What, marry you propose?'

'I've found the ring. I shouldn't have been looking but he was being all sneaky and–'

'Lisa! Does Bob know about–'

Her effervescent smile dispersed. 'What, you think I just dropped into conversation I'm still married?'

'Well, okay, but you can't marry Bob, can you? Lisa, if he asks you, you've got to tell him, you can't let him think–'

'Why not?' she snapped. She picked up her cup and drank again. 'Oh, alright, I know I can't marry him until it's sorted out, but he doesn't have to know anything about Red, does he?' My stomach turned over, the coffee taste sour in my mouth.

'Well, yeah–' I cleared my throat. 'But he kinda does, doesn't he? What you gonna do, go for a long engagement and hope Red gets a divorce anyway? I mean, two years, or five without contact, and then you can just apply–'

'No,' Lisa said. 'That's too risky. Besides, Bob will want to get married right away, I know he will.'

'Well, put him off,' I said. 'What's the hurry anyway, you're living together as it is.'

She slapped the air with her hand. 'That's not how it works round here and you know it. Only the other week at church, some of the neighbors started gettin' at him, saying how he ought to make an honest woman out of me.' That, I figured, was a thing well beyond the capacity of Bob Breslau, possibly even the good Lord himself. 'Lucy was real popular you know? Things have already been said about me moving in like this.' The dead wife was Lucy, that was it. Jesus, Lisa and Lucy – Bob sure had a type.

'Lisa, you sure you want all this? You wanna live where people give a fuck what you do, where they think they got the right to pass judgment on you like that?' But I could see from her expression that it was exactly what she wanted. She stuck her chin out and the little scar on her cheek showed white against her tan.

'These are good people, Rita, good people. It matters to Bob what they think, so it matters to me. And hell yeah, I wanna live somewhere where people look out for each other, where they give a damn, what the hell's wrong with that?' Yeah, I thought, mom 'n' apple pie, 'n' all.

'You are sure he's gonna ask you? I mean, you didn't just find Lucy's old ring or something?'

'No, I did not,' she sniffed. 'Besides, I saw the receipt.' She straightened her arm so she could pick invisible lint from the sleeve of her sweater with sharp, agitated jabs of thumb and forefinger.

'Okay, so, Bob's gonna pop the question. What then?'

She stopped pecking her sweater and smoothed her hands over her knees. She'd thought about a lawyer.

'I figured he could send the papers an'all, but then that's not to say that Red would even bother to sign them. But, then there's the whole ...' and she didn't say 'trying to murder him thing', but I guessed that was what she meant. 'I mean, once I make contact, even through a lawyer, he's got somewhere to look, he's got a way in, hasn't he?'

'Oh Lisa, he's not going to be bothered with all that, is he?'

'Really? Can you honestly say he won't come after me just because, just to get revenge?' She picked at the skin on the side of her fingers, the winding of hair not enough anymore. 'Sometimes, I get these awful dreams he's coming after me.' So did I, but I wasn't about to tell her that, or that I looked forward to them. 'I keep thinking he's gonna get me, or the boys - you know, I love those boys, really I do, and I'd never forgive myself if anything was to upset them.'

'You're just being crazy now. Red's not going to come after the boys and you know it. Hell, you've said that half of what you said he did, was all Paris's idea just to make him look bad.'

'You don't know what it was like.' She folded her arms around herself. 'He was plenty mean enough, even if I ... look, do we have to go through all that again?'

'Okay, alright.'

In the silence that opened up between us, while she built herself up to asking me what I knew she was going to, I tried to work out what I was going to say.

'I was thinking ...' Lisa began, back to the hair winding.

'I know what you're thinking,' I said, feeling too tired to pretend otherwise. 'You want me to sort this out for you, contact him or whatever. Get you your divorce.'

 **BROKEN PONIES**

'Would you?' she said. She let go of her hair and knitted her fingers together in her lap, sitting forward on the couch. 'He'll listen to you, I know he will.'

'No,' I said.

'But Rita!'

'What can I do any better than a lawyer? Just go and pay for one to send papers to him, or I'll pay for you to send the papers and–'

'I did it already!' This time there were tears in her eyes, real ones.

'What ...?' She picked up our mugs and marched into the kitchen with them.

'I got a lawyer to send stuff, okay? Ages ago. He ain't replied.' She began running water into the sink. I breathed out, a long, slow calming breath just like they'd talked about at the refuge.

'You could have just told me,' I said. 'I mean, from the get go.'

'Please, Rita. It's cost me nearly two thousand bucks–'

'Two thousand?'

'We sent it twice, okay?' She rinsed out a dish cloth and began wiping down the already clean kitchen counter. It was just like him, she said, keeping her waiting, torturing her even now at a distance. What right did he think he had to be that way with her? Squirt squirt, rub rub. All she was trying to do was make a better life for herself, to make a new start and put all this behind her, and what did he mean by trying to hang onto her like this, what the hell was in it for him anyway? 'You know,' she said, suddenly motionless and staring at the hood over the cooker. 'You know, one day last week, I just woke up, and went to the bathroom, and came and made Bob and me a coffee, and took it into him, and he woke up and kissed me and do you know? It wasn't until I came down later that I remembered everything. All the shit I'd done, all the shit that had been done to me and ... well, and that I was married to Red and all of the rest of it. That was twenty minutes, Rita, twenty minutes when I was just ... just normal.'

'Okay, look,' I said. She stopped scrubbing. 'I need to think about it, okay?'

'Is that a yes?' she said, her face all lit up.

'It's an I'm going to think about it, okay?'

'Okay,' she said, but when she returned to her scrubbing, there was a smirk on her face.

'I said think about, okay? Think about.'

Bob and the boys were back with the props for Lisa's perfect Christmas an hour or so later. I gave my vague approval when asked, and went back into the kitchen, leaving Lisa and Bob giggling to unpack. Brandon was there, leaning against the counter reading a magazine. He ignored me at first, then rolled his eyes sideways for a furtive glance. When I met his gaze, it was eyes front and back to the magazine.

'Had a good time at the fair?' I asked. Brandon shrugged. His magazine shrugged with him. 'What sort of thing was it, just decorations and sh ... stuff like that?'

'Spose,' he managed, after dedicating a lot of thinking time to it. Oh Christ, what did I expect? What teenage boy wanted to talk to a twenty-something female, especially when her sister was about to become his wicked stepmother?

'So, Christmas. Not really your thing then?' Brandon shrugged. 'I guess you're more into games, right?'

'Sure.'

'Cool. Hey, I met a guy who was a game designer. He ...' Brandon risked another sideways look at me. 'Well, never mind about him.' He went back to his magazine.

'I'm getting a PS3,' he announced.

'Awesome,' I said. 'That's ... awesome.'

'Hey Brandon!' Bob appeared at the back door. 'Can you go get the red tool box from the back shed? Got to rewire one of these little suckers.' He grinned at me, part of a Christmas elf under his arm. Brandon folded his magazine then placed it on the counter between us. Round-shouldered and head down, he sloped out past me.

''Spect you think this is all a big old fuss over nothing,' Bob said, once Brendan was gone.

'No,' I lied. 'It's ... cute.'

Bob grinned, his big, broad face foolish and so stupidly happy. 'You don't know what a difference she's made to me, to us,' he said. 'I know that's weird, right, because she's your sister an' all.'

'No, really,' I said, squirming.

'She talks a lot about you,' he said. 'Says how good you were to her when you were kids, you know?' A cold flash itched over my skin. In all my worry that she hadn't told him about Red, I hadn't thought that she might have told him about us. 'That's families for you,' he said, then clarified his assertion with, 'always there for each other.'

'Yes,' I said. 'That's families.'

He left, still grinning, like a big dog wagging its tail. Happy families, here we go - just how much had Lisa told him about us? Trying not to think of it, I picked up Brandon's magazine and flicked through a few of the pages. Words and images fluttered past, bombs and guns and explosions; immersive narratives enough for anyone.

'Hey Rita.'

I jerked my head up and was confronted by our brother, Frank. He was in Bob's kitchen, one hand on the edge of the counter, as if he had every right to be there, as if someone had let him in. Which, of course, they had.

CHAPTER SEVEN

'YOU'RE BACK from Mexico, then?' Frank said. It took me a second to realize he meant the cover story I'd concocted for everybody else in the world.

'Mexico, sure - what the fuck you doing here, Frances?'

'What, you can't even say hello? And no one calls me Frances anymore, or Franny, before you go there. It's Frank, and you know it. So, you're looking well.'

I closed Brendan's magazine and put it on the counter. 'You ... too.'

He wasn't. He looked as if he'd turned a lot older than thirty since I'd last seen him, losing weight along with hair.

'Rita,' Lisa said from behind him. She was standing at the threshold, gripping her hands together, those long nails catching the light. 'I know this is a bit of a shock and I'm sorry, but I didn't think you'd come if you knew. I didn't know how else to get you guys together.'

'Oh, I dunno Lisa,' I said, folding my arms. 'I mean, call me crazy, but perhaps you could've just asked me, or something?'

'Come on lil' sis,' Frank said. 'Don't I even get a hug or nuttin'?'

Lisa had gone all out with dinner. Tomato soup, which she said three times had not come from a can, followed by meatloaf with mashed potatoes and string beans. We were even promised peach cobbler.

Frank talked about the music venue he was now managing, the record store presumably not having worked out. As my soup got cold, I glanced up at Brandon, who was molding the inside of his bread roll in his fist. He caught me looking and smirked.

'They come with all these guestlist whatevers ...' Frank was saying. 'We only got insurance for three hundred. I mean, we only charge, what, six bucks a pop as it is, and they want us to be ... be ...' Frank's maths failed him as Lisa cleared his bowl away. 'Well, we got to make it back on the bar, start the night down already. It's crazy, this internet ...' Frank shook his head.

'Here we go!' Lisa put a large, floral edged dish on the center of the table.

'Now, that looks delicious, honey.' Bob beamed up at her.

'Do I got to eat the beans?' Caleb said.

'Yes, you do,' Bob told him. 'Greens gonna make you grow up big and strong like me.'

'Whatever,' Caleb muttered.

'So,' Frank said, recklessly helping himself to extra potatoes. 'How long you been back?' When I didn't answer, because I was thinking about the last time we'd eaten together, which must have been nearly ten years since, he knocked on the table and grinned at me. 'Earth to Rita? Lisa said you're livin' in Vegas now, what the hell you doin' there?'

'I work security,' I said.

'No shit!' Frank grinned, spoon in the potatoes again. Lisa winced.

'Frank,' she said. 'The boys?'

'Hey, no worries - there's a shit load of potatoes here. Knock yourself out, kids.' He took a pull on his beer and looked at me. 'So, you work, like, one of the really big places on the Strip?'

'No,' I said. 'One of the really small places, not on the strip.'

'Hey, I was only askin',' Frank said. 'Why you always got to be so mysterious? What you do there, work out all day or somethin'? What you think, Bob? You like muscly chicks or what? Be kind of like doin' a man, right?'

'Frank,' Lisa hissed.

'I don't think Rita looks like a man,' Bob said.

'I guess that's kind of a weird thing to ask anyway,' Frank said. 'I mean, seein' as you're with Lisa now. Hey, Rita, you know how these two met?'

'I ...?' Not sure what the company line was on this, I glanced over at Lisa, and saw Brandon slink his head lower into his shoulders.

'Well,' Bob smiled across at Lisa, 'I was just in this place for a coffee. I'd not been in for a while, but work sends me across state sometimes, you know? Anyways, I found myself passing and suddenly remembered that they did the best pecan pie in the world, so ...'

'That's right,' Frank pointed and clicked, the way he used to do when he thought he'd caught one of us out cheating at cards. 'It's crazy how like ... like two people can just find each other like that, am I right, Rita?'

'Yes,' I said, not sure what I was saying yes to.

'Are you alright?' Lisa asked.

'Peachy,' I muttered.

'So, Rita, what the fuck was Mexico all about then? You really back for good now?' Frank plowed on, regardless of the look Lisa flashed me.

'Yeah, I'm back now,' I said.

'What were you doing out there, building wells or some shit like that? Seems to me Mexico would be better off if they all stopped sneaking over here, and looked after their own, am I right Bob?'

'Well, I guess it's not just a–'

'So, Frank,' I said, looking at Lisa. 'How you get in touch with Lisa, after all this time?'

'There's this little thing called the internet and you can, like, send messages to people?'

'Rita doesn't use it anymore,' Lisa said.

'No shit,' said Frank. 'Well, Rita, Lisa sent a message through Facebook.'

'You messaged him, Lisa?'

Lisa pushed her half-empty plate away before she spoke. 'I did, yes. I want to get the family back together, Rita. It's important that we ... try and build some bridges.'

'Oh,' I said. 'Thanks for keeping me in the loop.'

'I sent you enough emails,' Frank said, cracking the cap off another beer. 'You could have replied, you know?'

'Why, were you asking for money again?' I said.

'Rita!' Lisa snapped.

'Nice, Sis, real nice – thanks for that. I was asking where the hell you were, actually, because we were worried to shit about you. You do know Mom never stops talking about you, asking where you are, why you don't get in touch no more? Just ask Lisa.'

'You've spoken with Mom?' I saw the flash of color across Lisa's cheeks even through her tan. She reached for her glass and put it down without drinking.

'We need to do this, Rita. We need to ... to put the past behind us.'

'I think Lisa just wanted to try and make things right,' Bob began, smiling, as if he knew what the hell he was talking about.

'What's wrong with Lisa's mom?' Brandon said, looking up from his plate.

'Oh, there's nothing wrong with her Brandon,' Lisa said. 'It's just that, well, Rita and I ... well, Rita finds it hard to speak with her, right now.'

'Why?' he asked. I bit back the answer that was pressing against my throat.

'Grown-up stuff,' Bob said. 'Why don't you boys clear the plates for Lisa?' Brandon dropped his head again and shrugged. Caleb, who'd eaten everything on his plate but a row of green beans, let out a long-suffering sigh and took his own plate into the kitchen.

'You been to see her yet?' I asked Lisa.

'Not yet. We've talked on the phone, that's all really. But it was nice, you know, to talk to her.'

'Good, well, send her my best.' I picked up my glass and drank. Brandon leaned past me to fetch my plate. He smiled at me and I smiled at him, and for a moment I wished so much I could be him it almost hurt. Or that I could be me again at his age, or someone else at his age, just not me.

'Fuck, Rita!' Frank slammed his bottle down. Brandon jumped.

'Hey,' Bob snapped, 'you just watch your mouth in front of my boys–'

'Jeez, I'm sorry Bob, but I just can't stand the way she's just sittin' there like nobody else ever had shit to deal with!'

'When I ever said that?' I said.

'You're sayin' it now,' Frank snapped. 'Sittin' there, like you was something special, like Mom didn't deserve the time of day from you, or some shit like that.'

'Boys, go to your room,' Bob said. When neither of them moved, he pointed. 'Now!' Brandon thumped my plate back down and dragged his brother out of sight.

'Oh, I'm sorry,' I said. 'I'm so sorry you all want to go play happy families.'

'It's not that, Rita,' Lisa said. 'But how the hell do you think we're going to rebuild our lives if we don't put the past behind us?'

'Lisa's right–' Frank stood up. 'I don't know what shit you're into, or half of what happened last year' – panic flashed across Lisa's face – 'but you don't know how much Mom's hurt, because you won't speak to her, speak to any of us.'

I stood to face him, anger shaking through me. 'They were the ones who sent her away and never let her come home, I never–'

'That was Dad,' Frank roared. 'You know that was because of Dad, and don't pretend like you were the only one hurt by that, or the only one he hurt, okay? You don't got the monopoly on a fucked up childhood, okay?'

'Alright, you folks need to calm down here,' Bob said.

'Well, hey, Bob,' I turned on him. 'Welcome to the family! This is pretty much as functional as we get. Sorry to burst your bubble, an' all!'

'Nice,' Frank said, arms folded, head nodding – the older brother again, the man of the house, when Dad was too drunk or too ill to boss us around. 'Lisa tries to make something for herself and you go put her down about it.'

'When was I putting her down?'

'Seems that way to me,' Frank said. 'Rita, you don't got the right to drag all this resentment around with you, because he never touched you, alright?'

'Shut the fuck up!' My throat seemed to close hard and tight, tears and heat beating behind my eyes. Oh Christ, I wanted to hit him. I wanted to smack that look off his face, like I had when we were kids, when he caught me smoking and tortured me with telling Dad about it. Then he'd hit me right back and pinned me to the ground and punched me, the way older brothers can and you can't do anything about it, because you're thirteen.

'Frank stop it, you know Rita was hurt just as much as–'

'Mom let him do it,' I yelled, 'She let him–'

'She never had no choice!' Frank bellowed. 'Don't you get it, Rita? He did it to her, what he did to Lisa, all the time.'

'But they were–' but what was I going to say? That they were married, they were adults, that meant it didn't count?

'Frank, that's enough!' Lisa said. I looked at her, her face painted that weird, orange color against her not-so-blonde hair and those nails, those goddamn shell pink and white nails like angel's claws.

'He did it to her, Rita,' Frank said. 'And when she was just too beat up or too sick for him, he did it to Lisa.' He looked up at Bob. 'Shit, I'm sorry man, we shouldn't ...'

'It's alright,' Bob said. 'Lisa told me.'

'You're lying,' I said. 'That's not how it was, that's not–'

'Mom sent me away,' Lisa said. 'We've talked, since I came back from the refuge, since I met Bob. There's so much we never knew then, Rita, she didn't know what else to do. But that meant he ...'

'You hated that school,' I said. 'You ran away from it all the time–'

'I know,' Lisa said, those nails clicking and clicking as she worked her hands together. 'Rita, I was angry and fucked up, and I wouldn't listen then, and I hated her as much as you, more so.'

'You wrote to me, you told me how she was to you, what she said–'

'Yes but–'

'No!' I pushed past her, strode towards the door, and snatched up my jacket from where it was slung over the back of the sofa.

'Rita,' Lisa said. 'Don't go, Rita!'

'You gotta know,' Frank called after me. 'You gotta know the truth, Rita–' He lunged for me, but I was faster and stronger than we'd been when he'd last tried it. I knocked his hand away like it was nothing, like I'd wanted to do when we were children.

'I saw it,' I hissed, 'I saw what our father did to Lisa - I was eight years old and I saw him–'

'Well, you know why, don't you?' Frank snarled.

'Frank – don't you dare!' Lisa yelled from behind him. 'We talked about this, you say a word and I'll–' but he was bigger than her, blocking out the light between us.

'Because you were his, Rita – his daughter – and Lisa wasn't.' Frank pushed at me.

'Frank, you swore, you swore to me you wouldn't say!' Lisa slapped Frank's shoulder. 'Rita, I'm sorry, I'm so sorry! I didn't know, I really didn't–'

'You're lying.' I stepped back from Frank.

'Oh really?' Frank said. 'Just how you figure that, why would I wanna–'

'I don't know what you want!' I snapped. 'What the hell do any of you want?'

'You're such an asshole,' Lisa said, pushing past Frank to reach me.

'Hey!' he spluttered. 'Jesus, so everyone's bustin' my balls now?' He stalked back into the lounge.

'Rita–' Lisa put her hand on my arm. 'I want you to talk to Mom, please, because you need to understand, then we can move on, then–'

'No.' I pulled away from her. 'What the hell is this shit about? Of course he was your dad, he was our dad, he was ...' I trailed off. She was crying, in the way only she could, tears rolling down her face like spilled pearls.

'I never meant you to find out like this,' she said, and she probably hadn't. She'd meant for us to get together and remember what good times we could, all of us behaving under the spell of her meatloaf. Only she'd been so sure it would work, so sure, she'd forgotten about just who we were.

'Get away from me–' I shoved at her. I hadn't meant to, not as hard as I did, not hard enough to make her stumble and catch hold of the door post.

'That's enough Rita–' Bob came into the hall after us. 'I know I don't rightly know what y'all went through, but this here's my house, and I don't want the boys hearin' all this. These ain't things they need know about.' His words buzzed about me, just static on an ill-tuned radio.

'Is anything you ever told me true, Lisa?' I demanded. 'Shit, is this even true, or is this just another one of your fuckin' games?' I could hear the thunk of bugs hitting the glass, the fall of bodies around her feet.

'Rita!' Lisa was really crying now, her face all screwed up and pink; sobbing, childhood tears like she'd never cried then. It made me angry. Something evil and black twisted and boiled inside me. I wanted to hurt her; I wanted to hurt her so much.

'Don't you think Bob should know everything too, Lisa?' I sneered. 'I mean, if we're all being so honest here?' I saw it in her, real fear to go right along with the real tears. She gulped for air as if I had my hand on her throat and I could hold her under, push her face down into the dark.

'Don't,' Margarita said. With her voice came a black water taste and a roaring in my ears. I snatched my words back from the brink, jamming my hand to my mouth as if they might escape despite everything.

'I'm gonna go–' I snatched for the door lock, yanked, but nothing happened. I slammed the flat of my hand against the door.

'Rita – Rita come back here!' It was Bob, not Lisa. 'I never meant for you to go, just–' Bob, striding over to me, his face kind, fatherly, trying to understand, to be the better person, if only I'd calm down, if only I'd stop acting all unreasonable. 'No, Rita, listen

to me–' He put his hand on my shoulder. 'Rita, please, you're upsetting your sister–'

Fear flashed through me, red and jagged and from all the way back home. Before I knew what I was doing, I smashed his arm away and punched him in the side of his face.

Lisa screamed as Bob staggered back from me. 'Rita, get off him!'

'Dad!' It was Brandon. His voice cut through me, the sound of it jerking me back from the darkness. Bob was on the floor. I was standing over him, and Frank was holding Lisa, who was screaming at me to stop. I couldn't hear them; I could hear nothing but a high-pitched whine of static, as if the world had turned down the volume and they yelled at me from behind glass.

'I'm sorry ... I'm so sorry, I–' All I saw as I made for the front door was Brandon at the foot of the stairs. I willed the door-lock to open and headed out down the front steps. I didn't look back.

'It's going to take time,' the counsellor at the retreat – they don't like to use the word *clinic* – had said. 'You're both hurt, you've both hurt each other, and you've got to expect this to take a long time to heal. There ain't no quick fixes, not in a bottle and not in a pill. You've both got things ... thing's you need to say to each other which are going to be hard to hear.'

That night I dreamed of Red. I saw him in the hot light of the swamp, with the crack and sigh of the place muttering about him and the lines of his face drawn by sun and pain. He touched me, took hold of me, and the roughness of his hands devoured my skin, scratching deep as a tiger's tongue, all the way to the bone. I could hear my heart beating, feel as it pulsed the blood through my body and I shook with it. I dreamed I was a fruit and he was eating me; each bite, each pull and tug as he peeled away my flesh, was wonderful. Then I hadn't been eaten at all; I was just lying on the grass beside him, the wet, rich earth beneath me and the sky above, as if I were a drop of water waiting to fall into it. I reached for him, to touch him, desperate to feel any part of him again, but he was gone. I was lying beside my father, and I was my mother. When I woke up, I cried.

I sulked for December, then I borrowed Ralph's car.

CHAPTER EIGHT

I PULLED UP outside the gates of Carillon an hour after passing the edge of the city. Everywhere was still half-dressed for Christmas, as if the world had only just woken up and was blinking through a hangover.

He'll turn me away, I thought. He'll get angry, start shouting. I'll just turn around and go. I won't look back, I won't argue. He'll know I'm here then, so when I send the letter I'll write at the motel; he'll be expecting it. He'll read it, sign it, and send it back to me there or at the Height's address, which is the only one I'll give him, and that will be it. If for some bizarre, twisted reason of his own he still refuses to sign, well, at least I can say to Lisa I tried, I did my best.

'Yeah, right,' Margarita said.

'All right,' I said. 'I need to see him, okay? I need to know how I feel about everything that happened, so I can move on.'

'For someone so keen on movin' on, you sure is standin' still.'

'Look, he's got to do this. I need him to sign the papers - I need to see him do it, to make sure this is all over.'

'Really,' Margarita said, 'then how come your heart's beating like a nervous prom date?'

'Because he might have me arrested!' I snapped back.

'Oh, sure,' she said.

I got back into the car, took my shades off and folded them into their case. In the rearview my eyes looked small and vulnerable.

I put the car into drive, swung it across the wide, grey road and pulled up by the squawk box. The security cameras above the gate bowed their head to look at me, like wet-eyed birds. I reached out and pressed the button.

'Can I help you?' The voice was metallic and distorted, could have been anyone in the world.

'I'm here to see,' I stumbled over the name and decided on the formal, 'Mister Levine ... Junior?' Well, that sounded way more hideous out loud than in my head. 'I've got to speak with him on a ... legal matter.' I let go of the switch with relief.

'Is he expecting you?' the box asked. This time I detected an accent through the distortion. Whoever it was, was silent for a while. The security cameras swung away from me as if they were already bored, and the gates flinched into life. I pressed the gas and moved slowly forward, feeling as if the gates were opening onto quick sand. Remember not to struggle, I thought, that only makes you sink faster.

'Whatever he says,' I told the mournful trees as they waved me through, 'whatever he says I'll just accept it, that's just the way it has to be. Zen, be fucking Zen about it. What will be, will be.'

'Que Sera, Sera. Que fuckin' Sera,' Margarita said.

The house was revealed to me as the drive swung round to the right; a white, bright, wedding cake of a place glimpsed through the garden piece by piece, until there it was, Carillon, fountain and all. There was a long, low black car outside the front steps and, as if they'd arranged themselves on the steps to wait for me, were three men. One, black suit, white shirt and ear piece, held the door of the car open. Coming down the steps in a camel-colored suit with a hat in his hand could be nobody in the world but Papa Levine, Red's daddy. He was not as I'd imagined and yet he was familiar – a tall, lean, older man, with a shock of grey hair swept back from his

temples and a slight stoop in his shoulders, too far away to make out the detail of his face or see if he was in any way like Red. Who was right next to him.

Red.

He was wearing a suit, casual jacket, no tie. While the other two remained where they were, he started down the steps toward me, not hurrying. I pulled up, unsure what to do as the blood pounded in my ears and a flush spread across my neck and itched at my shoulder blades. He turned to say something to the others, nothing I could catch, but the tone perfunctory - a 'this won't take a moment' throwaway line.

'Get out the car an' face him,' Margarita hissed at me. 'Don't sit there like a pussy!'

'Mornin'.' He didn't alter his expression. 'Now, you'll have to forgive me, but I quite forgot about our meeting.'

'Oh,' I said, because it was better than stuttering out 'Red, it's me, Rita,' which was the only other thing I could think of to say, apart from - 'Red, it's me, Rita, I got my hair done and ... well, sorry about that trying to kill you thing.'

'I'm so sorry you've come all this way,' he said, 'but we've double booked here. I've a meeting inside and–' It was Red, it was him, it was his voice, like cold syrup curled from the spoon on a hot day – but he was looking right through me. He held his hand out. 'So ... I'm gonna have to ask if you wouldn't mind coming back tomorrow, same time?' I looked at the hand. I didn't take it. 'That alright with you?'

'Rooster?' Papa Levine came down to the bottom step. The driver closed the car door and stood to attention. 'Everything alright, son?'

Son. Why did that make my stomach churn more than anything? Red was Papa Levine's son, heir to all this, all this Carillon, with its electric gates and endless grounds and security guards, and what was I? A lower pay grade than the man who'd opened the car door. What the hell was I thinking?

'What, no kiss?' Margarita sniggered.

'Everything's fine, Papa,' Red called back, turning to wave toward the house.

'Of course,' I said and got back into the car. 'I'm sorry to have bothered you.'

'Why, thank you.' And he looked at me, just for a second, a smile curling the corner of his mouth. 'But it weren't no bother. None at all.'

'Well, that's good then,' I muttered.

My face burned as I turned the key. I reversed the car around the fountain, refusing to let myself look at him. Fuck him, fuck all of them and their big white house and their elongated vowels and polite ways, fuck the goddamn whole sorry lot of them. He could go fuck himself, if he thought I was coming back here like this tomorrow, for what? So he could ball me out without an audience?

'Screw him,' Margarita said. 'Let's go get drunk, let's go get laid, let's go make trouble for someone. Come on, I'm bored of this shit already.'

'Like that's going to help,' I muttered.

'Well, it ain't gonna hurt none,' she said. Oh, what the hell did it matter anyway, what had I been expecting? A year or more after we'd tried to kill each other, and he could barely remember my name, well, boo-hoo me. I guess there were too many people in the world who'd had the same idea.

'You cryin'?' Margarita asked.

'Shut it,' I told her, as tears beaded the edge of my lashes. I wiped the back of my hand across my eyes and eased forward, car wheels crunching on gravel. The trees with their weeping widow's

embrace leaned down as if to console me - poor little Rita, come all this way to see the big bad wolf and nothing to show for it, not even a basket of goodies. 'Will you shut up?'

The white wings of the gates were folded shut as I approached. I slowed until I was forced to come to a stop. I waited, watching the gates, giving them a moment to remember what we were all here for. Still nothing. I sounded the horn. A flock of little grey-black birds took flight, wings thrumming in the air, until they were lost in the canopy above. Nothing else seemed to notice me.

'Oh fucking great,' I said to the steering wheel. There was a box on this side of the gate too, so I reversed back a few feet and lowered my window, praying only Red's housekeeper would answer it, anyone but Red. Please, God, don't make me go back there and ring the doorbell!

'Hey?' I said to the box, finger on the button. 'Hey ... hello? Can someone open the gate please?' Nothing. The wind billowed the tree branches above and brought the resinous smell of their leaves and the chatter of the birds. I swore and pressed the button again. 'Hey, I was just here and ... and the gate won't open?'

The box's silence was broken by an unintelligible blast of static. I squinted at it. 'Sorry, I didn't get–' There was the crunch of gravel, then the lock on the passenger's side door rattled. I spun around. Red was there, yanking on the handle.

CHAPTER NINE

'OPEN THE DOOR!' he demanded and when I neither moved or replied, he added, 'Come on, darlin', I know you're mad at me, but we don't got time for this!'

'Fuck you!' I snapped.

'Darlin'!'

I slapped the wheel, cursed him, then flicked the central locking control on the dash. Red wrenched the door open and flung himself into the seat.

'I flipped the gate off, 'n' said I'd go let you out,' he said. He held out a small black box the size of a cell phone, clicked a button on it, and the gates sprang obediently to life, opening with a resonant clang.

'What the fuck do–'

'Shit, darlin', you sure do pick your moments, just drive, for fuck's sake!'

'What the hell for? What, you gonna know my name now we're on our own n'all?' I said, heart beating and heat racing over my skin.

'I ain't got long, just get us away from the damn security cameras will you!'

'Fine.' I floored the accelerator, sending Red thudding toward the dash as the wheels scrabbled for purchase. A spray of stones spattered into the squawk box as we left.

'Holy shit, darlin'!' He laughed as he fumbled to fasten his seat belt.

'Oh, so back there you can't even crack a smile, and now what, you late for your flight or somethin'?'

'Jesus, not that fast!' He clicked his seat belt home. 'I just want a little privacy! There's a side road a little way down–'

'What the fuck is this?' The turning came into view. Still furious, I hit the brake and we juddered around the corner.

'This ain't no drag race, darlin'! Who you think's after us?'

'Make your fuckin' mind up!' I yelled. 'Christ Almighty, one second you don't hardly know me, the next you're going all getaway driver!' The road was empty but for yellow lines, which gave up the effort a few feet along. To the left, I saw what must have been Carillon's grounds, bounded in a high, brick wall. To the right, the land spread away in a sweep of wet blue-green. I pulled over under the shade of the nearest thing to a tree on offer.

'Get the fuck out of my car!'

'Well, I missed you too!' Red said. I thumped the seat belt release, wrenched the door open and clambered out.

'Fine – stay in the car!' I slammed the door, blood pounding in my ears.

'Now just you hold on–' Red slammed his door too, like it was a competition. 'What you got to be pissed at?'

'What the hell's going on?'

He came around the hood of the car toward me. 'You're the one who breezed into mine out of the blue like Hurricane Katrina's lil' sister' – I winced at his choice of metaphor – 'an' what, you think I'm gonna just introduce you to my daddy, an' make you ice tea?'

'Well ...'

'What I'm goin' say? Hey, here's the girl I was tellin' you about, the one as tried to kill me last year. I know you've been dying to meet her!' Unable to think of a single thing to say to him, I stalked off down the road. He came after me, his footsteps heavy on the dry asphalt behind me.

'Look, as I seem to remember–' when I rounded on him, he was closer than I'd been expecting. 'You did a pretty good impression of someone trying to kill me, actually.'

'I did?' Red pointed at himself in mock surprise. 'I guess it was all my idea to get handcuffed to a chair an' stick myself in the leg with a broken bottle?'

'I thought you killed my sister!' I yelled.

'Well, you was wrong 'bout that!'

'I know!'

The world crept in under the silence after my shout, the sigh of the wind in the trees above, the sound as a car passed us on the main road behind, as if it were nervously clearing its throat.

'I saved your life,' I said. 'You wouldn't have saved me.'

'You tried drownin' me,' Red said, hands on hips, revealing the red silk lining of his jacket. 'I wouldn't have needed savin', if you hadn't pulled me under.'

'You were shooting at me.' His shirt was open at the neck, no tie. Against it, his skin looked weathered, the lines that scored his cheeks stronger, deeper.

'I weren't tryin' to hit you ...' He shrugged. 'Just scare you up a little.'

'Bullshit,' I said.

'Scout's honor.' There it was, his smile lingering at the corners of his mouth, like it was creeping up on something smaller.

'Well ... well I don't think I was ever going to kill you, not really,' I said.

'That's good to know. Just the whole theft and torture thing then, huh? Never mind that now. I remember...I didn't have much else

planned that weekend, anyways.' The smile got me. I reached up and gripped the back of my neck and turned my face away from him, sucking my cheeks against my teeth to stop it happening, but there it was. Cold syrup on a hot day.

'You said we weren't friends or nothing,' I said. I let my arm drop. Red shrugged his shoulders under his jacket, let his hands slip from his hips.

'I ain't sure as how I've changed my mind 'bout that yet,' he said. The wind touched his hair as he stood looking at me, standing far too close for us to be friends. Then he pulled me into his arms and kissed me.

I'd been kissed before. He'd kissed me before. I'd been kissed by teenage boys at school proms who tasted of coke and hormones, and college boys who tasted of dope and existential angst, and men I'd wanted to use, and men I'd hated, and all the lost souls in restless Vegas nights, but I'd never been kissed like that before. It was a kiss that took all of me; it was simple and complete, and while it lasted, it was the first time in what seemed like half my lifetime, I hadn't thought about Red. Not who he was, or what he might have done, or what he was going to do, or what he might be doing, because I knew. In that moment I lived without wonder. In that moment, I lived.

'Yeah?' Margarita said. 'Just which one of us do you think he's really kissing here?'

Then the whole crazy-ass stupidity of everything rose up and smacked me between the eyes, and I broke away from him. 'What the fuck are you doin'?' To make myself feel better about it, I went as if to hit him, and let him catch hold of my wrist so as to stop me.

'Fuck me, darlin', but I've missed you!'

'What the hell you doing? You don't get to ... stop laughing, this just ain't funny. Oh Jesus!' Everything I'd meant to say, or thought I should say, or thought he was going to say, fought for pole position in my mouth. 'I'm so sorry!'

His grey-green eyes glittered as he grinned at me, half kind, half dangerous and everything I'd tried so hard to forget. 'Hell, darlin', I'm sure that's just foreplay twixt us, ain't it?'

'No, you idiot.' I put my palm to his cheek where I'd meant to hit it. 'I'm so sorry I tried to ... oh, you know, all that shit! I'm–'

'Don't.' And he took hold of me again, brought my face against his neck as I embraced him. 'Jesus, what I did, to the both of you–'

'No, please, I–'

'Darlin', there ain't ... we don't gotta do this now, we just gotta–'

'Yes, yes we do, I've got to, please, before anything else, before–'

'No, seriously darlin', we don't got time - I gotta go.'

'What?' I pulled back from him. 'What the fuck? I just apologised to you, and you gotta go?'

He leaned back enough to look at me again. 'Darlin', you are unbelievable at picking your moments, seriously. I got a meeting with Papa, we got some shit we got to see to - I really gotta go.'

'What?' He kissed me again and let go of me.

'Shit, darlin', you got no idea what went through my mind when I saw you, I mean ... Jesus wept, what the hell you doing here?'

'I came to see you,' I said, stating the obvious. He made to take hold of my hand, but I snatched it away and started walking. A car passed us, a dull, blood red color, its windows blanked out with sunlight as it turned down from the main road.

'Will you give me a moment?' Red yelled after me. 'Jesus, Rita, won't you–'

'Go fuck yourself, I don't care whatever shit you're in, I don't care about you, you asshole!'

Red stood still. 'Darlin',' he said, his voice lit with the smile that played across his lips. 'Seems to me as if you do.'

'He got you there,' Margarita said.

I closed my eyes, then I started to laugh. When I looked again Red was laughing too. I shook my head at him and walked back toward the car.

'I fixed the gate,' he said as he caught up to me. 'Said I'd just run down and let you out. Shoot darlin', you took the wind from my sails, I didn't know what else to do. I figured we just need some time here, where we don't got to explain ourselves to no one else.'

I paused, hand on the car door. 'Sure, whatever. You're right, I should have just called or something, or written.'

'Hell no,' he said. 'It wouldn't have been you, if you had.' He reached for my hand and this time I let him take it and let him kiss me. The wind picked up and scattered dried leaves at our feet, and a car passed us going the other way, back toward the main road. When we broke off from our kiss, I caught a glimpse of its red flank as it headed away downhill.

'Look at you,' he said. 'Will you just fuckin' look at you? You sure you're really, you, darlin'? You sure I'm not just makin' you up here?'

'How more real you want me to be?'

He grinned at me, reached into his jacket and took out a cell phone. 'Get into town,' he said. 'Go find yourself a hotel, soon as you're set, call me - here, give me your number.'

'Oh, shit,' I laughed and fumbled mine out of my pocket. 'I can never remember it, you know?' We stood there, phones in hand like people do, both of us putting in our security codes.

'One two three four?' I stared at him. 'Your code is one two three four? Are you serious?'

He shrugged. 'Look, put your number in there under–'

'Rita?'

He grinned. 'Whatever you like, darlin', think I'll know who it is.'

I pressed the digits and wrote in my name. When I handed it back to him he rang it and my phone lit up, vibrating with excitement.

'Call when you're set, stay anywhere you like, s'on me.' He kissed me. 'I'll come find you. We ain't got time to do justice to all of this shit, I really do got a meeting!'

'Sorry to keep you,' I said, thrusting my phone back into my pocket.

'Just get out of here.' He pulled away from me and set off, only to turn back again once the car was safely between us. 'Beggin' your pardon, darlin', but soon as I get where you's at, so help me God, but I'm gonna fuck you back till last Tuesday. That don't sit right with you–' he placed his hand on his chest with a mock bow, 'just don't pick up when I call.'

'Subtle,' I told him.

'As a land mine,' he said.

CHAPTER TEN

I LEANED AGAINST the car and watched Red jog away. He looked back once, waved, then was away down the road. I watched him while I walked round to the driver's side door, then as I got into the seat, and then in the rear view. When he was gone, I tilted the mirror so I could see my eyes.

'So this how it gonna be?' Margarita asked. 'Big daddy Red gonna click his fingers and you gonna come running, like the little bitch you are?' I turned the key in the engine and while it idled, picked up my phone and saved his number as 'Red'.

'Shut up,' I told Margarita. I put the car in reverse and swung it around to face the main road again.

'Oh come on,' she said. 'You go on pretending like you wanted him to throw you out, or hit you, or some crazy shit like that all the way up here, just to make you'self feel better. Now look, he's just gone and made your year for you.'

'Okay, shut the fuck up,' I said. The road ahead was clear now, not a car in sight – red, blue or any other color. When I pulled out, I glanced toward the gates of Carillon. The low January sunlight reflected off them, and they gave no hint that he'd gone that way, or that I'd just driven from there with the scatter of gravel behind me. They'd closed in on his world as completely as water after a stone has dropped.

'Well, I can't say as I mind, he was always my favorite. Now what, when we gonna get to play with him again? When we gonna–' I hit the steering wheel.

'Shut up, shut up, shut up! Leave me alone, get out of my head and leave me alone! I want all that shit behind me, I want to be free of it! Don't you ever think for one fucking moment that I deserve some peace, that I'm not sick of living like I do?' There was a long silence. I pulled out of the junction and headed back down the road that lead, after miles of hot, wet, dank woodland, all the way down to the city.

'I don't know,' she said, after a while.

Neither did I. I was going to a hotel to wait for the man I'd tried to kill, the man who had, least it not be forgotten, tried to kill me, and yet my heart was racing and I felt more stupid and giddy than someone half my age had a right to feel. But it wasn't him. Not really. Alright, it was him, of course it was…

'Damn right it is.'

'Oh of course it is, but not like that.' It was Lisa; it was because of Lisa and what she'd asked me, the last thing I could do for her. I could do it now; I could get Red to sign the divorce papers, and then Lisa would be free to marry Bob Breslau and the boys, to be Brandon's new mother when he didn't really want one. Lisa would have them all, and welcome it, welcome her greatest role of all, that of wicked step mother, well, that was what she wanted. She wanted a family all of her own, of course, and a family that was better and safer and cleaner than ours had been, and why not? I could give it to her now, could have given it to her all along, if I hadn't been so scared of myself. It was going to be easy, it was going to be something she and I might laugh about years from now, how stupid we'd been to be so silly about it, but most of all, it would be over. And if I did this then perhaps, just perhaps, everything Frank had said wouldn't be true after all.

'Talking of mothers ...' Margarita said. I pressed my foot on the gas pedal and the speedometer flickered up to fifty, then fifty-five, then sixty.

'You know, we could have a conversation too?' Bethany at the retreat said to me. 'Just you and I alone?' She was nice, in a professional way, in a way which made you want to talk. 'You're paying a great deal of money for Lisa to stay here.'

'It's our money; we earned it together,' I lied, though I supposed we had, when you thought about it.

'Even so,' she said, unlocking the narrow door to the therapy room, 'I know you come to the sessions with her, but you need to think about your healing too, Rita. This is about helping you both, not just her, because she won't ever get to a place of resolution without you, you do realize that?' She'd looked at me through her glasses before taking them off and letting them swing on their chain, mixed up with the brown and green beads she wore.

'Sure,' I said.

'Nothing you say to me goes any further, Rita. I'm not about to say anything to Lisa. You're very protective of her, even after everything. Why is that?'

'She ... she was there for me,' I said, 'when we were children, when ...' and I lingered long enough over the words for her to smile, for her to touch the glasses where they hung on their chain and eventually to say:

'When your father abused her.'

'I saw it,' I said, already back there under the bed, with the suffocating smell of dust bunnies and cobwebs.

'That was abuse,' she said. 'That was abuse too, Rita, what he did to you by making you watch.'

'No,' I shook my head. 'No, it was worse, worse for her always. He didn't know I was there, it wasn't about me.'

'That doesn't mean what he did to you was okay,' she said. 'It wasn't enough for him to choose not to abuse you.' I walked about the room, one arm clutching my chest, hand to mouth, biting the side of my finger.

'One time,' I said, when I turned back to look at her and saw that she was waiting, just waiting, for me to be ready to tell her. 'One time, when I was about nine or ten, and Lisa must have been twelve or so, that sort of age – he was angry at me, my father. And he went for me, I mean, he was angry and he got hold of me like he got hold of her, you know? His hand bunching up my t-shirt and he touched my face and ...' I could see myself reflected in the glass covering the picture on the wall. An abstract of lilies, falling.

'And she came in, Lisa. I remember the sound of her footsteps as she ran upstairs, like she knew, knew what was going to happen to me because of what happened to her. Like somebody warned her. And she came in and ... and she put her hand on his arm, and she never did that, never touched him herself. And ...' I didn't cry, but the words wouldn't come until the counsellor put her hand to her mouth and coughed, and I sat down, perching myself on the edge of the large, brown leather chair opposite her.

'And she led him away, away from me, into my parents' bedroom and closed the door. So he'd do it to her and not to me. She went away after that - Mom sent her away to school and all the time I was waiting, I suppose, but he never ... never touched me.'

The counsellor pressed her lips into a smile. She waited, and the wind blew the grass outside the long window, the window that came down all the way to the floor.

'He never touched me,' I said. 'Not in any way. He never held me, he never kissed me on the cheek, he never ... touched me. And then sometimes I'd see him looking at me, like when I was running down the stairs, only I hadn't got my slippers on like he always said I should. Like he'd say 'Rita, wear those goddamn slippers or I swear, you'll hurt yourself on those stairs,' – and I didn't wear them, and I slipped down the stairs, and I went right down on my ass, bump, bump all the way down, right down–'

All the way to the floor, and the wind in the grass, and the sigh and crack of the swamp.

'And ... I was crying and sort of laughing, because our brother Frank was there, and I didn't want to look like a baby in front of him, but it hurt, it really hurt, and I was crying and Daddy came running up to me with all the noise of it, and my crying and ...' the tears came then, for the first time. The first time since we'd come to the retreat, the first time I'd ever cried there. The first time I'd ever cried.

'And he didn't hold you,' the counsellor said, after a long time, after I'd pulled out Kleenex after Kleenex from the box on the table beside me.

'He couldn't. Not then, not ever, because of what he'd done, what he was. And I wanted him to, even after what I knew, what I knew he did. I wanted him to hold me, and pick me up so much, more than I'd wanted anything ever. I wanted him to hold me, because then it might have meant I was better than her, Lisa, who got all his attention all the time we were kids. Do you know how sick that makes me? How sick and disgusting and wrong, that all the time, even after that, even after everything I knew about him, I still ...' I gulped for air, forcing the word until it had nowhere left to hide. 'Loved him. Somehow.'

There was a long silence, the tap-tap of feet passing, the snatch of voices without words. It began to rain, and the rain pattered against the long glass window. I wanted to be them, the voices, one of them at least – walking away just sharing a joke, getting on with the day. Walking away from myself.

'What you're feeling is quite normal,' she said.

'Normal?'

'I'm sorry, that's ... that was a poor choice of words, Rita. But nevertheless, what you're feeling is ... it's a form of survivor guilt, really. People walk out of blazing buildings, or train crashes, or hostage situations and after a while, they just can't stop asking themselves the question – why me, why was I spared? The one thing you've got to do Rita, is try and resolve what happened and let yourself move away from it. Survivors who don't, well, they usually go on to hurt themselves or other people, they ... fixate on punishment and, as I say, that can manifest as self-harm, or drug addiction, or sex addiction, or some sort of revenge fantasy that just becomes all encompassing, and...'

Rear impact jolted me into the steering wheel. The airbag deployed. The world went grey, the breath punching out of my lungs. I stamped on the brakes and the Audi, already shunted off course, swung through the full three-sixty, deep green trees and high blue-white sky spinning about me. Then the car crunched into the soft verge and threw me back against the seat.

I stared at the world through the windshield, not trusting it was finished with me, with the dull, dark, sinking feeling that I'd been here before. This time I didn't seem to be that badly hurt, though the whiplash was going to kill tomorrow. I released the seat belt and popped open the door.

The car that rear-ended me was a good twenty feet away, the front of it caved in and the driver's side light all shot to hell. The phrase 'fender bender' repeated over in my mind in time with the on and off blink of the car's indicators. As I stared at the other car,

the door opened and the driver got out. It was a girl, no, a woman, but she was barely five feet two and whippet light, in a red plaid dress over denim pants cut off just below her knee. The red plaid seemed unnaturally bright against the grey road and the car.

'Oh my God,' she was saying as she approached. 'Oh good lord, Jesus, are you alright? Darlin'' – so she was a native, then – 'darlin', are y'all right?' She looked on the verge of tears, working her hands together and hanging back from me, a dog that wasn't sure if you were going to kick it. I pulled myself to my feet and glanced at the back of the car, hoping she hadn't damaged my case - gender neutral black with conservative and functional zips, giving nothing away to anyone.

'Hey, you walkin', that's good, right?' the driver asked, taking a step closer. She was wearing lipstick, and I found I was staring at it. The color didn't suit her and it had been applied as if she'd been looking in the rearview to put it on, at about the same time as she'd hit me. She seemed to take that I was looking at her car, not her.

'Oh hell, but don't you worry 'bout that, darlin',' she said. 'I'm sure the insurance will fix it, ain't that what they're all for? Anyways, main thing is, you ain't got no boo-boos, right?' She was peering at me, one hand shading her eyes and the other reaching out as if to touch my shoulder. 'Let me take a look now, did you hit your face there?'

'I don't think so,' I said, dimly aware of the sound of another car slowing and coming to a halt behind me. A good Samaritan, I thought, as the woman squinted up at me. She had dark hair pulled into little bunches either side of her head, like the ears of a ferret or some feral little cat.

'Now, yes you did, darlin', you got a real shiner comin' there– ' There was the sound of a car door opening; I turned to look, but she touched my face, drawing my eyes back to hers. 'Oh darlin', why … you look right fit to faint. Can you see me, can you see how many fingers I got held up?' Three, she was holding up three fingers; I squinted at them and they came into focus.

'Oh, hey, I'm fin–' A hand slammed over my nose and mouth. A man's hand, a man who threw his other arm across my chest, pinning my right arm to my body before he swung me off my feet. I cried out, kicked back, but he had me, keeping me off the ground so that I couldn't connect with anything or anyone. An overwhelming stench hit me, smothering my mouth and making acid rise in my throat – pear drops and tequila and acetone. The air bag seemed to blow up all over again, grey, soft, blocking out the light as my ears buzzed and sang as if I were being plunged underwater. Then down I went.

BROKEN PONIES

CHAPTER ELEVEN

WHEN I WOKE, I remembered everything; the man's hand closing over my mouth, the sensation of his arms tight around me and I had the good sense to keep my eyes closed. I began mentally crawling through my body, my legs, my arms, trying to gather what I could from sensations that lurked there. Pins and needles fizzed in my toes; I clenched my teeth and waited as the wave of pain burned up my legs, praying that it wouldn't turn to cramp.

My right arm was extended above my head, my hand limp against a restraint, left arm hanging free. I was not on a bed, or if I was, it was inches from the floor. The creeping sensation I was being watched, or the fear I might be, tugged at the skin on the back of my neck. I listened, playing dead, hoping to catch the sound of someone moving about, voices even, but there was nothing but the dry rasp of my own breathing and the wind. No, there was something else, the sense of an echo, that what sound there was, drip-dropped into a vast, hard space. And a smell – damp concrete, cold, steel, rust, gasoline and oil. It was cold, I was cold, a cold that had eaten into my muscles and inched under my skin; I was cold to touch.

I dared not think. If I started to think about why I was here, what had happened to me, then I would panic. I listened again but there was nothing to tell me that I was not alone. So I opened my eyes.

They were dry and claggy; my lashes peeled apart and water fogged my vision. The world refracted, a square of light dancing out of reach. I scrubbed at my eyes with my free hand, gulped a lungful of air, and looked again. There was a horse above me.

It was pawing the air, its teeth revealed in a grin, nostrils flaring as it bore down on me, hooves inches from my head. It wasn't moving. It was white, its hocks filthy grey over gold, flanks swirled and painted with flowers in loops of green and pink. It was mostly hidden in shadow, the edge of a weak beam of light falling from above and revealing the hint of gilding crusting the horse's muzzle. It was a fairground horse – a flying pony – and there was another beside it, lying on its side, hooves galloping in mid-air. There was another piled on top of it, and another, and more. Some were still impaled on barley twist stems of gold and black; others had broken free, legs snapped off at the knees, heads missing, flanks caved in and hollowed out, all of them dirty and broken.

I was in a warehouse, or a disaster-wrecked ballroom, or the third region of hell; alone in a dank, leftover space, stacked with carnival dead. I turned my head and came face to face with a clown. I yelped – there it was, inches from me, its dead-eyed face gruesome with a cavernous hole in its forehead. I flinched back, only I was trapped. My shackles rattled, metal against metal, and the sound cracked through the space gunshot loud. It was a head, just a clown's head, as if that made it a whole lot more normal. There were more of them, three or four, lined up alongside me. I could swear they were sniggering, that I could hear the grating 'haw-haw' of mechanical laughter.

'Keep it together,' Margarita said, her voice low and deliberately calm. I thrashed to sit up, jerking at my wrist but it would not come free. It was locked into a set of handcuffs, the other side snapped into a thick steel staple. I pulled at it again, the sound of

my struggle echoing. I was laid out on a wad of blankets on some sort of dais, a round, rusted expanse. I got onto my knees, tugging at the handcuffs while I stared about, trying to blink through the stars jumping at the edge of my eyes. It was the base of a fairground ride, the floor a thick steel mesh. I'd been locked to one of the couplings, that must have once tethered the flying horses as they turned. The central column of the ride and its housing was still intact, rising up to what was left of the canopy; a broken, bat wing umbrella, festooned with the guts of the wiring rig. I could imagine the music and the echo of screams.

I got myself into a squatting position and forced myself to breathe out, making each breath longer than the last. I stared at the nearest clown's head, taking in the cracked red paint of its cheeks and the thick screw end still protruding from its severed neck, then made myself count them. Seven heads, and the floor beyond scattered with a tide of detritus made monstrous by shadow. There were windows on the far wall, some twenty or thirty feet away, glassless, nothing more than grey-white squares offering no hint of what lay beyond. A path had been cleared in the scatter of rubbish on the floor, a sweep of bare earth overlaid with wooden planks. Breathe, I told myself, all you have to do right now is breathe. If there'd been a solid floor to the place once, it was gone; only shards of tarmac were left, standing proud over the ground beneath. Part of the roof above was open to the sky, and below it, in a pool of grey light. I saw the soft, wet earth had been disturbed before being overlaid with the wooden planks.

There were more clown heads at the foot of the ride, clustered together as if I'd arrived late for a beheading. The scribbles on the walls from other days and other visitors – love hearts and tags and initials – were all faded by darkness. Other forms I couldn't make out lurked in the shadows, vast shapes hiding from the pools of light, deep sea fish avoiding my gaze. I breathed out, I breathed in and tasted the cold, and the stench of flotsam.

'That's better,' I muttered, as my heartbeat slowed. I looked at the handcuffs again. They were standard issue, but that didn't make them any the less toughened steel, and any the less unpickable without something to pick them. The long horseshoe staple they were linked to was loose, but not the sort of loose that meant it would come free easily. I could make out two fat bolts on the underside of the floor, holding it firmly and frustratingly in place. I sat back on my heels.

'Ok,' Margarita said. 'Now you can think.'

CHAPTER TWELVE

I'D BEEN LAID OUT on a couple of blankets, each folded in half longways. They were thick wool cloth, a dull olive or grey, though it was hard to tell in the half-light. The edges were over stitched, the top corner of one unraveled and going into holes. Oh, and I was alive, which meant that they wanted me that way, whoever they were. For the time being, at least.

Then I noticed my feet were bare. I twisted round to look, but the sneakers I'd been wearing were nowhere to be seen. Socks gone too. Had they thought it possible I'd get free and so taken my shoes to try and keep me here? I ran my free hand over my heels – no trace of injury and remarkably clean, which meant that they hadn't just come off as I'd been dragged here.

'At least I got the rest of my clothes.'

The place was silent; no far-off sounds reached me, nothing more than the wind outside and the scratch and scuttle of things too small to worry me. I was a long way from anywhere and had been brought here so that I wouldn't be discovered while they - and I guessed that 'they' included the girl from the car crash and the man who'd grabbed me at least - were elsewhere. They'd left me where they thought I couldn't escape, in a place where it was unlikely I'd be found, because they were busy, or not bothered about watching me. So, if I was going to get free, now would probably be the best time to do it.

I worked my way to the edge of the dais, kicking the clown heads away and wincing as they rattled against the metal grid of the floor. I tested my weight against the cuffs; if I pulled against them, I could reach the edge of the dais and see the scatter of rubbish on the floor below.

'Give me a lever,' I muttered, 'and I'll move the world. Fuckin' Archimedes, I'd like to see him get out of this shit!' Then I paused. The word 'lever' stuck in my mind - lever, leverage - what the hell was I here for? 'Let's hope it's for good old money,' I muttered, 'because the alternative ain't pretty.' I ran through a list of possibilities, trying not to turn each into the title of a top shelf slasher B-movie.

Then I saw it, something that might be what I needed. It was a metal rod about a half inch in diameter, protruding from the tangle of broken machine parts and over-sized toys to the left of me, and completely out of reach. I'd no idea if it was free or sunk eight inches deep in concrete, but it was better than sitting on my ass and shivering.

I pulled on the handcuffs, swiveled round and eased my feet over the void in a vain attempt to reach it with my toes. Despite the chill of the place, sweat broke out on my skin as I hung off the cuffs, the metal gnawing into my wrist.

'Goddamn it!' I slumped back onto the base of the ride and sought the refuge of the blankets. The horse grinned down at me and the clown heads grinned up at me - the whole place having a huge fucking joke at my expense.

The blankets were rough to touch. I could make out something printed on them; I turned one round and saw it was good old army issue, going into holes at one corner. I looked back at the metal rod protruding defiantly from the rubbish pile.

'Shit, I really was a loss to the girl scouts,' I said.

I knotted the corner of the blanket, then eased my fingers into the hole nearest to it and worked at it until it was ripped out to six inches or so. It was not easy working with my right hand shackled to the floor, but then no one was marking me out of ten on my needlecraft skills. When it was done, I got as close as I could to the edge of the stand and narrowed my eyes at the rod.

I've never seen the appeal of fishing. After squatting in the semi-gloom handcuffed to a fairground ride and attempting to snag a metal rod from a rubbish heap with a ripped-up army blanket, I can't say it's grown on me any.

I threw and I missed. I threw again and because the blanket was gripped in my left hand, I threw it woefully off target and got it snagged on something else. When I pulled it free, a load of junk tumbled down the shallow heap, but the metal rod remained impassive. I tried again, and again; then I took some time to pick out squashed soda cans from the garbage with my feet and wrapped them into the knot at the end to add weight to the proceedings. They were worse than useless. I went back to the empty knot and tried again.

Why the hell was I here anyway? It unsettled me that the girl had let me see her face, because if Hollywood serial killer movies had taught me anything, it was that the moment the kidnapper revealed themselves, you were pretty much headed to the mortuary slab, after some excruciating and pointlessly elaborate death. Only that was crap; serial killers, from the little I knew of them, were nothing like the malevolent, intricate psychopaths the movies would have us believe. Most victims of serial killers were not chosen due to some long-held psychosis, or to relate to the precise chords of a Mozart symphony, in a way only an FBI analyst could decipher. Most were chosen because they were there, and because they could be taken, most of all because they would not be missed. Serial killers killed prostitutes and drug addicts and runaway children, and trailer trash kids, and homeless people. They killed people who everybody would expect to go missing anyway, who would not raise the alarm for days, if ever. There were rarely teams of investigators drawing the links between blurred photographs pinned to a wall, because the deaths were usually separated by enough time and geography, for nobody to care that much to bother. It was only when they took someone who'd strayed accidentally into their way, someone people cared about, that they were caught. Or that's what I told myself, as I sat handcuffed to a dead carousel.

I threw my blanket; it touched the metal rod. It slipped. I threw it again and this time it snagged. I froze, holding my breath as I tried to tease it forward and catch the rod more firmly, then the whole thing slipped free, leaving the rod smugly in place. I breathed out a long, slow breath, wiped my forehead on the blanket, and made myself focus on the rod again. Come on, chalk that up to a partial victory, I told myself.

Deciding to curtail my wandering through a back catalogue of slice and dice horror films, I concentrated on something else. If I wasn't the victim of a random encounter on the long, wet and lonely road, I was here for a reason.

'Hell, doll, I know where you're headed with this one,' Margarita said.

'Well, you got any better ideas?'

'Nope.' The knot of the blanket hit the rod, then glanced off it. I counted to ten and got myself onto my knees, gripping the chain of the cufflinks with my right hand. I leaned as far out as possible, refusing to dwell on just how ironic it would be if my weight worked the cufflinks free, only for me to plunge head first onto the floor and become impaled on the goddam spike.

 **BROKEN PONIES**

I was somehow here because of Red. He was the only connection that made any sense. For a while, strung out over the broken floor, I considered that perhaps Paris was behind all this, but it just didn't feel like him. It was too indirect, too mysterious – besides, he'd never liked getting his hands dirty, not when it had come down to it. I doubted he'd have been able to resist saying 'hi' by now anyway.

The hole in the blanket caught the rod. I was so surprised it was all I could do to stop myself reeling it in to have another go, and so losing my chance. There it was, the grey wool cloth stretched out between me and my prize, the one that until now, had got away. I wrapped the blanket around my fist and pulled, slowly tightening it against the rod. It held. I gathered myself, got back into a squatting position, and heaved.

Nothing happened. I pulled again, gripping the handcuffs on one side and leaning back against the blanket, gently at first and then more heavily, then tugging at it. Nothing. The blanket slipped, nearly coming free; I gasped and I eased up on it at once, terrified that I'd lose it again. Stretching round as far as I could go, I pressed my heels into the wide slat mesh of the dais and pulled.

The rod shifted. The room echoed with the noise it made, the grind of metal on metal. I could see now it was ridged, a long screw or a piece of armature from inside a building, and this meant it was more firmly snagged on the rubbish pile than I'd hoped. I risked another pull; it moved again, but as it moved a small rockfall of trash clattered down around it. It shifted toward me, straighter than before. Cursing, I relaxed my grip on the blanket, but the loop was already slipping up the shaft toward me. If I pulled it again, there was every chance it would slip right off the end; if I didn't pull, then what the hell was I doing with it anyway?

Just another few inches, I thought. If I can just get it to move another few inches closer, I might be able to grab it with my feet or push it back to the right and hook it again and this time really get some purchase on it and…the blanket slipped from the rod and went limp in my hand.

'God damn you mother fuckin' piece of shit!' The room threw my words back at me, bouncing them off the flying horse holocaust and the love hearts graffitied on the walls. I let myself collapse onto the remaining blankets, lay on my back and closed my eyes.

I was here because of Red. Which must mean whoever had taken me, had been watching him. It made a kind of sense. If he was the target, for whatever reason, if the girl and whoever wanted something from him, they'd got to me to get to him, and whatever they were after. If they'd been watching Red, they might have seen us argue, seen us kiss.

'I said he was trouble,' I told the room, knowing Margarita was listening. I ran my hand over the remaining blanket, then sat up.

It was growing dark. The light that had been washing pale grey into the room, was fading. There's nothing in the dark which isn't there in the daylight I told myself, but then seeing what was here in the daylight, that didn't help a lot.

Where the hell was this place anyway, what was it? A fairground, abandoned and all gone to shit. How far from Carillon and the city was I? What light remained showed me the walls and the odd way they'd been painted before the graffiti, pale above and darker below. No, it wasn't paint; it was a tide mark running at the same height all around the room. It had been in a flood, in the flood – it had been washed out when Hurricane Katrina had hit, and no one had touched it since. It still stank of river water, faint perhaps but there nonetheless. I glanced over at the horses and it seemed more obvious still looking at them, each with their long socks of

 **BROKEN PONIES**

grey over their white painted fetlocks. Well, I was still in the state which, I supposed, was something.

Now I'd stopped my futile fishing attempts, the sweat I'd worked up had cooled on my skin and my toes and fingers were numb. I pulled up one of the blankets and wrapped it around myself – God bless Uncle Sam, but it was warm, good old army issue.

Army issue.

I thought of the wedding ring in the ashtray – who'd choose army issue blankets? Sure, you could pick them up in a five and dime anyway, but people go with what they know. I closed my eyes, pressed the fabric to my nose and breathed in its utilitarian scent.

When I'd been alone in the shack with Red in a state of amnesia, I'd had a vision. Sat with him, both a stranger and yet not, warmed with bourbon on top of a head injury and an empty stomach, the world had slowed down in the dark, flickering at the edges. I'd seen what he'd remembered, or I thought I had – that dark, clanging space of iron bars and locked doors, and the fear that had marched behind him, snapping at his heels. I'd heard the relentless beat of the clock as the time had ticked out for him and for the man he'd lost to the desert. One of his men, one of his boys – his boy; taken on patrol only to be seen again on the screen of a TV, shredded with static as he was made to kneel. Red had killed to find him, had pushed and pushed, desperate to save this boy above all others, but he hadn't saved him. He'd seen the boy beheaded, and I'd seen his anguish through the flicker and shadow play of that night.

Or I thought I had. Afterwards, in the months in Vegas alone in my white room, I'd told myself that it was not a vision, but the research I'd done on Red before the shack, breaking through in place of my memory. Before I'd set him up, I'd spent hours trawling through veteran's chat sites and support groups and fundraising pages, collecting their stories like some ghoulish family researcher.

I told myself that I built this vision out of these scraps, and of what Lisa had told me of it in her emails, all knitted together around the few things Red had said. It had been a convincing argument, until it had started happening again. Not with Red, but with other people - with men like Tiki man.

It's not a vision, I told myself. It's not mystical; it's instinct. It's shutting off the part of your mind that thinks and letting the part of my mind that sees the connections come out to play, and that's Margarita. It's joining the dots that other people miss; it's a skill.

'Okay,' I said. 'Show me – come on. I'm in this scary-ass trash heap of a place, if you're gonna have a vision, then seriously, could you get any better? What do you need, you need me to be drunk or something, you need me to be half out of my mind? Well, I'm pretty much most of the way there - there's got to be something I saw, some hint of who's behind all this?'

Silence. The flood wrecked place closed in on me in shadow and silt, its rough edges smoothed by twilight easing into black. The clown's heads faded to cracked pearls in the gloom and the horses shied away from me into darkness, bowing their heads and backing away.

'It don't work like that,' Margarita said at last.

'Well make it work,' I demanded. 'There's something behind all this, I know I've seen it, I've seen something that might figure out all this crazy shit - so you just make it work, goddamn it.'

'I can't,' she said. She wasn't laughing at me anymore. 'Just go with it.'

'Go with it? That's easy for you to say, you aren't the one handcuffed to the floor!' I snapped, which was stupid, but I wasn't in the mood to be reasonable. 'Alright, you don't get out of here unless I do too, so you better make with the voodoo magic, whoever or whatever you are!'

'I'm you!' she hissed. 'Don't you get that? I'm you, I'm the part of you that you don't wanna face up to. You' spent the whole last year livin' in your clean white box, an' snooping 'bout memorials and dead ends, as so you don't gotta look the real world in the face, just so as you don't gotta own me. You ain't gonna see what you need to see, until you're me, or I'm you, or whatever the fuck way round it is, and that ain't gonna happen till you figure you is me, y'dumb bitch!'

'No,' I said, yanking my wrist against the handcuffs in fury. 'You're not me, you're just some psychosis that comes to the surface when I'm on edge and—'

Light blazed through the blind windows. The world jumped with grotesque shapes, their shadows dancing over the graffitied walls. Someone was coming.

'Who am I meant to be?' I hissed in desperation at the darkness. If I knew the connection, if I knew who wanted me here and why, then I'd know how they expected to find me. Did they just think I was Red's long-lost girlfriend, or a date, or his hairdresser – just how scared should I be right now?

Footsteps struck the ground, shoes scraping on gravel, quick march.

Light burned my eyes.

Should I cry out, did they expect me to cry out? Just who the hell have they kidnapped, Margarita, you or me?

'Hey,' a man's voice said from behind the light. 'You gonna do just what I says now. Or I'm gonna shoot you.' Oh, so it was her, then.

CHAPTER THIRTEEN

'DID Y'ALL HEAR ME?' I didn't answer. The flashlight blanked out my world as he shone it in my eyes again. 'Hey?'

'Go fuck yourself,' I muttered as I heard him move closer, because anything was better than the sob of panic which was building in my throat. I tried to look, but the beam was full in my face. I closed my eyes, colors tracing across my eyelids.

'You goin' do what I say, understand?' Un'er stand?'

'Yes!' I snapped. 'I understand, just get the fuckin' light outa' my face, will you?' He lowered the light. I felt its heat diminish, then blinked at him.

'You wanna make it hard on you'self, just you go ahead,' he said. I could make out the shape of him, lean, lanky, nothing but shadow and indistinct lines.

'What the hell is this?' I said, fighting not to raise my voice in case my panic bubbled to the surface. 'What the hell am I–'

'Hush up –' The flash light burned across my vision again. I raised my unshackled hand. When the light was lowered this time, he'd stepped closer, and something of his face swam into view.

'Alright,' I said. I guessed him to be about six foot or more, angular and long limbed; everything else obscured by darkness.

'I'm goin' give you the keys to them cuffs,' he said. 'You goin' open them, an' ...' He faltered, 'an' ... don't try nothin'.'

'Okay,' I said, deciding against dumb innocence at the prospect of getting my hand free at last. He raised his gun, its snub nose pointed directly at me.

'If needs be, I'm goin' carry you,' he said. 'You dick me around, I'm goin' shoot you in the leg.' The keys hit the army blanket to my side. I looked at them, then back at him.

'Can I have some light?' I asked. 'Or does that count as talking?'

He moved the beam to where my hand was chained to the floor, not so fast that I didn't catch a glimpse of his grin. Oh, he was loving this alright, dressed up and playing at prison guard, conducting his own Stanford experiment at my expense. I picked up the key and worked it against the handcuff, missing the lock, scratching at it.

'Open it up,' he said after I let the key slip and made out I'd nearly dropped it.

'I can't see what I'm doing,' I said.

'Get on with it –' he took a step closer to the edge of the dais.

'I'm trying,' I said, moving so that my shoulder obscured what I was doing with the key. I turned away, then I heard the click of the safety at the back of my head.

'You wanna try a bit harder?' he said. I wasn't sure if he'd guessed I was bluffing or was just trying to concentrate my mind. I could hear the slight rasp of his breathing and smell the sweat on him, the odour of dank fabric. I fit the key in the lock and the cuffs dropped open.

I sat back from him, keeping the blanket around my shoulders and massaging my wrist where the metal had chafed it raw. He was younger than I'd thought he'd be, sharp cornered and rat-faced.

'Ge'down,' he said.

'Can I have my shoes back?'

'Ge'down now!' The light blazed in my eyes.

'Okay, I got it!' I snapped.

I moved toward the edge of the carousel, keeping the blanket around myself. He stepped back as I paused at the void.

'You really gonna make me walk on all that crap?' He flicked the gun, then lowered the beam of light to show me the floor. I eased myself onto the mess of sharp edges and busted up concrete, the clown heads leering up at me. He stepped to one side, letting me draw level with him, and pushed his tongue into the side of his mouth before he spoke.

'Don't take this personal,' he said. Then he raised the gun. 'Hands on you' head.'

His torch threw my shadow ahead of me, so it rippled over the ground. They'd known what they were doing by removing my sneakers. The ground was rough and my progress painful; I was going to find it hard to run anywhere. Added to that, it drew the line between us more concisely than the gun at my side – he walked with a slow, confident stride easily keeping up with my submissive, barefoot creep. Despite the blanket, I was shivering as the damp gnawed at my hands and feet, inching toward the heart of me. His footsteps echoed as we crossed the wooden planks that had been laid on the floor, then the boom went dull and we were back on solid ground again, my toes feeling wet earth and gravel.

Outside the carousel room was a path. Night had fallen, and though I strained to make sense of what was ahead of us, I could only see jagged shapes and half-formed shadows dancing away from the light. There might have been buildings close to us, passing like great whales, invisible and massive, or there might have been nothing but a vertiginous drop. I paused, my breath billowing in the torchlight, white ink in black water.

'Keep goin',' he said.

'Where?' He came up behind me and thrust the flash light against my shoulder. I flinched, but he pressed the barrel of the gun into the small of my back.

'Now y'all get see what you's treadin' in, s'all,' he said. I could smell him, sweat, cigarettes, damp and coffee, and feel the breath in him as his chest heaved in and out. I knew that smell; he was the one who'd taken me at the car crash. I pinched the inside of my cheek between my teeth as the memory of the panic I'd felt flared up in me, then died away. He was breathing hard, too hard for someone completely in control, or who knew entirely what he was doing.

We turned left, him walking a pace behind me, dawdling his stride so as not to tread on my feet. The flashlight painted shapes for me, looming up either side of us in crazy Mondrian splashes of green and pink, dirtied by storm and night. The world was now alive with sound in contrast to the eerie scufflings of the carousel room, the crack and snap of trees, the wet wind as it tumbled unseen fragments before it. I could hear the rustle of things scurrying away from our approach, the call of birds and a rhythmic creak-creak pulse, as something swung back and forth in the dark, working rusted hinges. A face sprang out at me; I started at its twisted, skeletal smile, until the flashlight showed me it was just painted on a wall, jester's hat and all.

'Crazy shit ... right?' the man said beside me. Stupid as it might sound, I'd half-forgotten he was there, or why he was there, or that he was seeing all this too. I glanced at him and his face hardened, as if I'd caught him out. He pressed on my shoulder, urging me forwards, but I had the sense he was pleased with this place and just how strange it was.

'House proud,' Margarita whispered. 'An' he wants to show you.'

The flashlight beam caught the edge of a building; when we rounded its corner, I saw a square of light on the ground, faint and yellow, its edges distorted by scattered debris. There was a drift of plastic forks washed up against the edge of the wall, clutched together like bleached white finger bones, then a slice of light cut through the dark. A door, opening.

The man moved away from me to push me ahead, and I stumbled into a room lit by storm lanterns, and heavy with the smell of propane gas, smoke and damp. It was a cafe, or it had been once – the stems of tables were still anchored to the floor, tops missing and transformed into a forest of steel mushrooms. There was a locker washed up amongst them, lying at the edge of the circle of light; deep green metal sprayed over with white letters, spelling the word bitch. The walls of the place were hung with wet looking images of food, grinning cheese burgers and curly fries stained grey below the water line. In the far corner, on the other side of the light, was a flock of swan boats washed up and marooned, their necks clustered into inverted question marks. Over the counter with its empty salad bar and blackened surfaces, was part of a word, a name, which had once been picked out in neon letters. Some remained as dead glass tubes, but the rest had ghosted into rust stains on the peeling paint, filling in the blanks to spell out Carnival Kings.

The woman from the car, still in her plaid and jeans but now with a fleece jacket over the top, got up as we entered, pushing back the foldout chair she was sitting on. There was someone else too, sitting around the lanterns as if they were at a camp fire. He rose as she did, solid, square and folding his arms across his chest as he looked at me.

'Well, hey there,' he said. 'Nice to see you, darlin'. Hope you ain't got a sore head or nothin'.'

'So,' the woman said, approaching me with her hand on her collarbone. 'That there's who brung you's, Skeet' – names, not

good, names were not good at all – 'an' I'm Molly, and this here,' she glanced at the big man behind her, 'this here's Ethan. Just so's you know.' She ducked her head a little, as if we were being introduced at a whole other type of gathering. I risked lowering my hands.

'Okay, Molly, can you tell me what's goin' on here?'

'Oh, shoot, don't you worry 'bout that right now.' She took out her cellphone. 'Now, just you hold on.' Skeet thrust his gun into his pants, switched off the flashlight and threw it onto one of the few remaining tables that had its top.

'Skeet,' Ethan said with a nod of his head. Skeet looked at me, his cowlick fringe falling over his forehead.

'Don't make this hard on you'self.' He was going to get hold of me again. I felt the rush of adrenaline hit me before he grabbed for me. I got away from him, but he came after me, face impassive. I stumbled, got my balance and hit out, but he knocked my blow aside and caught my arm, twisting me round. I dug him hard as I could in the side with my elbow and heard him catch his breath.

'What's up with you, bro?' Ethan shouted. 'You need me t'give you a hand?'

'I got it,' Skeet said. He threw his arm across me, then pulled me against him, as he'd done when he'd snatched me on the road.

'Easy,' he hissed, as if he only meant me to hear him. 'Fuck's sake, make it easy on you'self!' He locked my arms above my head, crucifying me in his embrace as Molly advanced. I kicked out at her, but she was laughing, holding her cell up to me as its square of light blazed blue-white.

'Shoot, you're all heart, ain't you,' Ethan said, bigger, thicker set than his brother, if they were brothers. 'You wanna do it, darlin'?'

'Just a moment,' Molly said, not looking up from her phone.

'Get the fuck away from me!' I demanded. Ethan laughed, clapping his hands together.

'Oh, for Christ's sake, this phone!' Molly said. 'Now look what it made go'n say, Lord beg my pardon!' She thrust the phone at Ethan. 'Here, tell me when you's ready!'

I bucked against Skeet again, then made myself go limp, dragging on his embrace in the hope that my weight would pull me free. He staggered, then got control of me, heaving me back up the few inches I'd won.

'Quit it,' he said. 'You better.'

'Okay,' Ethan said, squinting at the phone. 'Daddy's set.'

Molly slapped me across the mouth with the back of her hand. The blow shook my teeth in my head; pain exploded and sang in my ears. As stars blurred my vision, the salt taste of blood flooded into my mouth.

Ethan let out a whoop of delight.

'Did you get that?' Molly asked. 'Did ya?'

'Sure did,' he said. 'All the way back!'

'You fuckin' bitch!' I spat, gulping back the tears that burned behind my eyes. Dear God, I begged, please don't let me cry, don't let me cry!

'Let me see,' Molly said, crowding to the phone. 'There - hit play back ... hell's teeth but I think I did me some damage with that one too!'

'I hope you broke your fuckin' hand,' I muttered.

'You know what?' she said, tilting her head to the side to squint up at me. 'Why don't we just make sure we got that?'

'I'm gonna fuckin' kill her,' Margarita said, as Molly hit me again.

CHAPTER FOURTEEN

I SAGGED AGAINST SKEET, my head ringing, spittle and blood bubbling over my lips as I fought to get my breath again.

'I got you,' he said.

'Thanks for that,' I muttered. Molly's second blow wasn't as hard as her first, but it was enough and hell, she hadn't even pressed the video button on the phone. All that pain for nothing.

'I think we got that,' Ethan said. 'Hold her up, Skeet.' Skeet did as he was told, and Ethan stepped forward.

'Get the fuck away,' I said, through the swelling of my lip and the bloody taste in my mouth, but he got hold of my head, hands over my ears and made me look at him. Close up, I saw he was older than Skeet, older than I was; already softening at the jaw with his hair receding. Ten years from now he'd be running to middle-aged, fat belly hanging over low slung jeans and chin loosening into his neck. He peered at me, pork roast before the pan, pallid and fleshy. What light there was caught on the cross he wore at his neck, simple, silver, made white against his dirty pink skin.

'You' be alright,' he said. 'You got your teeth–' which was more than he did. One was missing beside his front canine and there was a flash of grey where more were held in place by metal fretwork. Prison smile, I thought, the cheapest solution to the problem when the American taxpayer is paying.

He got up and went over to Molly. They stared at the phone, and I heard myself again - you fuckin' bitch!

'We got it,' Molly said, nodding. Then they looked over at me.

'Come on,' Ethan said.

'You're gonna love this,' Molly said, screwing herself up with excitement, almost dancing on the spot.

Ethan strode over to the grey-green locker. He flung its door open, took hold of what would have been the upper end and dragged it across the floor toward us. It screamed against the broken tiles, scattering spray cans in its wake. He let it go, then reached inside, rattling out a length of chain as he stood up.

'This be alright,' Skeet said to me. 'If you don't fuss none.' I twisted my head to look up at him, then back at the locker, as what they intended hit me harder than even Molly had.

'No,' I said, fighting against Skeet, lashing out with my feet and kicking at his shins.

'Well, you just don't learn, do you?' Ethan laughed. 'Don't you get all het up now, this ain't gonna be that bad.'

'Keep goin',' Molly laughed, dancing in attendance with her phone as Skeet hefted me up and advanced on the locker. 'You look real convincing, darlin'!'

'We're goin' put you in it,' Ethan said. 'Or, you can lie down and get in it you'self. Hell, I don't mind either way, I like it when they put up a fight!'

'Get her legs!' Skeet said, out of breath, struggling to hold me. I thrashed again, feeling his grip on me loosen.

'We only need you alive,' Molly said. 'Don't bother us none if we hurt you.' I couldn't, I couldn't let myself get put into that thing. What the hell were they going to do with it, throw it into the nearest river and watch it sink? I could feel the pressure of the water running through the whole state around me, as if it

 **BROKEN PONIES**

were the outlet pipe for the world and I was going to drain away with it.

'Please! You don't have to do this!'

'Thing is, we kinda do ...' Ethan stepped over the locker and grabbed for me, as I got my arm free and scratched at Skeet's face.

'God damn!' he exclaimed, snatching at me, his arm hard across my chest. 'Easy, I said easy!' Ethan let out another whoop of delight as I kicked him, as he batted my foot away and then got hold of me – first one ankle, then the other.

The two of them carried me over to the locker, strung out between them, Molly recording everything.

'I'll fuckin' kill you!' I yelled. Fear stabbed through me as the two men raised me above the locker, a dark rectangle below me, deep as forever. I twisted and bucked between them, then gave way to a scream of defiance as they slung me inside. There was a deafening clang, and the world went black.

'Let me out you fuckers!' I screamed when I could breathe again, hammering on the inside of the door with my fists. The chain rattled through the handle on the front, the noise echoing around my metal prison. They hammered back, the sound agonising as it boomed around me. I twisted about, trying to turn onto my side, but there wasn't enough room - there wasn't enough room for me to move. Not this, not small spaces!

'Just breathe –'

I slammed my hands against the door, the awful, suffocating pressure of it heavy as if it were a slab of stone on my chest.

'Breathe–' It was Margarita inside me again, a spark in the darkness. 'Don't do nothin',' she said, low, comforting, her voice something like Lisa's, like it had been when we were children. 'You don't got to worry, you don't got to go crazy here. You ain't alone, you're with me.'

'I am alone,' I told her, my voice small and from a hundred years back inside myself. I closed my eyes and she was with me, took hold of me.

'No you ain't, doll.'

I am under the bed, in the crawl space. There is a spider working its way along the skirting board. I'm not scared of spiders. It takes an elegant stride over a knot in the carpet, then pauses to sense the way forward with its feet, testing the path as if looking for traps. Lisa has gone. I have watched her from our bedroom window, only it isn't our bedroom anymore, it's just mine.

'I don't want to be alone,' I'd said, winding my fingers through the fringe of the shawl Momma kept over the chair in her room. Momma had been crying.

'You won't be alone,' she said. She wanted to hold me; I knew that she ached to do it but, if she did, she'd break apart into a thousand pieces. 'It's for Lisa, she'll be happier there, she'll be ...' but she didn't finish.

The spider sets off again, striding over the carpet with purpose, as if it's seen a friend in a crowd.

I'd been under the bed when I'd seen them, or heard them - Mom and Dad - after Lisa had gone. They were outside our room caught in the corridor, Mom's footsteps first, then his reaching her and he taking hold of her hand, and she pulling from his grasp.

'I've made my decision,' she said. 'She's not coming back, you understand me? You can make friends,' she said later, not knowing I knew what she'd said. 'Proper friends, at school. I know you're going to miss her, but maybe she'll be back for vacation.' Then she'd said it again, not as if she was talking to me but to herself, making it true by saying it out loud. 'You can make friends.'

 BROKEN PONIES

'What's your name?' I ask the spider. But it isn't the one who answers.

The chain rattled and clanged again. I jerked my eyes open only to screw them up again, as light burst in on me with the squeal of the hinges. Ethan leaned over me, hand extended to help me out.

'Said it didn't need to be so hard,' he said.

'Be angry,' Margarita told me.

'Get out of my fucking way.' I heaved myself from the cabinet, swatting his hand away.

'Whoa, I just tryin' to help here–' I pushed past him, getting my back against the wall before I faced the three of them.

'What the fuck was all that about, you just tryin' it for size?'

Molly looked at Ethan, who laughed and clapped his hands together.

'Well hell, we gotta make it look realistic,' he said. 'Sure, ain't that the whole point?' He sounded petulant, as if I really ought to have known this. Molly had been filming the whole time, just as Ethan had filmed her hitting me. God love modern technology – pay-as-you-go cell phone, harder to trace than a ransom note, less messy than a pinkie finger in a box. When it was all over with, a million hits on YouTube as a consolation prize. My legs decided they'd had enough of all this and I sank to the ground, back to the corner of the room.

Molly went and fetched something from the kit clustered around the storm lanterns.

'Like I said –' Ethan said, half in a yawn, stretching his arms up above his head. 'Like I said,' he let his arms drop again and focused on me. 'We got a whole lot of shit to get through ... you don't gotta take it personal or nothin',' just as Skeet had said before.

'Yeah,' I said. 'I'll try not to.'

'There we go,' Molly said, 'that's a can-do attitude!' She held my cell phone out to me. 'We're goin' need his phone number.'

'Who's?' I said. 'I don't know who you think you're gonna call, because if this is about money, I don't have any. I just work security in Vegas, and I came down here to sort out something for my sister. I don't know what this shit is, but there's nobody who's gonna pay up for me.' Molly was smiling, the way you do when you're waiting for a three-year-old to finish speaking.

'All we want is to unlock your cell,' she said. 'You got five missed calls from him, and three from your answering service. We just wanna let him know you's alright, that's all. What's the code?'

I put my hand over my eyes and let my head drop forwards for a moment. Well, darlin', I thought, your timing's pretty immaculate too, isn't it? If I'd thought I could bluff them that I was nothing more than his sister-in-law, out to secure a divorce from his estranged wife, Red had shot that one right out of the water. There it was, emblazoned on the front of my phone, 'Red' interspersed with 'voicemail'. I imagined him ringing the first time, just a little ego-bruised I hadn't rung him by the time he might estimate I'd find a hotel and check in. Then again, perhaps assuming I'd been in the shower the first time, then again; angry, hurt and more than a little humiliated, sure I was playing games with him. By the fifth time, was he worried? Starting to be concerned about where the hell I was? Come to that, was anyone else?

'The code,' Molly said again. 'The one goin' unlock your phone? I mean, we can hit you again if we gotta, but that seems like a whole heap of unnecessary, don't it? I'm sure you wanna get this over with, probably a whole lot faster even than we do.'

'I'll put it in,' I tried, but she just laughed at me.

'Now, just how stupid d'you think I am?'

'Okay ...' At least mine wasn't one, two, three, four. Molly keyed it in and the phone treacherously opened up for her.

She copied Red's number onto hers. 'Goodness me, you ain't lying - you don't got more than five numbers on here.' She glanced up at Ethan as he came and stood beside her. 'You wanna check your messages, hear what 'ole Red Rooster's gotta say for hisself?'

'Don't,' I said, before I could stop myself. Molly sniggered, and I felt my cheeks burning harder than when she'd hit me. She held the phone so that Ethan could hear also, her face a pantomime of anticipation. Behind them in the gloom, Skeet grinned then shook his head, turning his back on the others, hands jammed into his jean pockets before he went and sat down again.

'Wait ... wait. Here we go,' Ethan stooped his head to listen, the two of them close enough so that I could hear the mechanical voice on the line telling me that I had five new messages. I glared at them from the floor, feeling I was back in high school at the mercy of some snaggle-toothed head jock and his scrawny cheerleading girlfriend.

'Oh my goodness,' Molly said in mock surprise. 'He got plans for you, girl! Makes me blush just to hear it, my my! Who'd have thought old Rooster was such as dark horse?' I'm gonna fuck you back to next–'

'That's enough,' I forced myself up and made a grab for the phone. Molly snatched it away. Ethan drew his gun from his belt and levelled it at me. That at least was different; at my high school the bullies weren't often quite so heavily armed.

'Shut it off,' he said to Molly, his face serious. She did what he said, though I could see by the vicious way she ended the call, she didn't like it. You better watch out, Ethan, I thought - miss Molly's only letting you have those pants on loan.

'Well,' she said, stabbing her own phone with her thumb. 'Ole Red Roostersir's gonna get his answer, I suppose, stop him twisting in the wind 'n' wonderin' what happened to his missus. Absence do make the heart grow fonder.' Her face lit up in a smile. 'All gone.'

'He's gonna call the FBI,' I said. 'Why do you people even think he won't do that?'

''Cause if he do ...' Molly said, 'we're goin' kill you.' She said it just like that, as easy as she hit me.

'Really? You're gonna kill me, what, in Louisiana? You do know they've got the death penalty here, and they ain't above sticking it to a woman. Even if you turn it on the judge an' go all please sir, it weren't me, that big old nasty Ethan made me do it,' – well, that made him smile anyway, even Skeet laughed from his chair – 'Even if you do that, he'll be on death row before you finish, and you'll never get out again. You really gonna risk that for what, a few thousand dollars?' Because it seemed ludicrous to even suggest that I might be worth a million to anybody, even Red.

'Oh sugar,' Molly said, head on one side again. 'You his wife. He ain't gonna let nothin' happen to you, now is he? Not now you come back, n' all.'

The wind sent little scurries of dead leaves in at the door. The paraffin lamps popped and the sign outside creaked as it blew back and forth, working its rusty pulse. I went to speak, then caught the words against my tongue. They thought I was Red's wife. They thought I was Lisa.

CHAPTER FIFTEEN

'WE GOT MORE shit to do,' Ethan said. 'So you hush up and do as your told, or I'm gonna start shootin' off your pinkies.'

He turned and lumbered toward Skeet, who straightened up at his approach.

'Why am I not telling them who I am?' I silently asked Margarita.

'Because they won't believe you anyway,' she said. 'Not when they're all together, belivin' what they wanna.'

'Teach us to get our hair done,' I said, and she laughed.

'I'm not even sure how this works anymore,' she said.

'Hey–' Molly leaned in to catch my eye. 'Hey there – look, they gonna be a while, can I get you something, sugar?' She was back in hostess mode.

'I need to take a leak,' I said, without a word of lie. Molly glanced over to the doors to the left of us, and I saw they were labelled as bathrooms.

'Sure, only I got to go with you.' She flipped open her fleece jacket. 'So don't you go gettin' all uppity on me, because if I have to, I'll shoot you, same as Ethan.' Her gun was tucked against her side in a brown leather holster, a whole lot more lovingly than Ethan treated his. I could imagine her cleaning it the way other women might do their nails, everything spread out on a neat little cloth with hearts printed on it.

The bathroom was grey and water stained, carnival colors

washed over with river silt and decay. There were masquerade masks painted on the walls, their floral designs pock-marked and cracked; brass fleur-de-lys wept rust at the corners of stained mirrors. I could have done without the mirrors – I didn't need a visual reminder of why my lip hurt like hell.

'Now, don't go get all excited or nothin',' she said. 'But I'm gonna have to watch you pee. Don't wanna, but I don't want you gettin' no crazy ideas 'bout knocking me out and tryin' make a break for it.' I pushed open the nearest stall. There was a puddle of brackish water in the base of the toilet and a rising stench of bad drains.

'Fine,' I said, as I turned to face her, dropped my pants and sat down. She leaned back against the wall, propped the door open with her foot, then drew her gun. Closing one eye she aimed it somewhere above my head, at a faded poster on the wall instructing us to be careful of thieves and watch our purses.

'I 'spect you was thinking 'bout it,' she said, tilting her head and mouthing 'bang' as she sighted down her weapon. 'I would, if I were you. You're funny, ain't you? I think you're a bit like me. You ain't half as freaked out by all this as I figured you'd be.'

'You think?' There was even toilet paper, though it looked as if the roll had been soaked and then dried out years back. I got enough off it to be of use, all at gunpoint and without showing her more than I had to. Now that's decorum for you. I pulled up my pants, fastened the zip and Molly lowered her gun.

'I really thought you were gonna try and jump me,' she said.

'I figured now isn't the time,' I replied.

'You figured right.' She grinned. 'This place's pretty much miles from anywhere. Miles an' miles. You get out? Hell, I don't know exactly where you'd run to anyhow, not as we couldn't find you. You been away, ain't you?' When she saw the flicker of reaction on my face, she grinned. 'Oh, we know all 'bout you. How livin'

here didn't suit you none, so you took off. People like you never think as us little folks know what you're up to, but that's just where you're wrong. Bet you wish you never came back though.' She put the gun in its holster. I took a step toward her, but she didn't move. I had a good few inches on her, but she was wiry as hell, with the sort of hard, muscular strength that was deceptive.

'You goin' try hit me?' she asked. 'I mean, you could, but you'd have to knock me out cold. You'd never fit through the windows, on account of they're bein' real small. Don't know what you'd do after you put me down, even if you managed it.'

'I think I could,' I said. 'But you're right. I couldn't get past Ethan and Skeet out there. Not right now. I was wondering though ...'

'Yeah, darlin', what you wonderin'?'

'Just which one of them are you fuckin', or are they just not that into you?' Her face crumpled into a scowl. I wasn't sure which nerve I'd touched, but I'd got a rise out of her.

'Like I said, I don't wanna kill you, but that don't mean I won't hurt you. I ain't got no problem with that, bitch, none whatsoever.' She raised her gun again and indicated that I was to leave the stall. When I stepped to the door she didn't move. I eased out past her, pressing my back against the door frame. When our faces were inches apart, she barked - woof- and laughed as I jumped.

'Watch it, lil' doggy,' she said. 'I bite.'

I pushed the washroom door open. As Molly shoved me into the room, I saw Skeet and Ethan had manhandled the green locker up onto its end and dragged it closer to the entrance. In the yellow glow of the lanterns, the place looked more external than interior, a camp fire in the forest. The shadows of the broken tables stretched across the floor, then grew up the walls toward the ceiling, a moonless sky without stars or sanctuary. Ethan nodded to Molly.

'Now,' she said, letting the washroom door clang shut behind us. 'We're almost through. Then we'll get you something to eat and drink, 'n' you can get some sleep. You'd like that, wouldn't you?' I took a step away from her. 'It ain't much, darlin',' she said, slotting her gun back into its holster. 'All you gotta do is take off them clothes.'

My hair band had come loose, and my ponytail was half pulled out. I dragged the band free, figuring it was going that way anyway. I let my hand drop to my side then pulled back my shoulders.

'How much have you asked him for?'

'What you care?' Molly said, scowling. 'We ain't got time for that now.'

'Your clothes,' Ethan said. Skeet went to their kit bags, picked one up and brought it over. He held it out to me. When I didn't take it, he dropped it at my feet and shrugged himself away. Half turned away, he fished in his pants pocket and drew out a small knife, unfolded the blade and began to clean his fingernails. 'Now, you's a big girl. Don't say Daddy's gonna have to undress you?'

I looked at the three of them, Ethan with his arms folded across his chest, Molly with her thumbs jammed in her dress pockets and Skeet, two steps behind, pretending this was nothing to do with him. The wind was blowing through the windows, rattling the roof, rain 'plink-plinked' into the corners of the room. A smile spread across my lips.

'Suppose you got to hand it to those redneck mother fuckers,' Margarita said. 'That's pretty clever.'

'What you laughing for?' Molly asked.

'You don't look nothing like me,' I said. 'The moment he opens up that box, he's gonna know it's not me.'

Ethan glanced at Molly and said, 'What you gon' 'n said?' She ignored him.

'That don't matter,' she said. 'Only needs a moment.'

She was right, of course. They'd sent Red the video of Molly hitting me, now they'd sent him the one of Ethan and Skeet bundling me into the locker. If it were me, which it was once after all, I'd send him to a drop off point next with the money, observing him all the way, making sure he really was alone. Then I'd give him directions to find the locker, once I'd secured the money. Perhaps he'd make the logical assumption that he was being sent in the opposite direction from the kidnappers, but even if he had his doubts, he'd be too distracted when he saw the locker on the roadside, the word 'bitch' sprayed on the side. He'd be armed, of course, even if they told him not to be, but you need two hands to open a padlock and, desperate to make sure I was alright, he'd put his gun away to do it. When the chain came free and he wrenched open the door, for a second he'd see what he was hoping to see – me, in the clothes I'd been wearing in the video. Only it would be Molly, with her gun. Which meant this wasn't about the money.

'It was gonna be Ethan,' Molly said, as if she knew what I was thinking. 'We been watching the house, seein' when we could get a crack at 'ole Papa Levine.'

'But he always has his driver, I suppose?'

'Sure does,' Ethan said. 'But then you came home, an' ...' he grinned. 'Well, you did us a favor.' Ethan pointed at me. 'You ... you just get on now. Do what we ask, an' you're getting closer to this bein' over, y'understand?'

I nearly told them, nearly blurted out that I wasn't Red's wife and that they'd got it all wrong, just in case they might think I was of no use to them, but I didn't. They'd heard his messages, found his name on my phone – perhaps he'd even replied to them already. It didn't matter anymore who I was; I was useful.

'No.' I dug my hands into the pockets of my jacket. Ethan took a step closer, the trace of humor that had been playing over his face drained away.

'Daddy says take off them clothes. That's an order.'

Molly went to speak, but I cut across her. 'Orders, Ethan? Where'd you learn them? Say, were you actually in the army, or did you just watch a whole lot of TV and, like, pretend?'

The lines of his frown were back, drawing his face into a scowl. 'Prisoner will do as instructed,' he said, coming closer, raising his voice.

'Whose orders?' I asked.

'We don't need you alive no more,' Molly began. 'We got all we need from you and don't you–'

'Prisoner will do as instructed!' Ethan barked. I could feel the fury in Molly even from behind Ethan, could sense her bristling at being interrupted.

'You the big man here, are you, Ethan?' I pulled the zip down on my fleece, not dropping my gaze for a second. The air chilled my skin as my arms came free of the sleeves. 'You callin' the shots?' I let the fleece fall to the floor.

'Well, look at that. Seems as if I am,' he said. 'You ain't so full of you'self now, are you? Take off the shirt.'

'You heard him, bitch,' Molly said at his elbow. 'Bitch goin' do it – you gonna make her do it, Daddy!' He didn't look at her. Neither did I.

'This all your idea? All this clever stuff, you worked it all out by yourself?' I gripped the hem of my t-shirt and pulled it up over my head. The pendant Johnny had given me snagged on the neck and thudded against my collarbone. 'Thought this all out, did you, Ethan? Or you just followin' orders? Because that really matters, doesn't it, who's behind all this? You, or–'

'Shut your mouth,' he said.

'He gonna shut it for you, bit–'

'Molly, go get the collar,' Ethan snapped, his hand flinching at his side. She took a step back, glaring at me more than him. I couldn't decide if she just wasn't used to him speaking to her like that, or that she didn't want to leave us alone.

'Push it,' Margarita said. 'You've pissed her off, keep goin'.'

'Come on, Ethan,' I said, keeping my voice low, intimate, making Molly strain to hear. 'Where you gettin' your orders from? 'Cause if you're makin' then up, then you're in charge, aren't you? But you sound like you're not quite there, know what I mean? Come on, just between you an' me – what's this all about, Ethan?'

Molly bit her lip. 'Ethan–'

'Go fetch it,' Ethan said.

'Chain of command, Ethan,' I said. 'Who's in charge, Daddy?'

'Go get the fuckin' collar, Molly!' Ethan turned on her and she jumped, her cheeks blazing. Ethan drew the gun from his belt and pressed its barrel to my cheek. Panic burned through me, the muscles in the back of my neck and shoulders alive with fear, but Margarita never let me go, not for a second.

'Now, you gonna do what Daddy say, bitch. Take off your pants an' don't give me no back chat. I swear, I'm goin' kill you an' fuck your dead eye socket if you don't.'

'Don't you have a way with words?' I said.

I didn't break my gaze. Neither did he. I unfastened the button on my jeans and pulled down the zip. The gun on my face was cold, hard – a metallic thumb print. My heart crashed against the wall of my chest, my hands shook as I eased the jeans over my hips. I made myself look past Ethan, trying not to meet his gaze and not break it at the same time, and saw Skeet move toward Molly and touch her arm.

'Do it,' Ethan demanded. In the gloom behind him, the storm lantern light lit the edge of Skeet's arm as he touched Molly, as she looked at him, as she shook her head. Skeet dropped his hand. I refocused on Ethan.

'I gotta bend down now,' I said. 'You alright with that, Ethan?'

'That's better,' he said. He moved the gun back an inch and I slipped my jeans off. I knew Molly was somewhere over by their kit, heard her come scampering back to his side. I straightened up, his gun still in my face.

'I got it,' Molly said. I could feel the hate coming off her like heat off sunburn, but I wasn't sure which one of us she hated the most. 'Ethan, I got the collar. Ethan, I got it!' In the dark behind her, Skeet watched us all.

If he does it, I thought, if he touches me, it doesn't mean a thing. It's no worse than being hit in the face or shot, and I've already done both already and lived.

'Don't think about it,' Margarita said.

'Now look at that,' Ethan said, the words slow and thick in his mouth. 'You's all undone, ain't you?' Don't think about it!

There was a Greek club at my high school, attended by a weird bunch, the sort that made me look popular. Even the Latin club looked down on them, but they were hardly on the A-list either. I hung out with one of them for a while, a boy I kind of dated. I let him get a little closer than most, though not so close that I caught anything, other than a few Latin phrases. He was known to mutter them at moments of teenage angst, and when he tried to get his hand under my shirt. He taught me a few more the day I finally let him. Looking at Ethan, who I guessed had never been near anything so Catholic as a Latin phrase book, I felt laughter bubble up inside me at the memory of those words. Well, it was worth a try. Words are powerful things, superstitions doubly so. I formed my fingers into devil horns, index and little finger up, middle fingers held down by my thumb.

'Di immortales virtutem approbare, non adhibere deben ...' I let the words whisper through my smile. 'You heard me, Ethan?'

'What you say?' He lowered his weapon. 'What you grinnin' for?'

'Dabit deus his quoque finem ... you sure you know what you're doin' Ethan?'

'Well you're the one stood in your panties,' he said.

'You better be careful,' I said. 'Least the devil know your name, Ethan.' There was a hint of cinnamon in my voice.

He took a step back and tilted his head to the side, and I saw the nerve jump in his jaw. He was looking at me as if he ought to, because I was nearly naked and he'd made me strip at the point of his gun, but there was something unconvincing in his gaze.

I let the stupid Latin phrase touch my lips again, making no sound at all. The wind was getting up outside, hissing and breathing through the place, sending debris scuttling into the corners of the room. The rain was coming in waves, easing off and then coming again, harder, heavier. Ethan looked away.

Just for an instant, but he blinked first. I was trembling, as much from the cold as the fear and relief that the gun was not in my face, but I forced myself to stare at him. I pushed everything from my mind, apart from the faint consolation of remembering that today was one of the rare days I was wearing matching underwear.

'You goin' put this on now,' Ethan said, but there was something different in his tone, quieter. Molly held out a collar to him, black leather, the kind you see advertised either for teenaged goths or middle-aged swingers, a D-ring on the front locked into a length of chain.

'I'm gonna get dressed first,' I said. 'If that's alright.'

'Do it,' Ethan said. 'You ain't my type, anyhow.'

CHAPTER SIXTEEN

ETHAN STEPPED ASIDE, taking both the gun and Molly with him. I dropped to the floor and began to scrabble through the kit bag, trying to listen to what they were saying, my fingers clumsy.

'He didn't do nothing,' Margarita told me. 'An' you made him nearly shit himself - you're alright, just hang onto that. You're alive.'

Ethan was telling Molly off in a hushed voice, angry but trying not to let me hear - something about her not doing what he'd asked, about her showing him up. He wasn't used to this command thing, Ethan, not when it came down to it. Molly was livid, even with the volume turned down; she snapped something back at him and he shut up as if he'd choked on a fly. Then he said something to make her laugh, and she relented and let him kiss her. Skeet watched them, then took his seat by the lantern and turned his back.

Ethan took the collar from Molly and strode back over to me, just as I'd finished with the army issue track pants and was pulling on the ribbed, khaki vest. He threw the collar down onto the empty kit bag.

'That entirely necessary?' I asked.

'Just put it on,' he said. 'Or I'll let Molly do it. That right, darlin'?'

'Just give the word, sugar,' she said. I picked it up.

The tongue of the belt fitted over the D-ring. When it was on, it could be locked in place, and without the key, hacksaw, mirror and a whole lot of time and patience, it was not going to come free. The leather would be easier to cut, but even that would need a substantial piece of kit. Damn it, but I couldn't see a way not to comply, not one that wouldn't involve being hurt.

I fitted the leather strap around my neck and closed the buckle. I left it as loose as I dared, though I knew I still wouldn't be able to get my head through.

'You done?' Ethan knelt in front of me. 'Now, ain't it better when you do what you're told? Save us gettin' all up in your face. Hell, that looks kinda right on you, know what I mean? Sorta suits you.' He took hold of my arm and pulled me up with him.

'See, that weren't so bad,' Molly said brightly. 'All you gotta do is sit tight and shut up, an' this will be nothin' but a bad dream.' Ethan looked at her, his wide forehead creased into a frown. 'Oh yes,' she said. 'An' you get to sit in the duck. Won't that be jolly?'

'Come on,' Ethan said. 'You can pretend like your daddy's takin' you on vacation–' which was not an image I needed right then.

The plastic swan boats remained impassive as we approached.

'This really is just all too goddamn surreal,' I muttered, as Ethan made me step up into the nearest boat.

'Sure is real,' he said, 'hundred percent real.' I thought better of saying anything and sat down on the wooden bench that passed for a seat.

Molly approached with chain in hand. 'Now, just you hold on…' she leaned in and clipped it into a padlock through the D-ring on the collar. 'There,' she said, and bent to lock the other end into a hole in the side of the boat, where once there'd been pedals.

'Well don't you look snug,' Ethan said. 'Like a princess in a story book, what's that swan lake thing?'

'It's a ballet,' I said. 'The swans win.'

'Then you better look out, hadn't you?' he said.

It was cold shackled to the swan boat. The head of the plastic craft next to mine lowered down at me, its yellow beak faded and its once black eye cracked and mournful. It would have been funny, only it wasn't. So much for putting all this shit behind me.

'You're alive,' Margarita said.

'Thanks for reminding me.'

'Come on, bro,' Ethan called out, stretching his arms above his head.

'She gonna be alright?' Skeet asked, nodding toward me as he stood up.

'She ain't goin' nowhere,' Ethan said and turned to look at me. 'Go on, darlin', you just give that chain a good yank for me, just make ole' Skeet here happy.' I flipped him the finger. 'Now that just ain't nice,' he said. 'What you reckon, bro?' He clapped Skeet on the back. 'While we gone, you want her make you happy yankin' on something else?'

'I'll get the locker,' Skeet said.

'Oh come on, bro!' Ethan laughed. 'It's gonna be a long night, I don't mind if you wanna take a ride on that - sure, ain't we at the fairground anyways?'

Well, he's real brave, I thought. As the two of them walked toward the locker, Skeet looked back at Molly and she looked at him, though I couldn't make anything of what passed silently between them.

'Come on Skeet,' Ethan barked. They picked up the locker between them and carried it out of the restaurant, Molly going ahead with the flashlight. I saw its beam arc through the blackness outside, catching on the window frame and showing me the rain like static across the night. They must have a vehicle to transport the thing in, one bigger than the cars they'd been driving before. I fingered the padlock at my neck, testing the resolve of the hasp, but it held.

A noise roared up from outside – more lights, and with them, the chug and splutter of a reluctant engine, sounding bigger and older than anything I'd seen them in before. They could have dumped those already, and what about my car? Or should I say Ralph's car - he was going to be pissed. Though he wouldn't miss it until the day after tomorrow, so if it had been found, it would be logged, but nothing more, not if Red hadn't called the police.

Before I could speculate any further, the three of them came bounding back in, shaking the rain from their clothes.

'Hell of a night,' Molly laughed. 'Better hope it stops raining a'fore you gotta put me in that thing!' She looked over at me. 'I better go get myself dressed. Let's just hope it ain't all too big for me.'

While she was gone, Ethan sat down with Skeet, fumbled in one of the kit bags, and took out a beer. That's just what you need, I thought, alcohol on top of adrenaline and lack of sleep. And you're armed as well, great stuff!

'What you reckon to the show?' he said, looking over at me with all the subtlety of a twelfth grader. When Skeet didn't respond, he nudged him. 'Come on bro, don't be shy - she ain't bad lookin' is she? What say we take her with us when we're through, so as you don't get all lonely?'

'Never mind that,' Skeet said.

'Oh, come on, you ain't goin' faggot on me, is you?' Ethan said, as if the only true mark of a heterosexual male was rape and abduction. 'I ain't seen you with no one since 'fore I went away. You still seein' that girl with the teeth?' Now that left a whole heap to the imagination.

'I ain't seein' no one,' Skeet said.

'Older brothers are all the same, aren't they Skeet?' I said. 'You should meet mine some time, he's a real asshole.'

'No one's talking to you!' Ethan snapped. Skeet reached into his pack and passed something to him. Ethan grinned at me, got up and sauntered over, whistling between his teeth, then slapped a bread roll shiny with cling wrap on the edge of the swan boat.

'Now don't say I don't do nothin' for you,' he said.

'It's not cheese, is it?' I said. 'Because I'm, like, lactose intolerant.'

'You don't wan' it,' he said, bending to pick it up again. 'Don't have it.' I put my hand on it.

'I'll manage,' I said.

'That's my girl.' Ethan walked back over to Skeet, glancing toward the bathroom door before he sat down again. I was still trying to work out if the filling was pressed ham or squirrel, when Molly came back in, dressed in my clothes. She didn't look like me, though maybe through driving rain and darkness, if you were desperate for her to be me as you clawed open a beat-up metal locker, she might fool you. Looking at her – her being the 'me' Red had last seen, I had a stupid spike of guilt. I thought of him calling me and getting no answer, until his phone vibrated with the footage of Molly hitting me in the face, as if somehow I'd stood him up and this was all my fault.

Molly pulled up the hood of my fleece, then took out my sunglasses.

'Suit me?' she asked, as she slipped them on. 'We got them out of your car when we snatched your cell.'

'Look at you!' Ethan laughed. 'Could take you for sisters!'

'What you think?' she asked, letting him take her hand. He pulled her onto his lap and she squawked with laughter as he wrestled her into a kiss, an over-eager Labrador dog slobbering over a polecat. 'Get off me!' she laughed, and I saw how she glanced at Skeet, busy with his kit bag rooting for the world's most elusive sandwiches.

'Come on, darlin',' Ethan said. 'You gonna give Daddy sugar?' I was with Skeet on this one; I picked at the cling film on the roll, rather than watch Ethan pawing Molly.

'Ethan,' I heard her say, and looked up to see her disentangle herself. 'We got company.'

'What you gettin' all precious for?' Ethan asked, grinning as she tucked her shirt back into her jeans. My jeans. He put his bottle to his mouth and drank as if someone was going to take it from him.

'Hey,' Molly said to Skeet. 'You got one for me?'

'Sure.' He held out a sandwich, not quite looking at her.

'You goin' get me one?' Ethan asked.

'They're just in the bag,' Molly said.

'So get me one,' he demanded. Molly pulled her lips into a thin line. 'Go on, woman! Man's gonna starve to death round here.'

'They's just there, bro–' Skeet went for the bag again.

Ethan fixed on Molly. 'Come on, baby girl. Daddy's hungry.' I couldn't decide which I wanted more, her to spit in his face, or give him his sandwich on bended knee. As it was, she glared and threw one into his lap. 'That better,' he laughed. 'What you got that face for, we're all good, ain't we?' Molly continued with the face as she sat down. She unwrapped her sandwich as if she were pulling the wings off a fly.

'Hey,' Ethan leaned forward toward the other two. 'Come on, we're doin' it!' He clapped Skeet on the arm. 'Get you'self a brew, bro, come on. We goin' drink to us.'

Despite everything, Skeet smirked and pulled out two bottles from the bag. Even Molly relented and they drank, united like some grim little khaki-colored coven.

'Seems as we should be drinkin' to that, what they say ... absent friends.' Ethan looked over at me, as if I should have known who he meant. Then he asked Molly, 'He ring yet?' She shook her head.

'You checked it?'

'I'd a heard it, wouldn't I? He ain't replied yet, okay?'

'Alright woman, Jesus, just askin.' He tapped his bottle on his leg. 'Absent friends ... yeah.' He slumped back in his chair and looked at me. 'You know, I used to admire ole' Captain Levine. Straight up. Used to won'er 'bout him too, mind, seein' as what he was. You ever think 'bout that?'

'About what?' I said, as he clearly wasn't going to continue without a prompt.

'Well, he done his time, you know?' He waved his bottle. 'Was in all that ... that stuff over in Europe, Africa or whatever, then Afghanistan. You think an officer like him be sat behind a desk somewhere's before now, a lot higher than Captain. Or, maybe you don't ever think 'bout it?' he sniffed. 'He ever tell you what happened, why he got sent home all sudden like? I mean, they tried t'cover it up n'all, but he must'a said somethin'? Late at night, pillow talk,' – which he rhymed with stork – 'Didn't he never open up to you?'

'He never talked about it,' I said, deciding against explaining to him once more that I wasn't Red's wife.

'I bet he didn't,' Ethan said, grinning as if he'd won. He drank, and I shifted against the hard seat, pins and needles dancing in my feet. Skeet got up and shuffled off behind the broken counter into the depths of the kitchen, and Molly ate her sandwich.

'I bet he didn't say nothin',' Ethan said, starting up as if someone had dropped a quarter into his slot. 'I bet he never said as how he made us his ... his escape goats.'

'His what?' I couldn't help myself. Ethan focused on me.

'What, you laughin' at me?'

'No, really–'

'You laughin' at me, ain't you?' he said, almost as if we were

sharing a joke, him shaking his head. Molly looked up from staring into the lamplight but didn't speak. 'Laughin' at me,' Ethan said again. 'I got a funny story for you, you wanna hear it?'

'No,' I said, but he wasn't listening. Skeet stepped back into the ring of light and took up his seat at Ethan's side.

'Time was when I thought ole Captain Levine was the man, y'know?' He belched and went on. 'I mean, he'd been there, done his time. S'what he used to say, where we was, that was easy street for him.'

'I need the bathroom,' Molly said and got up all of a sudden, knocking over her beer bottle.

'Y'alright, baby?' Ethan asked.

'Fine.' She nodded and scurried off, boney arms folded about herself, head down.

Ethan watched her go, face brooding. 'You know what,' he said, rolling the liquid in the bottom of his bottle, watching as it swirled against the glass. 'When we was out there, some of the men used to play that British sort of football with the kids. Soccer, or some such. They like it out there, so it seems.'

'Hearts and minds,' I muttered.

'Damn straight,' he said. 'Know what? Couple of our boys were on the gate.' He pointed at me with the beer bottle. 'One of them kids, the ones they used to play with, come up to them with the football. Our boys weren't supposed to, but eventually one of them says somethin' to him on account of he's just standin' there.' His voice lightened up a half tone. 'Hey kid, you know we're on duty, go on back now an' we'll catch you later.' He drank. 'Guess what? Some fucker blew him up, the kid. Right there in front of them.'

'Oh, God!' I was shocked by it, by way he said it like that, just a throwaway line. Skeet hunched his shoulders, shaking his head. 'Shit,' I said, not seeing the funny side at all.

'S'right,' Ethan said. 'Took one of our boys with him, took the other one's face off, an' his arm. I'm surprised you ain't heard it afore from Levine, but then, like you said, I guess he didn't talk 'bout it much.' He pointed the bottle at me, holding it by his neck. 'You go tell shit like that to all them bleedin' hearts sayin' as how we should never have been there.' A few feet away from him, Skeet shook his head and picked up one of the kit bags to reach inside.

'It wasn't his fault,' I said. Ethan frowned at me. 'Look, what you said, that's terrible, what happened. But ... Red didn't do it, he didn't make that happen, and–'

'You think I'm that stupid?' Ethan's chair yelped against the concrete floor as he jerked forward, one hand clamping onto the arm rest as if to hold himself back. 'I know who done it, I was goddamn there, an' I goddamn saw it!'

'I didn't mean that–' I started, but Ethan got to his feet.

'You think I makin' that shit up?' he demanded. Skeet dropped the bag he'd been rooting in, alert to his brother's anger, watchful, waiting.

'No, that's not what I meant,' I said, keeping my voice low, calm, trying not to make it into a contest. My hand gripped the seat, my heart beat faster. Somewhere inside me Margarita became alert, dangerous, pushing at me to stand up and face him.

'Well, what did you mean, you callin' Daddy a liar?' Oh God, why did he say it like that, why did he–

'Hey, Ethan! We got him, he's on the move!' Molly came bounding out of the washroom, phone in hand, the screen a triumphant square of light. I realized I was gripping the seat of the swan boat, my hands wet with sweat.

Ethan's mood evaporated at once. 'There we go, front an' center,' he yelped. 'Let me see!' He took the phone from Molly and squinted at it, his face split open in a leer. I let out the breath I'd been holding and forced myself to let go.

'Told you,' Molly said. 'Told you he'd go for it, I tol' you!' She grinned over at me, exhilarated. 'Why the long face? You goin' get home soon, well ...' Oh how she worked that pause, shrugging her shoulders and giving a little tilt of her head. 'Let's just see what happens, shall we, lil' doggy?' And there it was, the threat Ethan hadn't delivered before. 'Now, you be a good girl an' sit tight. Skeet's gonna look out for you, make sure you don't spoil the fun or nothin'. I'll see you when I get back.' She laughed and walked back over to Ethan.

'Come on. We got ourselves work to do.' Ethan stood to pull on a waterproof jacket. When he turned, I saw there was something slung around his neck. I thought it was a gas mask, then realized it was a pair of night vision googles.

'You ready?' Molly asked, and Ethan kissed her, lifting her off the ground in a bear hug.

'Daddy's born ready!' He bellowed. Molly whooped with laughter; Skeet looked, then turned back to the storm lanterns. 'Skeet,' Ethan said. 'She's all yours – whatever floats your boat, just don't fall to sleep, now. I'm countin' on you, bro!'

'Whatever,' Skeet replied, batting the air with his hand, shoulders hunched. As they passed him, Ethan with his arm around Molly, she let her fingers brush Skeet's shoulder. He flinched, turning his head to look, but she didn't look back. The dark maw of the broken door swallowed them both. Moments later, the engine roared; lights coursed over the ceiling flooding the broken windows, then they were gone.

CHAPTER SEVENTEEN

SKEET WATCHED the door for a while, one arm bent up behind his head, hand holding the back of his neck.

'So,' I said. 'This wasn't quite how I saw my day going. How's it working out for you?' He huffed a laugh, then turned his back on me to sit down.

Moving so as to make as little noise as I could, I began to run my fingers around the inside of the swan boat, looking for anything that might help; a flake of metal, a broken edge, something that might cut leather if I worked hard enough at it, all while keeping my eye on Skeet. He was taller and stronger and faster than I was, but for the first time since he'd brought me here, I was alone with only one person. That made two less people to deal with.

While I moved through the swan boat, finding nothing, Skeet sat with his back to me. He bent to one of the kit bags by his feet, took something out and set it up on the floor in front of him. I saw him reach into his pocket for his pen knife and use the blade, then a blue flame sprang into life. He sat back, folding the knife into his pocket. Hoping he was absorbed in his cooking, I saw how far I could step from the boat and move across the floor without being heard, which wasn't far and wasn't enough to find anything useful. I sat back down again, my feet itching from the concrete and the cold.

'Hey,' I said. He didn't look up from his stove. 'Hey, Skeet? That your real name, or is it short for something, like a nickname?'

He glanced back at me, the stove light catching on his eyes and turning the shaggy outline of his cheek to a silhouette. Then he reached down to his feet, straightened up, and took a long drink from a cup. I smelled coffee.

'Hey, Skeet,' I tried again. 'I'm real cold, you got a blanket or something? I've only got this shirt on, you know, the one Ethan gave me, and it's real thin. Please? Skeet?' He continued to ignore me, drinking his coffee. Fine, I thought, be like that.

'Skeet, I'm cold–' I slapped my hands on the side of the swan boat, the sound echoing through the hollow form. One thud, two thud, making a beat. 'Skeet, I'm cold, I'm fuckin' freezin'. Come on Skeet, give me a break,' – thud, thud, drum, drum – 'Come on Skeet, don't be ...' I paused, my rhyming dictionary failing me. '... Don't be a creep.' Well, that didn't scan, but never mind. 'Come on Skeet, I–'

He stood up, his boots scraping on the floor, the hollow steel frame of the chair clattering after.

'If I get you something, will you shut the fuck up?'

'I'll stop singing,' I said. He looked at me without expression, his eyes narrow slits in the shadow of his face. Then he strode behind the desolate food counter, bent to retrieve something, and stalked over to me with a bundle in his arms. He dropped it into the swan boat.

'Now shut up.' It was a sleeping bag that smelled as if he'd been sleeping in it for some time, army green waterproof exterior, fleece lining. Refusing to think about when it had last been washed, I unzipped it and wrapped it around myself. Skeet sat down again and reached for his coffee.

'That smells good,' I said and saw his shoulders drop. 'I mean the coffee. This smells like shit.'

'You don't want it, don't use it,' he said.

'You got another cup?' I asked. 'I mean, this roll's pretty dry, I could use a drink. If you don't got another cup, I don't mind sharing. Hell, I feel we've shared something here already, Skeet, so I don't think we need to stand on ceremony. We could have a nice chat, seeing as it's just you and me. Youngest kids together, you know, bitching about older brothers and how it sucks being the baby of the family, shit like that?'

Skeet slapped his hands on his knees and stood up. He picked up his folding chair, marched over to the swan boat and slammed it down in front of me. He returned to the circle of lamp light; I heard him pour, then he came back over with a beat-up plastic mug in his hand. He set it down on the edge of the boat, then threw himself into the chair.

'Okay,' he said. 'You're goin' drink this, an' we can talk, then you're gonna shut your mouth. If you don't, I got some duct tape in my bag, un'erstand?' I looked at the coffee. 'Go on then,' he said, hooking one leg over the other, resting his ankle on his knee. 'You ain't got long. Start runnin' your mouth.'

'Alright,' I said. 'What's your cut?'

'Of what?'

I raised my eyebrow. The plastic cup, when I touched it, was too hot to hold. 'Oh come on, Skeet. What's your cut of the ransom money? I mean, I'm just spit-balling here, but what the hell else you in this for? The other two, Ethan and Molly, they're up to some devious shit all their own, right?' He was looking at me, head to one side, his eyes narrowed in his rat-like face. 'But you? I figure you're just here for the money. So ... and call this professional interest, how much you willing to go to jail for?'

'I ain't goin' jail,' he said, smirking.

'Oh please,' I said. 'You can keep tellin' yourself that, but we both know this never ends well for the bag man. That's you, right?

 BROKEN PONIES

I mean, Ethan's the boss, isn't he?' Skeet's smile hardened. 'Big brother, been in the army, done time already, right?' He didn't answer. 'Either way, you're not looking so good right now either, if you don't mind my saying.' The coffee, when I fit my finger through the cup's handle and raised it to my lips, was still scalding, and smelled mostly of hot plastic.

'I ain't goin' jail,' Skeet said again. The chair creaked as he flicked the hair from his eyes and glared at me.

'Oh well, let me see ...' I looked up at the ceiling as if making a mental list. 'We got kidnapping, assault, false imprisonment, erm, conspiracy to defraud–' Skeet's smile was back. 'Oh, yes, and let's not forget, I got your DNA under my fingernails.'

'What?' He sat up, both feet on the ground. I put down my coffee and held up my hands.

'You know what DNA is? I got your skin from when I scratched at you, all stuck up here waiting to be found. Oh, you've been a real gent, sure, but thing is, Skeet, you got to see how this might go.' He scratched the back of his neck. 'You get a prosecutor with something to prove, starts hinting at goodness knows what, an' you're looking at fifteen, twenty years hard time. Between you and me, I wouldn't choose this state for a long stretch, nice lookin' young fellow like yourself.' If you like that sort of gap-toothed, rat-faced look, of course. 'I mean, most of the prison population's black, right? And, you're white as ice-cream, bro, so the only option for you's gonna be the Aryan brotherhood, lettin' some big ass Nazi stick it to you just so as you don't get jumped in the shower by–'

'That's enough,' he snapped. 'What you goin' on like that for, runnin' you' nasty mouth?'

'Oh gee, I don't know?' I sipped the coffee. 'Maybe I don't feel like being gentle with you, seeing as you kidnapped me, and let your girlfriend hit me in the face, an' all.'

'She ain't my girlfriend,' he said. 'You go on much as you like, there ain't no FBI or that shit comin' for you. I ain't worried.' He began picking at his nails.

I drank some more of the coffee, which was starting to cool. 'You never answered my question,' I said. 'How much you doin' all this for?'

'Enough,' he said.

'Well, if it was me–' Skeet left off picking his nails. 'If it were me, and I didn't want Red to call the FBI, I'd make sure I asked for enough money so as to make it look real, but not so much that he might have to go to the bank, or get some transferred, or some such. Not enough to make him think I knew what I was doing. So, that would be what ... seventy-five thousand?' Skeet didn't flicker. 'Okay, so lower then, fifty? Because, split three ways, that would mean you're prepared to go to jail for what, about eighteen thousand? That's pretty cheap, Skeet.' He chuckled, then leaned forward, resting his forearms on his thighs.

'You know what this place is?' he asked.

'Erm ... Disneyland, Hell?'

He grinned at me. 'This was gonna be an amusement park, alright. Started buildin' it 'bout ten years back. My daddy used to work construction here.' I noted the way he said 'my daddy', not 'our daddy' – only a mother in common. 'Least ways, didn't matter much in the end, 'cause ole hurricane Katrina come right though here, took it all out. You weren't here then, was you?'

'No,' I said.

'Oh, I know you weren't, because we know all 'bout you. You folks always think as we little people don't know squat about what you get up to, but that ain't so.' He said it the way Molly had, as if he'd taught her the phrase, or she him. 'Mamma wrote Ethan all the time he was away, told him 'bout ole Red Levine, when he got

himself hitched n' what not. Young trophy wife, what upped and left him soon as the shit hit the fan. Not that he didn't deserve it.'

'You do know you're wrong about that,' I said. 'I'm not Red's wife.'

'Yeah you are,' Skeet assured me. 'We got your picture.'

'You've got my picture?' The coffee was growing colder, enough that I could hold the mug in my hand and miss its warmth.

'Momma clipped it out the local paper, she do shit like that. When we fixed on this whole thing, I took it from her.' He shrugged, pleased with himself. 'When you' tracking something, you gotta learn all 'bout it. You gotta watch where it lay down, n' what it lay down with. You look right pretty on your wedding day too.' So that was it, a picture in the paper of a happy couple, and me looking just like she had then, enough in a faded newspaper picture anyway. Skeet wiped the end of his nose. 'Sure, I seen you myself,' he said. 'I seen you with him. Truth be told, the way you two were fightin' were more of a giveaway than anything. Only married's gonna argue like that.'

I remembered the flash of sunlight off the windows of a red car as it passed us on that side road. I imagined the three of them watching Carillon for hours, days even, waiting to snatch Papa Levine, and getting more and more restless and frustrated when they couldn't get near him. By then, it wouldn't have mattered who I was; they'd have just wanted to do something, because the tension must have been killing them. I looked down at the swill of coffee at the bottom of the cup.

'He's gonna call the FBI,' I said. 'They're gonna be looking for me. Why d'you think they won't look here? This place has got to be on all the maps, there can't be anything the hell else out here for them to bother with?'

Skeet shrugged. 'Rest of the country never bothered much with us after the storm anyhow. They don't know shit 'bout us, an' care less. This place …' he let his gaze roam around the dead restaurant. 'They just let it go to shit, like they did everythin' round these parts. Then, someone reminded them they'd sunk all that money up this way, so they come an' cleaned out the place.'

'They repaired it?'

He frowned. 'This look like it been repaired? Place were full of hobos and the like, us kids gettin' high and so on.' Oh, so it was yours once, was it, Skeet, I thought? With his friends, if he'd had friends, or maybe only Ethan, his big brother, until he'd gone away to war and Skeet had been all alone, the rat king pushed out of his kingdom. 'Big city men brung a load of guys down to beat them out, kicked our asses, on account of some deal or other comin' this way. Know what they did then?' I shook my head. 'Built a goddamn fence round the whole thing, ten feet high an' all ...' he waved his hand. 'All 'lectrocuted and what not. Time they done with all that, deal fell through, an' nobody give a shit no more. Big city company? They just make do with a one-man security team to watch the place, swing by, see no one's inside.' He crossed his foot over his knee again.

'A security team?'

He grinned, a lazy, self-satisfied grin. 'Not so much of a team. Just one man's all they need, seein' as it's gone to shit an' nobody knows what to do with it. Just one man...' He tapped the side of his boot with his finger. 'An' his brother, o'course.' I looked up at the swan boat next to me. It looked back as if it had known all along and was pleased with itself for knowing.

'That would be you and Ethan.'

'Damn right it is.' He stood up and took the plastic cup from me. 'I been livin' here for over a year or more now. I know this place. Anybody wants to come lookin' round here, police, FBI or whatever, they gonna buzz me up to let them in, matter of course.'

He threw the last of my coffee on the floor.

'I wasn't finished,' I said.

'I don't give a shit.' Cup still in hand, he pointed his finger at me. 'People think it's a cryin' shame what happened to this place. I don't. I kinda like it, all fucked up and broken like this. You better hope your husband ... or whatever the fuck he is to you, ain't called the police. First sign of nothin' much? You think I don't got somewhere I can put you where you won't never get found? You think I can't put you there, an' get clean away?'

He turned away from me, picked up his seat, and sloped back to the circle of light, letting the chair legs scrape and jolt against the floor.

'Where you gonna go, Skeet?' I said.

'I got somewhere,' he said. 'We got somewhere. Never you mind.' He dropped his chair and bent to the kit bag.

'That'll be cosy,' I said. 'Just the three of you. Nice little nest egg to set you up, just you ...' He came back over to me. 'You and Molly, oh, and Ethan of course, which will be real-' He ripped a strip off the duct tape. 'Awkward.'

'You take the tape off and I'll put your hands behind your back.'

'Oh come on Skeet, we don't need to do this, do we?' I tried.

'Momma used to do this to us when we was kids,' he said, 'so she could watch the TV in peace.'

'What you doin' this for, Skeet?'

'So y' shut up.' He held up the strip of tape.

'Not that, all this kidnapping and shit. Why you doin' this to me, Skeet? What the hell I ever done to you, because it can't be about the money? That really all you worth, Skeet?'

'It ain't about the money-' he hesitated, then lowered the tape. 'Ethan's my brother, we look out for each other.'

'An' what about Molly, who looks out for her, Skeet?'

'You don't get t' talk 'bout her–' Skeet snapped.

'I saw how you looked out for her, Skeet. Your brother's wife?'

'She ain't his wife.'

'No? So, why's she with him then an' not you? Hell, you're a darn sight better lookin' than he is, you got those kind eyes n' all, so what's she doin' with him? You like the thought of him all on top of her, do you Skeet?'

'You got a filthy mouth,' he spat. 'Someone ought close it for you.'

'Or maybe that ain't it,' I said. 'Maybe you already had a crack, an' she knocked you back.' Or maybe she hadn't.

'Shut up!' He grabbed hold of the chain where it joined my collar and jerked me forward. 'Shut your mouth.'

'Wonder what they're up to now, all alone together?' I gripped the chain where he did, staggering forward to try and ease the pressure at my neck. 'Wonder what's gonna happen when you head off to the hills together?'

'You wanna know why I'm doin' this?' Skeet got hold of the collar, then clutched at my neck. I grabbed his arm, but I couldn't stop him, couldn't do anything but hang from his grip, grabbing at his wrist, unable to speak.

'People like you's why I'm doin' this,' he snarled in my face. 'Now you gonna shut up an' listen. This whole place got fucked over, your sort been fucking us over from the get go.' He was lifting me onto my toes, his body rigid with anger. I scrabbled at him, one hand grabbing his belt while the other snagged on his pocket. 'All we is to you is cannon fodder n' trailer trash. If Katrina done gone fucked Washington DC, all hell would'a broke loose. Down here? It damn near finished us, an' they couldn't barely crack a smile. That what they want, flush us in the ocean, then they ain't got bother with us no more.' I tried to speak, to breathe, flailing against him as he twisted the collar against my throat. 'Day's gonna come when we take back this country, an' when that day comes, I'm gonna be right there.' I clutched at his jeans, my foot sliding against his shin as if I might climb up him and break his hold on me. Too far, I'd gone too far ... then my fingers touched cold metal in his pocket. 'You say it ain't so – you say it ain't like that!' I was choking; he was choking me, and the stars were fizzing into the edge of my vision, the sound booming and roaring in my ears. I was going under.

'You say it ain't like that–' then the world closed blackness over my head.

I am underwater. Dark, thick like molasses, then clearing to blue. Not the swamp, but the pool, chlorine bright and hard with echo. I'm waiting, held by the tension of a second hand, screwed up tight like a watch spring under the surface.

Under glass.

The world holds its breath, yellow-white sunlight refracting around me. At the bang of the starting pistol I'm free, underwater, hands, feet, body, in a crystalline rush. This is my element; this is where I belong, underwater. I'm aware of bodies beside me, then behind me, an arc of bubbles in the corner of my eye. This is my race. Ten feet, twenty, thirty, forty, no need to breathe, no need to think. I break the surface, rising into the wall of sound to taste the air before I slip back into the blue.

'Breathe, goddamn it! Wake up, you better not be shittin' me ...'

Underwater and free, I hit the end of the pool and turn, bubbles in my ears and my eyes, and the sky a second sea above me. On my back now, skin glazed with water, my vision liquid as if I'm under glass.

Under glass.

My heart should be beating fast, should be pounding, but it's not; it's slow, each beat a luxury to be indulged. Time is slowing with the caress of water on my skin, a tail of bubbles trailing out behind me. Little mermaid.

Under glass.

I am ten.

It is the end of summer, and Lisa has gone away; Mom has sent her away because she's too much trouble. That's what Lisa said; she was too much trouble and so they're sending her away.

I am ten.

I'm lying on the grass under the tree that overshadows the front yard. It is September, nearly October, and yet the sky is high as June, stitched blue between leaves of rust and red. Lisa has been gone for weeks. There's a letter; I saw it and knew it was from her for me, only Mom hid it in her purse.

'Is that from Lisa?' I said when I saw it, the looping handwriting so familiar, our address sprawling over the envelope. Mom put her purse on the table in the kitchen when she had to answer the door and it poked out and I saw it. There's a pink heart drawn on the envelope, a pink heart that looks like a strawberry. I reach for it, only Mom snatches her purse back before my fingers close around it.

'That's nothing,' she said, but she flushed.

The sky above me is blue, water blue; high and clean and clear. Under the tree it is calm, peaceful. I can hear the cars as they go by, the swoosh of their engines falling into a nice, regular pulse. It merges with the song I'm singing, eyes half-closed, holding onto Mr Pooter. I finger his dirty white ears, touch the chill of his black glass eyes. Then I hear the car.

I peer through my lashes and see it pull up to the curb. The sun flashes on its window as the door opens and a woman gets out. I don't know her. She's tall, dressed in blue slacks and a grey sweater, with her hair cut short. She's pretty, and somehow, I know she's a police officer.

'Hey there,' she calls out, her face bright, friendly. She has a nice voice, not shouty or harsh, but warm somehow, as if the colors of the tree are speaking. 'Hey, how you doin'? But it's hot today, isn't it? You'd hardly think it was nearly October.'

I get up and go over to her, keeping the fence between us but wanting to talk. I know we aren't supposed to talk to people we don't know, but surely that always means men, and I know she's a cop, and so that makes it okay? She asks me about what school I go to, what I liked best about it, was I good at math?

'No,' I say. 'I mean, it's okay, but I don't like it much. I like running, cross country, and swimming. I made the swim team last semester.'

'No kidding?' she says, and her smile makes me feel good. 'Maybe you could try out for the cops when you're older? We got to be fit you know, catch all the bad guys.' I think about it, and it seems possible that one day I really could do something like that, drive a car and hold a badge, because she's said so.

'Hey,' she bends down and I lean forward, because I sense she's going to ask me something and I want to hear it; I want to be good and helpful for her. 'Is your mom home?'

I look down at Mr Pooter where he's tucked under my arm. I have on red baseball sneakers, and the white rubber toecap is coming loose. I nudge at it with the good shoe, revealing the little margin of deeper red beneath.

'Well,' the cop says when I don't answer. 'It don't matter I suppose, but ...' she reaches into her jacket and for some stupid reason I think she's got something for me, and she's come all this way to give it me. 'Perhaps you could give her something for me?' She's holding out a card, a little white oblong. 'I bumped into her the other night, that's all. Thought she might want to give me a call sometime. Hey, I never did get your name?'

I take the card and fold it into my hand.

'Rita,' I say.

'That's pretty.' But she doesn't say it like she means it, just like it's something she was going to say whatever my name was. 'Rita, you know ... sometimes, when people are in trouble, they find it real hard to ask for help. You know, if they're scared? You know what that feels like?' Not looking at her, I nod. 'So, if your mom wanted to talk sometime, she could call me, you know?'

I look up at her. She's smiling, but it isn't a smile for me. She straightens up and looks over my head at our house.

'Keep doing good at school,' she says.

I am ten. We are in a diner, not Lisa and I, but Frank and I, though he's Franny then. He still hates it. Daddy has taken us to a diner, because Lisa's gone away. He's bought us each an ice cream, a big one, my favorite, caramel and chocolate with slices of strawberries that make fat, heart shapes as they press against the glass.

Under glass.

Underwater.

My heart beat slows, red against glass, each beat a luxury, each beat a gift.

I am ten, and Daddy has bought us ice creams. Frank is not eating his; he's playing with it, turning the spoon over and making a mint green ooze leak down the side of the dish to puddle at its foot.

'How would you kids like to go away with me sometime?' Daddy asks. I look up at him, then down at my ice cream, pushing

my spoon in for a strawberry, a strawberry behind the glass. A red heart. A heartbeat ... and then.

'Breathe, goddammit, breathe!"

'How would you kids like to go away with me sometime?' Daddy sips his coffee, the one he always gets with the foam on top. Sometimes he lets me eat the foam with a spoon, and the spoon is hot when it touches my lips.

'Can Lisa come with us?' I ask him. 'Can she come back from school, can she come with us?' Because I want to go, I do want to. Frank kicks me under the table and it hurts, though I know better than to react. Why does Frank have to come? Why can't it just be me and Lisa and Daddy or me – just me and…

'No, honey–' Daddy scoops the foam from his coffee, carving a wet channel across the top. 'Mommy wants her to go to school now, big school, away from home.'

'Frank doesn't go to big school,' I say to the ice cream. 'Why can't Frank go away to big school?'

I am outside, behind glass. Outside of myself and the world and time. I am outside the window of the diner, watching the little girl I was with her ice cream. I see her and her hair, that color which is neither blonde nor brown, mousy and tied up in bunches either side of her head. I want to scream at her, tell her that she doesn't want to go away with him, doesn't want to be alone with him, doesn't she remember what he does, can't she remember? But I don't want to remember, not then, not with my ice cream. I want it to be just like he says it will be, just me and Frank, well, not Frank, not Frank at all, just Daddy and me alone somewhere and safe, before Mommy sends me away like she did Lisa.

'Come on, Rita,' Frank says. 'We're going.'

'I don't want to go,' I say.

'Come on, we're going – we'll get the bus home.'

'What?' Daddy says, putting down his coffee so it spills onto the saucer. 'What the hell's up with you? I drove us here, I'll drive us home.'

'No,' Frank says. 'Come on Rita, we'll get the bus.'

'Come on,' says Daddy. 'Don't be like that, I'm gonna drive us home. We'll stop off somewhere, spend some time, just you and me.'

'We're getting the bus,' and Frank takes hold of me. I drop my spoon.

'You want a ride home, don't you?' Daddy says to me and I do, I do want to ride home with him; I don't want to get the bus with Frank, bossing me about and giving me a dead leg or an Indian burn.

Frank gets up all in a rush. He pulls me so hard that I fall and upset my ice cream dish. It crashes onto the bright, clean table top and the ice cream and the strawberries go everywhere, a sticky, cold mess. The dish rolls to the edge of the table, then hits the floor.

'Now look what you done!' Daddy gets up, furious; Frank has made him angry at me again. 'Look at that goddamn mess, boy – so help me but I'm gonna tan your hide for you–'

'I don't want to go!' And now everyone in the diner is looking at us, at Frank dragging me out of there, chocolate ice cream spilled all over me, and Daddy shouting.

'I don't want to go!' I cry.

I am underwater.

I strike the end of the pool and burst into light. The world roars at me, the water buoys me up, throws me into the air. I've won.

The girl next to me finishes behind me, and even she cheers as her arms clatter me into her embrace.

I am under the bed with the spider. I hear Daddy come home and his footsteps as he mounts the stairs.

He's coming to find me, so we can go away together, like he said.

He's coming to find me, he's coming to find me, so we can go away together like he said, and there's no one to stop him, not now, not now Mom sent Lisa away to school. I close my eyes and my friend closes her eyes too and we are together, under the bed.

But he doesn't come in.

We say the song that Lisa taught us to say, we count up to twenty-one and when we're done and nothing has happened, we open our eyes. My friend listens, and then she says that I mustn't look, she'll look, while I keep my eyes closed.

We creep from under the bed and we go to the bedroom door, then across the hall to their room. We can see in, just enough. We can see Mom and Dad like we shouldn't, like we know we're not meant to. They are facing each other, caught in a moment as if trapped underwater. He has his hand on her throat; I think he's going to hold her, to embrace her, but he isn't. He has his hand on her throat, then he lets her go, only she stops him. She catches his wrist and puts his hand back on her throat.

'That's it, come on back to me now.'

Mom put his hand on her throat. There will be a mark there later, a red mark in the shape of heart. And the policewoman will see it, when Mom has to go to A&E, and she will find out Mom's name and come over to give me her card. And I will let it fall into the storm drain. I will fold it up as she drives away, and I will post it through the black slit mouth of the storm drain on the sidewalk, and I will watch it, a white fold like the wings of a moth, falling into dark water below.

'You can do what you like to me,' Mom says. 'I don't care anymore, Harold. You can do whatever the hell you want to me, but you won't touch Lisa again and so help me, if you lay one finger on Rita, if you hurt her, I will kill you.'

I will fold up the card, I will lean over the storm drain, I will let go of the card and watch it spiral away. And I will know that I have done a bad thing without knowing why, and so to punish myself, I will push my friend away and down into the darkest part of me until I forget her. Until I need her again.

I am eighteen.

In the pool, I look across to the front row where I know Daddy is watching. He's standing up; he's put his stick down so he can applaud me. He has to sit almost at once, because the cough is coming and will shake through him and make him fight for air on dry land. He is dying, drowning, but he is applauding me, because I've won.

I am underwater, I am fighting for air. I break the surface, and I breathe.

CHAPTER EIGHTEEN

AIR SLAMMED BACK into my lungs. The shock of it bucked through me, and I coughed, pain burning in my throat as if Skeet were still holding me. I was on the floor. I tried to twist on to my side, only I couldn't, because Skeet was astride me. The smell of him flooded my nose and I hit out at him.

'Get the fuck off of me!' The chain, still attached to my neck, sawed and rattled against the side of the swan boat as he stood, and I was able to move, to curl up onto my side then onto my hands and knees, retching.

'You all right now,' Skeet said, to himself more than me. I blinked my eyes open, clearing away tears. I must have collapsed, and he'd caught me and laid me out on the floor. I could smell the stink of his hands even as I spat my mouth clear.

'What the fuck was that?' I asked as glared up at him. 'Touched a nerve, did I?'

'You had it comin',' he said. I was shaking, my arms and legs alive with cramps as life crawled back into them. I reached for the side of the boat and pulled myself up, wanting to get back to it as if it had become a refuge. I couldn't seem to unclench my fist, then I slipped, and he moved as if to catch me.

'Get back,' I hissed and got hold of the boat with my other hand. 'You get the hell away from me.'

'Suit yourself,' he said, flicking his fringe from his eyes as if I'd really hurt his feelings.

'Get away from me,' I said, finding the seat at the back of my legs. 'An' if you ever touch her again, I swear I'm gonna cut you balls to chin.'

'Touch who?' he said. 'What you mean?'

'Rita,' I said. 'Don't you ever touch her again.' I grinned at him, the dank, stale air of the place breathing through me. He shrugged and sloped back toward the light. While his back was turned, I slipped the knife I'd pulled from his pocket past the waistband of my pants and into my briefs.

'How did you get that?' Rita asked.

'When old Skeet was busy tryin' choke the life from you. Now hush a moment, I gotta think.'

Mary Jane, the tattooist on the strip, had a bosom which she claimed could hide a quart of vodka.

'Damn straight,' she said. 'I just tuck the neck up under the band of my brassiere and no matter even if they pat me down, they don't find it.' Looking at her as she scrawled her exquisite doodle on me, I could believe it, but I doubted I could hide much in mine, so that was out. Skeet was going to notice the knife gone any second, seeing as he seemed to play with it more than he scratched his balls. I wrapped the sleeping bag around myself and reached around for it. It was about two and a half inches long, smooth when it was folded into its red casing, with a ring on the end that might have made it a key ring, if you'd ever gotten caught with it.

Now, I thought about this real fast and real hard, while I stared at the back of Skeet's head, because I did not want to go where this was headed. He was busy scratching about with his stove or something, and it occurred to me he was fixing us up another coffee. Well hell, Skeet was a whole lot more shaken than he'd like

to admit about what had just happened. He'd scared himself half to death when Rita passed out on him, and must have been shitting himself that Ethan, and more importantly Molly, were going to be mad as hell about it. So now he was fixing up another coffee to say sorry to me, which was really sweet of him, but he was going to notice his knife was missing any second.

'I'm so sorry about this, hun,' I muttered. 'Just don't think 'bout it and it'll all be fine.' I slipped my hand into the front of my briefs, turned the knife end on, and pushed it inside myself. It fit pretty neat, truth be told, hardly touched the sides. Soon as I was done, I sat down, perching on the edge of the seat, easy as a whore on the back pew in church.

Soon as I was set, I saw Skeet feel for his pocket. Then he looked, then he looked again. Then he turned out the pocket, and got up to hunt about his feet, lifting up the kit bags to look under them. I kept my head down, drawing the sleeping bag tight about myself, trying to act as if I was terrified and still in pain after our necking session. Which I was.

Skeet got up and came over to me, pausing to pick up the flashlight and click it on.

'What you want?' I said, starting back from him and wishing I hadn't, what with the knife and all. He shone the beam on the floor, turned about himself and squatted down to search under the boat. Then he looked at me.

'Dropped my knife,' he said.

'That'll be tryin' to kill me,' I said. 'Hope you lost your pocket change too.'

'I weren't tryin' to kill you,' he said, hurt sounding, as if there I went, making shit up about him again, which was real unfair of me. 'Did you pick it up?'

'Pick what up?' I gripped the sleeping bag closer around me.

'My knife, you got it?' He stood up. 'You fixin' on sticking it in me? Go ahead, it's only a pocket knife.'

'I don't got it,' I said.

'Stand up.'

'Oh please, can't you just leave me alone?'

'Look, just stand up, will you?'

'Fine.' I stood and held the sleeping bag out as if it were a cloak, Count Dracula style. 'You wanna frisk me?' I dropped the bag and kept my arms out to the side. 'See something you like?'

'Goddamn, girl! Think you almost want me to, you's like a she cat on heat. If you were my wife, I'd chain you up in the yard.' He reached out and patted each of my pants' pockets in turn.

'If I was you wife,' I said. 'I'd chain my goddamn self up in the yard.' He paused, I saw him swallow, then he ran his hand over my breasts. I guessed he must have known someone like Mary Jane, too.

'That do it for you, Skeet?' I asked.

He looked at me, eyes narrowed to slits. 'Open your mouth.'

'Seriously?'

'Open it.' He shone the beam full into my face, peering into my mouth, then he lowered the beam. 'Lift up the sleepin' bag.' I did, and he swung the flashlight beam about the inside of the boat, under the seat, in the swan's ass, even up in the neck end. Then he ran out of ideas and clicked off the light.

'You better not got it,' he said. Well, it seemed that his grasp of female anatomy had failed him.

'Well, you know what they always say? Go look in the last place you had it, an' you're sure to find it.' I said, safe in the knowledge that his knife was very much not in the last place he'd had. It kind of amused me, and it took quite an effort not to start laughing. He glared at me, then went back to the storm lamps. I pulled the

 **BROKEN PONIES**

sleeping bag around myself again, thrust my hand between my legs and removed the knife. Everything considered, I'd had worse first dates.

Skeet messed around with his fire for a while, then had another look for the knife, kicking his foot across the floor and lifting up the kit bags again. Eventually he came back with another coffee just as I thought he would – sorry I nearly killed Rita, here's a plastic mug of cheap-ass instant.

'Well, thanks,' I said. 'That makes it all better, don't it?'

'I'm goin' get some sleep,' he said.

'Sweet dreams, Skeet.'

The circle of light threw his shadow lank and angular against the wall, then he picked up a lamp and took it behind the counter with him. There was a flicker of movement, then everything went quiet. Skeet had gone to bed.

The pen knife had two blades, one long, one short, and one of those Allen key things about an eighth of an inch in dimeter. I had two locks to choose from, but I only needed to open one. The longer, thinner blade would not fit into the padlock at my feet, so I got to work on the one at my neck. My flesh was bruised and tender from the collar and Skeet's little outburst, but I refused to think about it. First rule of picking a lock – don't think, feel. Second rule? Try not to get padlocked into a collar in the first place.

I fingered the padlock at my neck, then eased the point of the thinner blade home, turning so my back was to where Skeet lay, just in case he was a light sleeper. Then, I had to not think.

Think of something else. Think of Red, was he even coming? What time was it anyway, how long since they'd sent him Rita's screen test? I'd no idea, but if it were me, then I'd keep him guessing. I'd send him to a half-dozen locations before I sent him to where I wanted him to leave the cash, making him think I was watching him, which of course I would be. I'd no idea what sort of training Ethan had, though I doubted he was special ops – catering core would have been more his scene – but he'd gotten himself a nice new set of night vision goggles for a reason. You can't hardly see shit in those things, and they make you clumsy as hell, but if he was smart - and though he wasn't, Molly was - he'd have been spending his time practicing. Night driving, lights out, ready to follow Red's tail lights far enough behind so as not to be heard, and presumably not in that noisy-ass van. They'd keep sending Red messages, delightful little haikus of malice, bouncing him back and forth across the parish. Hell, it was what I'd have done, jabbing at him, winding him up, turning him round and round, hoping even he didn't remember where he was.

The padlock clicked. Nothing. If I'd tripped one of the tumblers, then there were more I hadn't reached yet. My hands were sweating; I had to balance the knife with one hand in order to wipe my fingers on my pants, flexing the life back into them. Then the knife slipped, thudded past my knee and impacted into the bottom of the boat. I froze, listening through the relentless drumming of the rain and the rattle of the wind in case Skeet had heard it. Nothing. I picked up the knife and tried again.

Thing was, I was starting to doubt Red even would come. Why the hell would he? What was I to him, really, when all was said and done, the bitch who got away? And what about Rita? She deserved better than him, better than the mess we were going to make of each other. Please God he'd called the FBI or the sheriff's office, and not done exactly what I was damn sure he'd done – set out alone to be the hero he'd failed to be before.

The padlock clicked, one tumbler, two ... two again, or was that three? I held my breath, closed my eyes, then let the air from my lungs seep from between my lips. Three.

CHAPTER NINETEEN

THE PADLOCK OPENED. I closed my hand around it to stop it falling, then I plucked out the knife and folded it away against my thigh. I unthreaded the hasp of the lock and set it down on the sleeping bag to cushion the noise, then coiled the chain up beside it, then the fucking collar itself.

Sweet Jesus, it was good to run my hands over my neck. I was free, even if I was alone and barefoot in Walt Disney's nightmare. I smirked to myself, well, not quite alone. I guess you're never really alone with an imaginary friend.

There was a little light from the one remaining storm lantern, showing me the kit bags and the stove. The coffee Skeet had left me was still plenty warm, which meant he wouldn't have been asleep long, if at all. Grandmother's footsteps it was.

I stepped from the boat. First thing I did was mound up the sleeping bag so it looked as if I were still wrapped up in it. Then I made my way towards the kit bags, knife in hand. Skeet was right about its potential; it wasn't much above a pencil sharpener, but it was good to have something other than nothing in my hand. I squatted down beside the kit, not wanting to touch any of it unless I had to, in case I made a noise. I looked at the windows, at the pock-marked surface of the glass wet with rain. Dawn was coming. I'd no idea if that meant anything to Ethan and Molly, but it meant that the cover of night was receding. It meant I could see more of what was out there, but I wasn't sure if that was a good thing or not. My heart thudded dully in my chest, but Rita was with me, keeping me calm, keeping me focused, telling me it was not a good idea to stick the two inches of Skeet's knife into the side of his neck, just to show him how much damage you could do with it.

'Just get out,' she said. 'Get out, get to a phone, call the FBI. Don't fuck around, don't try and be the hero either.'

'You never let me have any–' then I stopped. In the top of the second kit bag I opened, was Skeet's gun. 'Well look at that,' I grinned. 'Now that's just plain careless, leaving shit around. It's asking for trouble.'

'Don't go there,' Rita warned.

'Yeah, well right now, why the fuck not? Goddamn it, look what the hell they put you through? I'm sick of being the girl tied up in the corner, when the fuck was that me?' I clicked open the magazine; it was full.

'Don't!' Rita said.

'No sweat, I'll be gentle–'

'No,' she said. Crouched in the gloom, aware of the creeping dawn behind me, Rita pulled me back, made me think. 'Do this, and you're lost.' I closed my eyes and rubbed my hand across them.

'Calm down,' I muttered. 'I'm just messin' with you.'

'Get out,' she told me. 'Get out and get help, you can't handle this alone.'

'Wait a moment,' I said. 'I'm not gonna blow his brains out but think about it. If I run barefoot and alone cross this place, an' manage to climb a ten foot fence, an' run down miles an' miles of road, how long d'you think it's gonna be before I find another livin' soul with a phone? Hell, there might just be pay phones here, an' they might, just might, still be connected, but this here's the

rat king's castle and he's gonna come after me soon as he sees I'm gone. Quickest way to summon help's gonna be a cell phone, and I can't see yours anywhere, which means the nearest one is Skeet's. I'm guessing he sleeps with it under his pillow in case Ethan, or more importantly Molly, call for help. So, let's go get it from him.'

'That's crazy,' Rita said, but I couldn't feel her coming up with a better plan. I was already poking through the third bag when she said, 'And you're sure you can't find my phone anywhere?'

'Can't seem to. Besides, we gotta make sure whoever we call don't ring Skeet first – he's the key holder, remember? We could sneak his cell an' slip out, but what if we dial 911 an' they go call Ethan when they can't reach Skeet?' I picked up the duct tape.

'Not if we tell them he's the one holding us captive.'

'Yeah, good point, but we don't got no cell yet, so right now, it's kinda moot.' I looked toward the counter, once a bright red paint and shiny chrome affair. I slipped the roll of tape onto my wrist and stood up.

'I know you want to run,' I said to Rita. 'But I don't.'

'Fine,' she said. 'But you promise me, we get a chance, we go.'

'Alright.'

I clicked off the safety, drew in a deep breath and let it all the way out. Then I stood up.

Skeet was on a put-up bed, no more than a canvas sheet strung between a folding metal frame, one arm bent up over his head, one leg trailing on the ground, boots still on. His eyes opened and he tensed as if a jolt of energy hit him.

'Rise and shine,' I said.

'What in the hell–?'

'Don't move–' I took a step toward him. 'Not a muscle.'

'How d'you get out?' he asked, not moving a muscle. 'My knife, where the hell you put it?' I arched my eyebrow. Skeet's frown of confusion lifted into one of comprehension. 'You're shitting me.'

'Needs must, Skeet. Needs must.'

'Goddamn it, my daddy gave me that!' I bit back five smart mouth replies. 'Won't do you no good.' He sniffed. 'Ethan an' Molly are on their way, they got old Red on board—' my stomach lurched. I'd been half hoping he'd not come after all, or that he'd brought the national guard and the place was about to go all seventh cavalry. 'So, just what you fixin' to do here?'

'Well, here's the thing, Skeet. What's that phrase, you know, the one 'bout Mexicans? Like, when both sides of an argument got something the other wants? Mexican ... oh yeah, dat it, stand-off.' I slipped the duct tape off my wrist and threw it onto Skeet's belly. 'Rip you'self off a strip, would you, lover?'

Not talking his eyes off me, he uncoiled his arm, picking up the tape as he sat up. He held it out and peeled off an inch.

'Well now, don't sell yourself short.' I flicked the barrel of the gun. He tore off a good foot of the stuff, not cracking a smile. I made him put his wrists together, then wrapped them together, getting him to do as much of the work as I could so as to keep him at arm's length.

'This ain't gonna do you no good,' he said. 'Case you don't remember, there's two of them an' only one of you.'

'Yeah? That's all you know,' I told him. 'Now, throw me your cell.'

'I don't got one,' he said.

'Bullshit, how else were they gonna to call you? You said you'd already heard from Ethan anyways.'

Skeet swiveled sideways and flipped up his pillow. There beneath it was a walkie-talkie, with a range of about a mile. Well, I suppose I'd guessed where it would be at least.

'Where's mine?'

'Maybe Ethan got it?' He grinned.

'Well, let's go look for it,' I said, mentally swearing at Skeet, fate and anything else within reach. 'Get up, hands on you' head.' I stepped back from him, getting the counter between us.

'I bet they's almost to the gate,' Skeet said. 'Maybe they's already through – hey …' and he listened, tilting his head like a dog cocking its ear. 'Well, fuck me.'

'Master's voice?' I muttered, but Skeet was too pleased with himself to even pretend he heard me. The noise began to build, the rattle of a large vehicle with a badly maintained engine. I grabbed Skeet's arm and pressed the gun against the side of his neck.

'Shooting someone through the skull's a real shit idea, Skeet,' I told him. 'Bone's pretty hard stuff, you'd be surprised how often people survive, even a shot from an inch away. But the wind pipe? That shit's all soft an' squishy, rips out real easy, an' there ain't no puttin' it back together. You got me?'

'I got you,' he said. The sound of the engine built to a roar, then shuddered to silence, filled only with the sound of rain.

'While we got a moment, why don't you level with me, Skeet? What's all this about, why you doin' all this?' He could have said anything then; for the money, for the hell of it, for shit and giggles, but the one thing I didn't want him to say, was what he did say.

'Justice. An' on account of Ethan asking me too.' He looked sideways at me. 'That's what you do, when it's kin. You an' me nearly kin,' he went on. 'You know that?' There was the hard crack of a car door slamming outside and boots on the ground.

'How d'you work that out?' I asked, 'or are you gettin' metaphorical on me?'

'Ole Rooster an' us cousins, of a sort.' Another door slammed, louder, larger – I braced myself, nudging the gun barrel against Skeet's neck again, concentrating his mind.

'For the last time,' I said. 'Red and I ain't married.'

CHAPTER TWENTY

ETHAN CAME IN FIRST. For one sparkling moment, I thought he was alone and that it had gone wrong, or Red had never come, or that the FBI had Molly in their van and Ethan had been sent in to talk Skeet down. Ethan's broad, conquering smile froze as he took in his brother, hands bound in front of him, and me with the gun at his throat.

'Well now, what-in-the-hell's this happy horse shit?'

They'd put a bag over Red's head, a pillow case or something, a red smear blooming on the front. Oh Christ, I should have run, I should have taken the five miles barefoot option, because seeing him like that sent the blood hammering through my body. I pressed the gun into Skeet's neck just to stop it trembling in my hand.

Molly's little white face appeared in the gloom behind Red's hooded figure.

'Skeet!' she said, before she could contain herself. 'You bitch, what the fuck you doin'?'

'Hello, Ethan,' I said. I saw Red flinch toward the sound of my voice. 'You wanna put your gun down?'

'What the fuck you think–'

'Do it! Or I'm gonna paint this place a whole new shade of hillbilly red.' Ethan raised his gun along with his free hand.

'What the hell happened, Skeet? She hit you with her purse?'

'S'way it goes, bro,' Skeet said. I jabbed him in the neck with the gun.

'I'm gonna put you down, bitch,' Molly said. 'So help me, I'm gonna do it.' Goodness, she really was upset.

'Let's all just calm down here. What exactly you fixin' on doin', girl?' Ethan asked.

'Don't see no gun on the ground,' I said.

'No, no you don't.' He bent and placed his weapon on the floor. 'Now, I can't speak for Molly. She's kind of a law unto herself, ain't you, darlin'?' Molly grinned and pushed her gun against Red's head.

'That's right,' she said.

'Well, here's the thing,' I said. 'I don't much care what's behind all this shit, but I've had enough. You give me Red, an' I'll give you lil' ole Skeet here, an' we'll just walk away an' pretend like it never happened. Kind of like prom night.'

Red lifted his head. They'd tied his hands in front of him, rope or something; his pants were muddied and soaked through with rain water. Through all of it, through the look that Ethan shot Molly, and the cold gnawing at my hands and feet, I could sense something else. Red was looking at me, toward my voice. And he was trying not to laugh.

'Well now,' Ethan said. 'You know, I kind of like you, an' I'm real sorry you got mixed up in this. But, we got unfinished business with your husband here–'

'He's ain't her husband,' Skeet said. Ethan glared at him.

'Well, whatever the fuck he is, we ain't done with him.' He held his hands out at his sides. 'Besides, look at all the trouble we gone to gettin' him here. Be shame to let that all go to waste, now wouldn't it?'

'Fine,' I said. 'Why don't I just kill this piece of shit, then?'

'No–' Molly began, but Ethan hushed her.

'I don't think you're goin' do that, girl. But I tell you what, you've had one hell of a night already, why don't you take off? Seein' as you two are so cosy now, my brother can walk you to the gate, an' once you's through, you can hop down to the cross ways and thumb you'self a lift. By the time you get anybody to believe you, we'll be long gone, but you'll be home an' dry.'

'No,' I said.

Ethan pulled a face, turning his mouth down. 'Now come on, can't be fairer than that, now can I? Seein' as you ain't his wife, n' all, what you care what we're about?'

'Do it,' Red said, that dry, laconic voice turning him from a faceless scarecrow into the man I'd come here for. 'Please, darlin', you don't got to be the hero here.' Well, great minds and all.

'Now ain't that sweet,' Molly said and nudged him with her gun.

'Well, isn't it?' I said. 'But we're kind of like the marines, we don't leave a man behind, and–' Skeet stamped his heel down on my bare foot. I felt the bones crack against the concrete floor, then he punched my gun arm up with his bound fists. I fired, screaming in pain as he ground his boot into my foot, but the bullet failed to take off the top of his head and impacted into the ceiling, showering us with plaster. My legs gave way as Skeet forced the ring of his arms over my head, and the gun spun from my hand. Pain burned through me as I gasped for air, drowning again as a sob broke from me.

'You son of a bitch!' I heard Red over the noise of the others, over Molly's gleeful cackling and Ethan's war cry. Skeet let me go, let me slump to the floor, where I lay pinned by the pain. I felt the impact of footsteps, heard the scrape of them on the floor and tried to force myself away, fear making me cry out again. Only it was Red, breaking free of Molly and pulling the bag from his

head. He knelt beside me and heaved me into his arms the best he could.

'You fuckin' son of a bitch – darlin', I got you, I got you …' I could smell him, through the dirt and the rain and the blood – the scent beyond cologne that was all his. I closed my eyes. 'Fuck me, Rita, what the hell you doin' here?'

'I don't know,' I said, and his laughter warmed me, curled into the base of my spine despite it all; despite everything he was and everything I was, or because of it. I raised my head and looked at him, at the blood crusting on his nose and mouth and the lines drawn on his face by concern. 'I'm not Rita.'

'Oh, really …' And there was a smile at the edge of those animal eyes.

'What the fuck happened here?' Ethan demanded of Skeet. Skeet held his bound hands up in front of him.

'She got the drop on me, s'all.' Ethan punched him in the arm.

'How the fuck she do that? I said you could fuck her, not get fucked by her!' Skeet pulled away from his brother; I could hear the hangdog in his stride without looking.

'She got my knife,' he said.

'Yeah?' Ethan slapped him, then slapped him again. 'You fuckin' retard, I ask you do one thing, one thing, s'all.'

'Ethan, don't–' Molly said, but the man rounded on her.

'Don't you speak up for him, he only got one goddam thing to do an' he fucked it up.' He turned on Skeet. 'How she do it, huh?' Slap. 'Huh, bro?' Slap.

'Tell him how, Skeet,' I said. 'You gonna tell him how?'

'She picked my damn pocket,' Skeet yelped, hands up, trying to deflect Ethan and stand up to him all at once.

'How she do that, eh?' Ethan slapped him again.

'I lost my temper,' Skeet pleaded. Oh big brothers, when ever do they grow out of giving you hell? 'She picked the lock, when I went t' lie down, hid it from me.' He pulled from Ethan's grasp and turned his shoulder to him, flicking his hair from his eyes.

'Didn't you search her?' Ethan demanded.

'Please, can we not go there?' I muttered.

'What it matter?' Skeet snapped. 'S'all good now, ain't it?'

'Ethan!' Molly tried again, but neither of them paid her any mind.

'I should a' let her blow you' brains out–' Ethan shoved his brother in the shoulder. 'You were suppose' watch her, not get your beauty sleep. You jeopardized the mission.' Red laughed at this; Ethan spun on his heel to glare at him. 'You got somethin'?'

'Oh please, you carry on, officer,' Red said. 'Don't want to get in the way of your briefing, or whatever this is.'

'Laugh it up,' Molly said. 'You're time's comin'–'

'This my command,' Ethan barked. 'This my command, an' you goin' do what I say, Captain Levine. You hear?'

Together they picked us up, Red clinging to me as best he could. They had something to do, something to make ready, now all the gang was here, and to that end they locked us in a closet in the empty kitchen behind the counter. I was in too much pain to take a great deal of notice, other than of Skeet fumbling in my pocket - 'want my knife back–' and extracting it with thumb and forefinger. That, and the agony of trying to walk. For a short amount of time I gave into despair and let them manhandle both of us inside without protest. I wanted nothing more than to be alone and think, and if that meant being shut in a cupboard with a storm lantern, that would do.

'I want a medkit,' Red demanded, bound hands on the door as Ethan went to slam it. 'An' water. Even you know you're not within your right to deny us that.'

 **BROKEN PONIES**

'We ain't exactly playing by the Geneva convention no more,' Ethan said. 'You lucky I got you some light in there.' Nevertheless, a second or two after the door closed, it opened again and Ethan dropped a plastic bag on the floor. 'Hold out your hands,' he said. Red did, and Ethan cut whatever they'd bound him with, before shoving him back and slamming the door.

CHAPTER TWENTY-ONE

ONCE THE KEY rattled in the lock, Red knelt beside me. He ripped fragments of duct tape from his wrists, then brought the lantern light to bear on my foot.

'I don't want to look,' I said, as we both did.

'Can you move your toes?'

'Yeah, but it fuckin' hurts – shit – no, not that one, not the little one, it's fuckin' broken!' I took hold of his jacket lapel. 'Tell me you called the police, tell me you didn't just set out here alone with a bag of money?'

'Lie back,' Red said. 'We need to strap this up, try and get some pressure on it. Sweet Jesus, that son of bitch done a number on you.'

'That's nothing,' I said, shuffling backwards so I could lean against the wall. It was graveyard cold in there, the floor bare concrete and rust stains. No windows either. If Skeet hadn't been so pleased with his twisted wonderland, he'd have seen sense and locked me in here rather than the swan boat, but like I'd said before, house proud.

'It's cold as hell in here,' Red said. 'Look at you, you're shivering.' He pulled off his jacket, the same good make he always wore, and fed it behind me and around my shoulders. Then he went to the bag Ethan had given him and looked inside.

'Least one of you around here knows how to treat a lady,' I said, my laugh chattering through my teeth.

'What the hell else they done to you?' Red twisted back round from the bag. 'Darlin'–' he slid over to me. 'Now, darlin', I got to ask you ... Jesus ...' He touched his hand to his forehead. 'Did they do anything of ... of a sexual–'

'Oh no you don't,' I snapped. 'Fuck sake Red, they hit me, an' they half choked me to death, not to mention the whole kidnapping thing, that's more than enough, thank you. Goddamn it, don't you go gettin' all territorial over me just because you think you've staked a claim. Jesus, you wanna come over all moral defender? There's a thousand women in this state gonna wake up in their own beds and get raped this mornin', you go worry about them.'

'Look, I had to ask,' he said, hands up. 'It might not make no difference to you but–'

'Of course it would have made a difference to me, but it shouldn't get you riled up any more than what has happened, just because you wanna go there yourself. What about the police?' Red reached for the bottle of water Ethan had allowed us and ripped off the cap. Then he ran his hand along my shin, before gently moving my foot toward the light. 'The FBI, tell me you called the FBI?'

'Darlin', I'm not sure as you understand as' how things work.' His hand was warm on my ankle, his fingers firm and familiar as he worked over my foot where it was swelling and discolored.

'Oh snap, Red! You're tellin' me you really didn't call anyone?'

'Local police about as much use as a teacup in a rain storm.' He poured water into his hands and ran them over my foot. I winced, biting my teeth together. 'No bones sticking out, that's a blessin'.' In the bag there was a roll of bandage, mercifully still in its plastic wrap, and some sticking plaster. He ripped the bandage free and peered at my foot.

'Isn't it though? An' here was me thinking it was a bad day.'

'When you turned up at the house, you wonder why I got you clear the moment I saw you?'

'I guessed you were just pleased to see me.'

'Well, that too, but look- Papa an' me? We knew as we were bein' watched, they ain't that good. We just didn't know who it was. Papa thought it was one of them home invasion things, isolated place like ours, what people think ... what they say 'bout us, any road. We were just about to have a meeting with the head of our security firm, hence the suits an' the blacked out windows, when you come breezing in.'

'Shit – that fuckin' hurts!' He stopped, bandage pressed against my foot.

'An' it's gonna hurt if you don't sit still. This was a whole lot easier the last time, when you was unconscious. You want something to bite on?'

'Don't tempt me,' I muttered. He ran his tongue over his teeth and began again.

'When they sent me your picture, they made it clear you'd be dead the moment they got hide or hair of the authorities. I had an idea who they might be, and trust me, professionals they ain't. Professionals know you'll call the Feds, an' how long they got. They make the drop fast and clean, and this was not that.'

'Besides, it wasn't enough money,' I said, then pressed my hand to my mouth as pain flared in me.

'You think you worth more?' he said, not looking at me. 'Besides, I know what this is about, an' I don't want to have to explain myself to no one.'

'Oh fuck–' I slapped my thigh with my hand. 'Red, you goddamn idiot!'

'There's a GPS tracker in my car,' he said, concentrating on where he was tying off the bandage at my ankle. 'I left everything

to be found if I weren't back by dawn, an' set the alarm off moment I stepped out to get you.'

'Get who you thought was me, you mean?' Still holding my ankle, he nodded and sat back on his heels.

'Got to hand it to them, that was a nice move. I could have sworn it was still all your idea of a first date, 'till she took the bag off her head.'

'But you set off the tracker?'

'Alarm bells ringing all over the state. They ain't so bright, last stop was outside the door. I pulled up a way before an' walked down to the locker.'

'So your private security firm, they're the cavalry?'

'Hundred thousand a year, they better be darlin''. I flexed my foot against the binding and regretted it as the now familiar agony raced up my leg. When it had washed over me, when it had shivered to the ends of my fingers, it left only a moderately excruciating throbbing in its wake.

'Oh damn it, Skeet's the key holder to this place, the goddamn gate keeper. He's already said as how the first thing they're gonna do is call him to open up an' let them in.'

Red picked up the water bottle, drank and then offered it to me. 'Let's stay optimistic,' he said. He stood up and began testing the strength of the door, running his hands around the frame, then along the walls. I had the feeling that there was a lot he wasn't saying, like just how much this security team of his knew, and how long it might be before they turned up.

'So ...' he said. 'This here's a bit of a hole, but there's no need to be downhearted. First thing we're gonna try an' do, even if I can't get this door open, is get you away from here.'

'Red, no–' I began but he cut me off with a look.

'Don't go reading me the wrong way, darlin', I ain't being a gentleman here. Like I said, I left my car parked up a little way back from this place. Added to that, that's where my GPS tracker is, so that's where the cavalry's headin'. I couldn't think of a way of tellin' you before, but I wish you'd taken Ethan's offer and let the other one escort you out, you could have found it by now an' called up the world an' his wife to come get me.' He looked at the door lock again and ran his fingers over it.

'Where d'you leave it?' I asked.

'Out the main gate, then you gotta limp no more an' half a mile left an' you'll see a side road marked with a–'

'A half mile? It'll take me till Easter to get there like this.'

'Well, limp harder, then.'

'And how do I drive it?'

'Key's in the ignition darlin'.' He grinned at me then turned back to his inspection of the door. 'What, you think if we gotta jump out under fire, we stick it in neutral and flick the central locking?'

'Red, what the hell's this all about?' He looked down, hands still on the door frame. Then he came and sat beside me, his back to the wall next me. He reached into his pocket and took out a quarter.

'Like I said, I've always wondered about this catching up with me, though they never showed such initiative when I knew them 'afore.' He turned toward me, his face half lost in shadow. He was looking at me the way he did, as if he was trying to see more of me than skin allowed. I saw his gaze fall to the bruising on my neck, then to my mouth where my lip was split. Then he looked down at where his hand held the quarter, and didn't say what he was thinking, didn't add words to the pain in his expression.

'This is Iraq, isn't it?' I said, thinking that if he showed he was concerned about me again, I really wouldn't be able to stop from crying. 'Something about what happened ... the boy that they killed, on the video? You know I saw it ... when we were alone that

first time, in the swamp, when I didn't know who I was, let alone which me I was–'

'Oh, so that's what you meant before,' he said. 'You're ... so where's Rita?'

'Oh, she's alright–' then I found I couldn't meet his gaze. I'd gotten used to being, well, inside, and I'd never had to explain myself to anyone before, because when I wasn't inside, I wasn't ever around people who knew Rita well enough to notice. 'It was when Skeet put hands on her, she kind of blacked out and, well, it's what I was trying to say about the swamp, sometimes it happens. I don't know why, but she ... we ... see shit.'

'You tellin' me you ... what, read minds?' he asked.

I shrugged.

'I dunno. Maybe we're just joining the dots, you know? This time Rita ... Rita saw some shit she'd tried not to remember, not to see, an' she's gotta take time out to deal with that' – I could see by his face that Red was struggling with this – 'but before, in the swamp, I saw what you'd seen, in Iraq. I saw the world slow down an' ... an' you're laughin' at me.'

'No, no.' But he was, looking away from me, shaking his head.

'Look, I'm just tellin' you, that's all. An' Lisa told me stuff too.' Red tapped the coin on the floor and then began rubbing it against the concrete, back and forth, working at it. 'I don't know if all I did was remember all the things I'd found out, and somehow imagined the rest, but what I saw, when I saw it before, was that you had a man taken, you know, hostage, an' you went all ... all out to find him and someone–'

'Died,' he said. It was dark in that closet; the ceiling stretching up into a void of shadow above us. Red didn't look at me as he spoke, but kept working the coin back and forth, scribbling nickel into the dirt. 'Specialist Rockwell was a good man.' He pulled his mouth into a line somewhere south of a smile. 'It was ... not meant to heat up like it did out there. We were stationed at a base to the north, watching over the supply lines, but war's like that, like a dead old fire, you think you've got it, but turn around and a spark catches and–' the coin tapped. 'Up it comes again.'

'They were there, Molly an' Ethan?' Red nodded.

'I was used to havin' a team about me, just habit I guess ...' Like a wedding band in an ashtray by the bed, like a knife slipped into the right-hand pocket of your pants. 'Out of the blue, we lost three men on the supply road, came under fire. Same week, we lost four more.' He got up and went over to the door lock. He tried the edge of the quarter into the screw heads, rocking the coin from side to side to try and slot it home.

'They can't blame you for that, Ethan and Molly, that weren't you.' Red grimaced at the lock then came and sat down again next to me.

'Oh, hell no, that ain't it.' He pursed his lips. 'They blame me for their going to jail.' He held up the coin again and squinted at it. 'After ... after Rockwell was killed, I found my ass on the first plane out. Should have been an inquiry, an' I wanted there to be, trust me.' He looked at me. 'That might sound like a crock of shit to you, but it's God's own truth. I wanted to stand up and be counted, hell, I weren't ashamed. I seen worse, a hundred times worse.'

'All's fair in love and war, Red?' I said.

'Well ... I wouldn't go that far. Neither would Ethan and Molly I'd guess, seein' as they got sent down, an' I got off scot-free. Or so they think.' He tapped the coin again before carrying on. I was going to ask how come they'd gone to prison and he hadn't, but I could work it out. I remembered Skeet, hand to my throat, saying that all they were to the likes of me was cannon fodder. Ethan and Molly would have been easier to blame than an officer who might have

 **BROKEN PONIES**

made things difficult. Easier to offer them a deal, scare the shit out of them and tell them that it would be better if they did as they were told. Who the hell would have listened to them anyway? Ethan was hardly the type of poster boy a left-wing media could get behind.

'It don't make no odds,' Red said. 'But there was a lot more goin' on than Ethan Sprat and Molly Dent ever figured.' Hearing their full names like that made them seem more real, less like the cartoons they'd become in my mind.

'Skeet said you and he were related,' I said, and Red laughed.

'If you wanna call it that, but his folks aren't exactly on our Christmas card list. You know what they say about blood, a little of it goes a long way.' He held the coin up, pinched between his fingers. 'You reckon this might do it?'

'Only one way to find out,' I said.

The light from the lantern was fading. Its flame was dying down, the hiss of the kerosene growing louder as if it was struggling against the inevitable and whistling in the dark. I looked toward the door and saw it was reduced to a dull red circle encroached by shadow.

Red didn't get up. The coin flashed, then he folded it away into his pocket. What light there was glazed his eyes and etched out the lines of his expression. He was looking at me as if I were something he might just translate into his own language, if only he looked long and hard enough. I wanted to touch him. I wanted him to touch me and to feel the flex of his muscles under his skin and where his bones pressed under the surface and the beat of his blood under my fingers.

His lips resisted mine, then he gave into the kiss. He tasted of iron and smoke, of rust and heat and darkness. His fingers brushed the side of face, then he slipped his hand through my hair to the back of my head.

'Which one of us do you think he's kissing now?' Rita laughed inside of me.

'Oh, shit,' I muttered. 'What the hell we doin'?'

'Fucked if I know,' he said, and we laughed. He kissed me again and I closed my eyes and he kissed my throat where it hurt, where the flesh was bruised and where it stung at his touch.

'Not now,' I said. 'We can't do this now–' His fingers plucked at the fabric of my shirt; my lips found the hollow of his collarbone.

'I know, Jesus, I know darlin',' he said, his words breathing against me. 'What was it you said last time, that old sex and death thing? I don't much care if that's the truth, hell, maybe it be better if it were. Last wish, n' all.' The jacket he'd given me slipped from my shoulders as I let him ease me back against the floor. There was not enough room for us, for him to hold himself over me as he kissed my neck, my shoulders, my mouth, as my hands traced his ribs and clung to the roll of his shoulder muscle.

'Stop it,' I said. 'Please, it's fuckin' insane.'

'I know,' he said, and he relaxed against me and I felt the laughter in him. 'Part of me's still thinkin' as this is just your idea of the perfect first date.'

'Hey, fuck you!' I said. 'I'm actually quite romantic. You should try it some time, a few roses, an' I could stand a meal or two, once in a while.' He laughed and went to rest his face against my breasts, only as I moved, the pendant or whatever it was that Johnny had given me rolled over and I felt him catch his cheek on it.

'What's this?' he said, lifting his head to look at it. 'You got a rock round your neck?' He propped himself up on his elbow and picked it up, peering at it in what light there was.

'It's just a thing some crazy guy in a roadside shack gave me.'

'What guy?' He sat further up, turning it over in his fingers.

'Oh, for fuck's sake, Red! Don't tell me you' getting jealous over

that? How many more times I gotta remind everyone? We ain't married an'–' The key turned in the lock outside.

CHAPTER TWENTY-TWO

RED DROPPED the pendant and scrambled up, as if we were teenagers caught making out. He was on his feet before Ethan's silhouette was revealed by the door and pale light washed over us.

'Alright,' Red said. 'You gonna let Rita go now.' I pressed my back against the wall and snatched at him to heave myself up.

'You think as you's still the boss of me?' Ethan said, laughing. 'Look at you, actin' the big man in front of the lady.'

'Well, sure, you got me,' Red said, slipping his arm about me to pull me up. 'You got me, sure, but you don't need her. Do what you said before, let her go.'

'No,' I said. 'Not without you–'

'No,' he said, to me as much as Ethan. The man folded his arm, resting his gun in the crook of his elbow and standing with his weight on one hip, looking at us both as if we were the cutest thing he'd seen since Easter.

'Well, like I said before, I do kind of like you, girl, an' I'm real sorry as you've ended up in all this. But fate's cruel like that sometime', you always gonna have yourself innocent by-standers. But hey, I tell you what?' He straightened up and stepped back from the door. 'You come along with me now, and we'll see how it goes. If he asks me to let you go one more time, maybe I can find a way to make that happen for you both?' At least he didn't call himself Daddy.

Dawn had broken over Disney Land, Hell. It didn't help none. The sky was a soft, dirty orange; sunlight filtered through the night's rain, clouds building to rain some more. You could feel the air as if it were something damp and dirty pressed against you, a stray cat crept into your room and curled up on your pillow. Outside, the restaurant was carnage a world of snagged-up, broken-down colors and faded jollity, twisted and overgrown. It was fuzzing at the edges, green and growing, seeping plant life inching remorsefully over everything. A children's fun house was dressed as if for sleeping beauty, already looking as if a hundred years had passed. The dandelion clock structure of a burnt-out Ferris wheel was drawn black against the light. Everywhere was busted up rigging and half-standing scaffolds, draped and twisted in vines and creepers; fairyland stamped under the heel of a storm, then washed up and hung out to dry.

As we stumbled along in front of Ethan, Red half-lifting me as I struggled to walk on my broken toes, I knew we were headed back toward the carousel room. Now it was light, I could see that it was housed in a great, grey box of a place, what was left of its sign jutting from its roof. There were cracked murals on the walls, great slabs of plaster missing, and half-remembered fragments of painted ponies and carnival clowns remaining, a hoof here, a lurid smile there.

'You remember this place, don't you?' Ethan said to me. 'This is where she woke up after we took her. It's my brother's favorite place.' Daylight lit a path to where Molly was standing. I thought how small she looked, lost, a tiny figure washed-up and left behind like all the other junk. I should have hated her, and though I did, there was something else I felt for her. My eyes fogged with tears from the chill air and light after my confinement, then a sound came to me, that dull crackle, that flicker, as if I were aware of the film of reality and where its edges wore thin. I took a step forwards, caught my foot and winced at the pain. When I looked up, blinking to clear my eyes, I didn't see Molly. I saw Lisa, Lisa with the janitor at her school, who'd been ever so nice to her and got her pregnant; Lisa with the drama teacher in Vegas, who'd been ever so nice to her and then gone back to his wife; Lisa with Red; Lisa with Paris; with Bob. Lisa with that dark, endless ache inside of her for someone, some man to be nice to her, just like our ... my Daddy never had been. I saw Molly, running after her brothers, barefoot across dry ground, and in the army, running to catch up yet again. Always having to be faster and stronger, and louder, and fiercer and more like them, but never quite, never quite like them. And Ethan, the one who'd turned back for her, who'd waited for her, because he needed her to wait for him.

As Red went to move I grabbed his arm, made him hear my whisper.

'Skeet loves Molly. An' he's only here because of that, an' because he believes in Ethan, but only just, only because he has to.'

'Come on,' Ethan said and pushed us forwards.

The gaping hole in the roof of the carousel room was an amber-white square in the early dawn, the sunlight faint as the cloud cover rolled back over. There was still enough light through the windows to throw the horses into relief, a black, burnt-out mess of hooves pawing the air, beetles on their backs. The carousel itself took up the left-hand corner of the room, its broken, light-smashed canopy sheltering the last few intact horses, white in contrast to the fallen.

The planking on the path, which had echoed as I'd walked over it before, had been pulled aside. Beneath it was a pit, six by six foot. Skeet and Molly were standing together to one side of it and moved apart as they saw us, Molly coming forward and

 **BROKEN PONIES**

Skeet hanging back, turning his face away into darkness. Red was holding me up, my arm about his shoulders and his around my waist, but Molly, gun in hand, came and took hold of me.

'Sorry t'break you up an' all, but you're gonna come and sit with me, darlin'. All girls together, don't you think?'

'You sure about that?' I muttered.

'Takin' control, Private Dent?' Red said. 'You steppin' up now?'

'You don't get to call me that no more,' she said. 'Like I don't got to call you Sir.'

'No,' I said, but Red shook his head almost imperceptibly, then let me go. Molly went to support me; I pulled away, only my foot wouldn't take my weight and she had to catch me after all.

'Don't get all stupid, an' cut your nose off to spite your face, darlin'. Let me help you.' Well, that was real nice of her.

One of them had brought a chair out from the restaurant and had set it up at the head of the pit. Ethan strode over to it and sat down, gun in hand. Molly manoeuvred me until we were standing on Ethan's left, both of us facing Red, with Skeet off in the background, hands in pockets.

'He not joining us? He don't look too happy about this, your boyfriend.'

'Shut up,' Molly hissed, making me stumble and knowing it would hurt. There was something there, but I couldn't see what it was; something between them, or rather, something getting in the way of her and Ethan. She wasn't looking at me; her eyes darted between the two of them, Skeet and Ethan, and she was chewing her lip, had chewed it quite to ribbons.

'You know why you's here, don't you?' Ethan said to Red.

'I got an idea.' Red folded his arms. 'I mean, an idea what an ignorant son of a bitch like you thinks you're about.' Ethan leant forward in his chair, leaning his forearms on his knees and letting the gun hang between his legs. He shook his head, a smile playing over his lips.

'You just the same as you always were, like all of them. You think as we ain't worth the time of day – you think–' A blare of static erupted from Skeet. He grabbed for his walkie-talkie and turned to answer it. I shot a glance at Red, feeling my heart thud at the base of my throat. Skeet muttered into it, pressed the button, and listened for the reply, head cocked. He spoke into it again, words muffled, then hooked the handset back into his pants. Only then did he notice we were all looking at him.

'S' Earl, that's all. Likes to wake me up an' get me to do my morning walk through. Ain't nothin'.' Ethan narrowed his eyes at me.

'She thought it were,' he said, flicking his gun in my direction. 'I seen the way you looked at Red Rooster there. You tellin' me you called the feds anyways, after all I said to you?' The gun in his hand moved casually, until it was aimed at my head.

'No,' Red said. He spoke as he usually did, his voice low, languorous, no need to hurry. 'There ain't no one coming. That was just what I said, so as Rita here would leave if she got the chance. I knew she wouldn't, lest she thought there was a reason for her to do so.'

'What?' I couldn't help myself. 'You're shitting me, you never called no one?' Ethan was smiling again, though his gun hadn't moved.

'That I did not,' Red glanced over at me, but not long enough for me to read anything in his face. 'I've been expecting you, Ethan Sprat. I knew you were coming for me, that your ... your mind was such that it would do nothing but fester. I knew you were watching me, you ain't that good. Only shame of it, you don't got the balls to come face me like a man, that you got to drag her into all this.'

'I got my reasons,' Ethan said. I felt the weariness in my limbs

as he spoke, as his gun dropped and his face went all Cheshire cat pleased with itself.

'You're here on account of Specialist Rockwell,' Red went on. 'An' on account of you thinkin' you and this here solider' – he nodded toward Molly – 'you think you were most sorely put upon.'

'Damn right,' Ethan said.

'We did time for what happened,' Molly said. 'You know that. You went home an' we got hung out to dry.'

'What makes you think that was what I wanted?' Red fixed his gaze on Molly, and I felt her stiffen, felt her jut her chin out to face him, drawing her shoulders back. 'Well now, Molly Dent. You never struck me as one as would believe everything she heard.'

'Ain't nothin' what I heard,' she said. "S what happened.'

'That so?' Red asked. Molly looked over at Ethan.

'I got two years,' he said. 'Molly got half that, an' both of us dishonorably discharged. Neither of us got no trial.'

'An' just who d'you think would have spoken up for you, had you gotten your day in court?' Red asked. He raised his hand, went as if to point at Molly, then let himself smile and scratched the back of his head instead. 'I wonder what they said to you? Take our advice, make the sensible decision? You don't want to go to trial an' stand up in front of the press an' TV, all them ...' He waved his hand, spiraling his fingers. 'United organization of whatever, with their conventions of this and that? Told you to be sensible, I imagine, advised you to make the wise decision?' Red let his hand drop. 'An' you believed them.'

'Ain't no one standin' by us to say otherwise, was there now?' Ethan said. 'You were back home with your nice new wife, in that big ole' house of yours, even 'afore they got round to speakin' with us.' He slammed his fist against the arm of the chair. 'You know the shame got brought on us?' It was Ethan's turn to point at Molly.

'Why, her folks wouldn't even have her back home, she had go stay with Skeet an' our mamma, comin' cross country on a bus with her case, an' nothin' else.' Poor little Molly, thrown out with just a bag and the burden of guilt; my heart could have bled for her. 'An' puttin' her up's all I could do for her, where I were. You ever think about that?'

'How un...fortunate,' Red said. Molly and Skeet, I thought, all alone in some big old mess of a place, papered with take-out menus and pictures of folks cut out of the newspaper, both of them waiting for Ethan to get out. Ethan the hero, Ethan the big brother, so sorely treated by the world, and Molly waiting for him with his mamma, whatever the hell she was like, with her duct tape and her television shows. Molly, so damn grateful to Ethan for taking her in, when her own family wouldn't give her the time of day, waiting all that time with Skeet, the rat king, to keep her company.

'It ain't even just that now, is it?' Ethan went on, not seeing the way Molly looked over at Skeet, or how he turned to meet her look. 'Rockwell's blood's on your hands, sure as you killed him you'self.'

'You see me arguin'?' Red said. He took a step closer to Ethan, held his hands out to the side. 'You think I don't blame myself much as you blame me, Ethan Sprat?'

'Like hell you do,' Molly snapped.

'He ever tell you 'bout Rockwell?' Ethan looked at me from under his brow. 'What happened to him, an' how he should never have been there in the first place?'

'Should any of us?' Red said. 'Not ours to choose, Ethan. You know that.'

'He was sick,' Molly exclaimed. 'He'd done a tour down south, an' you know what he was like.' I could feel the anger in her, feel it snapping through her. Ethan didn't like her interrupting him; he

was enjoying himself, sat up there on his fold-up throne, but he let her continue. Perhaps even he had to admire her passion.

'He'd already gone to them and said as how he couldn't sleep nor eat or nothin', an' all they did was give him pills, and say he was gonna be fine. He was this close goin' AWOL, this close.' She held up her thumb and forefinger, just so as we could all see how close he'd been.

'Cannon fodder,' Skeet muttered. "S all we are, rich girl.'

'We were in Germany,' Ethan said, before Molly could go on. 'An' we had this ... this angels wall. You seen it, ain't you Captain?' I saw Red's jaw tighten at that, at Ethan using his old rank. 'What we did? One wall for the woman as did right by us, and one for them as didn't?'

Red smiled. 'The army life's not kind to the institution of marriage.'

'Rockwell had this girl, you saw her, saw her picture?'

Red nodded. 'I saw.'

'Few days before we shipped, he said as how she'd been onto him. She were Chinese or some such, pretty lil' thing – artist or something. He said as how she were too good for him, always on the side of the angels. Rockwell said as how she'd come to him an' said she'd found a way he could get out, through church people, what could get a man away if he wanted.'

'There were always such rumors,' Red said. 'I'm surprised he sat down an' told you all this, Ethan. I never figured you for the listening type.'

'He told me,' Molly said.

'He told you, did he?' Red cocked his head to one side. 'Caught him at a low ebb did you, Molly Dent? They do say a man will seek a woman's comfort when he can. Better than a confessional.' He flicked a glance toward me.

'I told him not t' do it,' Molly said. 'He was one of us, he'd never let us down, never run out on us, an' he didn't. He told that girl he couldn't do it, and she never wrote to him again, lil' bitch.' That was from the heart, what heart she had, Molly Dent.

'Not like you, Captain,' Ethan said. He stood up, the foldaway chair rocking back as he moved. 'You know it, what you did. Six fatalities in two days, whole place on lockdown, an' you send him out anyway. What the hell were you thinking?' His face was flushed, the anger rising in him. 'He got no reason to be out there – hell, you didn't even send him out with us. I never knew he was gone till he was out, an' you know what happened then, don't you?' He jabbed toward Red with his gun. 'Don't you?'

There was a silence, while the echo of Ethan's words boomed around the carousel room and the horses pulled back their gums and bared their teeth at us. Then, the rattle of the rain intruded, crackling over yellow earth, swelling into dark rivulets.

'Yes,' Red said, his voice little more than a whisper in the face of Ethan's fury. 'I know what happened.'

'Stop it,' I said. Both men looked over at me. 'Red didn't kill him.'

'Oh, you think that?' Ethan turned on me. 'What you think you know?' He looked back at Red. 'He know, he know what I'm sayin'. Rockwell were never meant to be there, were he, sir?'

'D'you wanna know?' Red said. He shrugged his shoulders, rolling them under his shirt. 'I mean, I don't got to tell you, but I will, if you've a mind to listen.'

'Listen to what?' Ethan said.

'You seem to think as there was nothing behind what I did, other than some sort of ... of contrary nature.' He walked away from Ethan, turned his back on him, and drew his fingers through his hair.

'Come back an' face me,' Ethan demanded. 'I don't want to listen to this shit.'

'Let him,' Molly said.

'What you care?' Ethan spat.

'I wanna know what he gotta say,' she hissed. 'Sure an' what else we here for?'

'You want me to remind you?' Ethan said, but Red turned back to face him.

'You remember, Ethan Sprat, you remember how all that mess over there started, this time round?' Ethan squared his shoulders but didn't answer. 'This weren't ever a war of us an' them, it was always a war of us an' them an' the next ones, an' them over there.' Ethan went to speak, but Red raised his hand, a little hint of their once deferential relationship giving him enough power to carry on. 'You know why Rockwell was a better man than you, a better solider? On account of he understood that. D'you have cause to remember that man we had in the cells at that time, the one you an' others used to call Ali Baba, because you never had the sense to think much above children's books?'

'Sure,' Molly said. 'I remember him. Spoke English, sorta.'

'What about him?' Ethan said. 'That whole place full of ragheads waitin' to cut our throats an' bein' nice as pie to our faces.' I expect they were, I thought, after a few weeks with you.

'Rockwell took time to get to know him, this ... Ali Baba. D'you know what he was?' Red smiled, as if over a memory, as if feeling pride in a solider who was a cut above the rest. 'This Ali, he was one of them as was glad to be behind bars, under our jurisdiction, because he was a whole lot safer there, than out on the street.'

A little town, I thought. Somewhere on the edge of nowhere, hot and dry with the cracked ground and the sound of wind in the trees. It crept in on me as I pulled away from Molly and sank to the floor, drawing my arms about myself. They didn't notice me; they were hardly looking at me anymore, and I was moving away from them to someplace else, where the air smelled of heat and gasoline and dust, and the stench of raw sewage and sweat, sweat that bleeds from the skin, sweat that is blood and burnt flesh and memory.

'You remember the museum, Ethan? Or that never figure large in your life? You even know what one is?'

Smoke, black against the sky, a sky higher and dryer than this one.

'They used to call it Saddam's piggy bank.'

Cordite and charcoal and the crack of gunfire.

'You hear how soon as we turned up, museum got took apart? Iraq's just a name that place got given, been people there four thousand years 'fore that. It had time to gather up the sort of treasure you only gonna find in them story books of yours.'

Gold, behind glass. Faces from another time, another world. Gold, not behind the glass anymore.

'They were stealin' it?' Ethan asked, interested despite himself, despite being the one with the gun. Red shook his head.

'They were covering up what was already took. They torched the place, thinking we'd not notice it were near enough empty already. We'd been trying to find all the lost artefacts, some here, some there. We got a lot of it, but not all. You know that one, the one you called Ali Baba? His father was one of them, one of them as went down with Saddam, an' he'd already got his, strung up on a street corner for his trouble. This Ali knew as his was comin' too, the moment we let him go, just like his father. He wanted out too, like Rockwell, like all of us.'

Two of them, I thought, talking in the dead of the night, in a night that was deader and deeper than most. The American and

the Iraqi, the one who could speak enough English, sorta. What had they found to talk about, in that clanging, desperate space, with nobody else to hear?

'You know what wins wars when you fightin' in someone else's back yard? PR, Ethan – what they think of you, what they don't. PR saves lives, Ethan, hearts an' minds, an' funnily enough, they don't much like us over there.'

The wind was getting up again, blowing the rain before it, bringing the scent of the trees, of earth and decay. The rain had soaked my clothes and darkened the blue cotton of Red's shirt to his skin, rain hitting the ground heavy as the fall of dead bugs drawn to the light. I thought of Lisa, far away and lost, sitting on the floor of a phone booth, feeling the power of her silence on the line, feeling that she had power for the first time.

'The American government don't make deals,' Red said.

'What you sayin', what deal?' Ethan snapped.

'You're right, Ethan. Rockwell should not have gone out into that night, but it was his call.'

'What you mean?' Molly demanded. 'He never wanted to be there, you made him go, you–'

'Fuck's sake – he was on a mission,' I said.

'What you mean? What the hell you know?' Molly glared at me as if she'd forgotten I was there. I folded my good leg under myself and swayed to my feet.

'Was it to... to get somethin'?' I said. Red nodded, his smile that of a professor. I could imagine it, the two of them in the gloom together, Ali waiting to be sure he could trust Rockwell, picking him over the others because they were of like mind. What had he done? Got word out and shown his new friend a little taste of what his father had hidden? Just enough to put the idea in his head, enough for him to go speak with his Captain, Rooster Levine, in confidence.

'She knows more than you, Ethan Sprat,' Red said. 'Course you never knew the men Rockwell went out with, you weren't meant to. One of them was Ali Baba, all dressed up in fatigues an' looking the part. What, you think we don't got brown soldiers in our ranks, you think you'd even have looked at him twice?'

'Shut your mouth,' Ethan growled. 'You think you clever? You think I give a shit about what you got him doin'? It don't make no difference to what happened.'

'Hell, that's worse,' Molly said. 'Just for the sake of some ... some shit from a museum?'

'Hearts an' minds, Molly Dent, hearts an' minds,' Red said. He was smiling, the kind carved into his face by time and experience.

'Like Ethan said,' Molly folded her arms, 'don't make no difference to what you got coming.'

'No, no it don't,' Red said. 'That's why I'm here, ain't it.' His smile faded, his expression becoming almost weary. Then he walked toward Ethan. Molly and Skeet went as if they meant to stop him, but Ethan waved them back. Without breaking his gaze, Red came to stand before him and reached for the hand that held the gun.

'Don't!' I said, but Red stepped forward until the barrel of Ethan's gun was an inch from his heart.

'I'm sorry, darlin',' Red glanced at me for a moment, just a moment, before he fixed his gaze back on Ethan. 'But like I said, I've been ready for this since before you, even. It's time.'

'You know it,' Ethan said. 'You sent him to his death, didn't you?'

'Stop it, you don't got to do this, you don't–' But neither of them looked at me. Skeet put his hand on my shoulder. 'Get off me–' I shook it off and glared up at him. 'You really wanna do this, be part of this?'

'Shut up!' Molly said, but she looked at me, and I saw it in her face, the fear in her. It was what they were here for, sure, but faced

with it, looking at it – well, maybe it just didn't look quite how she'd pictured it.

'That's right,' Red said. 'I've sent men to their death, but Rockwell was the last, an' he were ...'

'Johnny,' Molly said. Her voice was small, hard, a dig of flint against the ground. The rain washed over her little white face, the sprouts of her hair dripping, dark rat tails sticking to her cheeks. The edges of the two men, Red and Ethan, almost seemed to blur with water as if they were drawn against the ruined back drop in accented strokes. Then Ethan shook his head to clear the rain from his eyes.

'No,' he said, and pulled his gun back from Red.

CHAPTER TWENTY-THREE

'COME ON,' Red barked as Ethan turned away. "S what you here for, ain't it?'

Ethan bellowed a laugh. 'No sir, Captain Sir, you don't get it that easy.'

He strode over to me, his boots oozing through the yellow mud. Skeet went to get hold of me and I thought he was in on it, only when Ethan grabbed my arm and jerked me toward him, Skeet tried to yank me back.

'No,' he yelled. 'I ain't doin' this.'

'Leave her!' Red snarled, hands out, taking a half-step toward Ethan. 'It's me you want, me you got!' I stared at the rain hammering into the ground, the water gathering in pot holes and running over and filling the pit behind me. The pit, six inches in water, six foot deep and wide.

'You steppin' up?' Ethan said, his face inches from his brother's, and me trapped between them, struggling to get my balance and gripping onto Skeet, my last, most unlikely of champions. Red started forward, but Ethan jammed his gun against the side of my head and pulled me over to him, my injured foot turning and pain blazing up my leg as I fell to my knees.

'Fuck!' I bellowed.

'Ethan–' Molly's voice cut through the roar of agony in my head. 'What you doin', this ain't–' Ethan lashed out at her with his gun hand quick enough to hit her and get the damn thing back against my temple in an instant. Molly yelped as Ethan dragged me back through the mud and I tumbled after him, a broken doll hanging from his grasp, my own words running through my head – it's a really bad idea to try shootin' someone in the head – the throat? That's all soft and squishy, rips right out and there ain't no coming back from that!

'Put her down,' Red demanded. 'Fuck's sake, Ethan, this ain't her, this is between you an' me, you an' me!'

'I always said as how it was a cryin' shame she got messed up in all this,' Ethan laughed. 'But you know how it goes, Captain Levine, shit goin' happen.' The mud under my fingers was ochre yellow, the color of it seeming to burn into my eyes.

'Think!' Rita hissed inside me.

'You get to watch someone else die again. Because of you, because of what you did – you gonna watch her die 'cause of what you did to us, an' what you did to Johnny Rockwell. Then, I goin' kill you too.'

I was hardly there, with the rain pouring over me and Ethan grabbing the back of my shirt, dragged me up onto my knees. I was staring at the yellow mud on my hands. I know something, I know I do–

'Think!' Rita begged me.

'No,' Molly yelled. 'No, Ethan!' And she went to stop him, tried to grab at him, but Ethan shouldered her away, sending her scudding into Skeet. Red dared a step closer to Ethan.

'Me, you got me! Christ, you don't got to do this – Ethan! Ethan, look at me, you don't got to do this you–'

'No!' I screamed. 'You don't gotta do it, 'cause Johnny ain't dead.'

CHAPTER TWENTY-FOUR

MY SHOUT cracked through the room, loud enough to stampede the carousel horses. Its energy burned within me as I ripped from Ethan's grasp. I scrabbled away from him on hands and knees until Red caught me.

'Johnny's not dead,' I said again, scrubbing wet hair and dirt from my eyes as the rain poured over my face.

'What the hell you mean?' Ethan barked, turning his gun on me, on Red, on Skeet, on Molly.

'You know–' I jabbed my hand toward him, fingers in the shape of horns again. 'You listen to me, Ethan Sprat. You think I'm lyin', when I'm through, an' so help me but I'll shoot myself for you.'

'What the hell you doin'?' Red muttered.

'I saw him–' Molly broke from Skeet. 'I saw him die, we saw him die!'

'Johnny Rockwell,' I said to Ethan. 'Did they find his body? Did they give you back his body? Come on, Ethan, you ever stand over his coffin, you ever see it carried on board – did you?' There was another blast of static from Skeet's walkie-talkie as he went over to Molly, loping dog at her heels.

'Answer me!' I bellowed at Ethan. 'Did they find his body?'

'No,' Molly said. Ethan's face was running with water, his clothes soaked to the skin, his gun still trained on me, on Red.

'So what,' he said, 'so they never gave him back to us? I seen him die, we all seen him die. Captain Levine saw him die, didn't you?'

I pulled from Red's embrace and lurched toward Molly. 'I seen him too–' and I saw the pain on her face, the flash of hope. 'I saw him standin' on the roadside outside a shack made of trash, not four months ago. Johnny Rockwell, six-foot, dark hair, dark eyes–'

'I seen him die!' Ethan roared across me.

'Tattoos,' I went on, not talking to Ethan but to Molly, Molly and Skeet, who was stood behind her, the two of them half-lost in the shadow of the carousel room. 'Two tattoos, one on the right of his chest, here,' I thumped my fist into my collar bone. 'A heart, a heart with a dagger an' wings, an' underneath his number, his serial number. It started with a ...' I screwed up my eyes, tried to make it come, to be back there, to feel the heat of Nevada on my skin and the sweat creeping down my back, and the flash of light from CDs as they turned in the wind. 'It started with a one, an' a three an' ...'

'No,' Ethan said. 'You some fuckin' witch, you don't–'

'And a cat, Molly, a cat – you know it, don't you?' I saw from Molly's face I was right, that she knew I was right, and Ethan knew it too. 'A cat on the other side, with the words, the words ... lucky to die, an'–'

'That's bullshit,' Ethan bellowed. 'He's dead.'

'Oh, he's dead,' I said. 'I mean, he might as well be. He's livin' on the roadside, out of his mind, he won't even talk to his mother.' Because she was his mother - Martha. I only saw it in that second, or I'd always seen it, but only knew it then. Martha, watching over Johnny from the other side of the road, Johnny who thought he was dead. Martha, with her dog and her artists and her son, named for his father. The father whom she'd not married, the father who'd gone when he thought Johnny was dead, or been killed, or whatever, but had left his painting on the wall, signed 'J.R Well'. I could see all of it, enough of it anyway, even the picture of the girl in the washroom, the pretty little Chinese girl dressed up as Red Riding Hood, with four kisses for Johnny, a picture he'd sent home to Martha, so she might know he wasn't quite alone, that he wasn't without the comfort of a confessional.

'No,' Red said from behind me, quiet, just for me to hear. 'Don't.' He was shaking; I could feel it as he held onto me again.

'You were there, you bought Martha his things,' I said to him. 'You paid her your respects–' He had a nice way with him, old-fashioned. 'An' you ordered breakfast an' left her with five thousand dollars and never ate. I know you went there, it was you–'

'Don't,' Red said again. 'Please, Rita, please, don't do this. Let him–' Furious, I wrenched myself from his arms.

'Stop this, stop it now – this don't got to happen, you don't got to do this, Johnny's alive, he's alive!' I gripped the pendant Johnny had given me, ripped its cord and held it out to Molly. She jolted back from me as if I had a gun, then her face crumpled into tears.

'What fool thing's that–' Ethan began. 'Don't touch it, that thing's some voodoo shit, Molly!'

But she reached out for it and took it from me. She knew what it was, like Red must have known what it was, or at least where it was from. Molly had seen it and I knew where. She'd seen it on Johnny Rockwell, round his neck too, given to him by Ali Baba, perhaps?

'He said for me to give it you,' I told Molly.

'Weapons down – weapons down!'

Three men burst in on us from the rain. Red lunged for Ethan and hit him in the face. The big man staggered backwards, crashing into the fold-up chair. Through it all, through the rain

and the running feet and the arms that took hold of me, not to hurt me, but to make sure I was safe, I saw Molly's face, small, white, twisted, as she stared at the pendant in her hand. Then she looked up at me.

'Run,' I breathed, and she and Skeet ran. Like a pair of skinny jackrabbits they were off into the depths of the carousel darkness, Skeet turning to pull her up after him, once he'd vaulted onto the metal dais. He was heading for the windows at the back, and he knew the way. This was his place, after all.

'Stay where you are–' The security man was fair, his hair swept back from his face and darkened with water, his nice suit ruined. I saw the coil of the wire at his ear, the white of his shirt cuff; I watched him as if he was something I'd made happen, something not quite real.

Ethan, still with gun in hand, careened after Molly and his brother, feet slipping on the wet ground. He skidded into the gloom, legs flailing as he made for the horses, grasping for the carousel's dais. Only he slipped, stumbling over the cascade of rubbish and twisted debris. He seemed to spin in mid-air, caught for a moment with his arms up as if surrendering, then he fell. His body impacted onto the rubbish pile where he hung, impaled on the metal rod I'd so spectacularly failed to pull free earlier. I stared at him through the curtain of rain, and felt Red against me, and that he was shaking with the effort not to cry. Or laugh.

The hospital faced the bay and gave me the kind of view that you had to be both rich and sick to enjoy. I was neither, but Red was paying. My foot was X-rayed, reset then strapped up and I was given a healthy dose of antibiotics and a delightfully convenient morphine drip, which let me slip off into the kind of sleep I'd been craving for more than a year.

Somewhere, in the depths of unconsciousness, I floated free of earthly concerns and found myself in another place, another time. As both of my personalities were otherwise concerned, I didn't question it. I wasn't exactly a stranger either; I'd been there before, after a fashion. It was that space, the one that clanged and rang, hollow as a tin drum, with the walls creeping with damp and half-heard mutterings. It was night, and in that night, two men were talking on either side of the bars. At first, there was the mere exchange of glances, the one curious, the other defiant, with a strength the first envied. Then, there was a night when more than a glance was exchanged, a word, a cigarette between the bars. A light flared, a light was shared.

Had there ever been a treasure? Something of incalculable value hinted at, then more, a glittering trail of breadcrumbs toward an idea? Johnny wanted out and so did his new friend, perhaps more than either of them wanted gold? There needed to be proof, of course, but a message could be taken by the boys who played soccer in the sand, not that much younger than the Americans they played with, who made them think of all the younger brothers they'd left behind. The proof was found; the proof was brought to those that needed to be convinced, to Red and others. They must have talked about it, alone together in those hot, dry, rust-tainted nights. Which one of them suggested it first, which one lit the spark that blazed between them? And oh, the keeping of the secret. The gut-churning, sweat-breaking fear of it, that secret. Could he do it, could he pull it off, dare he do it? He'd wanted to share, tell someone, tell anyone, but he had to wait for his shift, for his time in the darkness. He'd nearly told Molly, once, catching her looking at him as she did, as she tried not to, because she'd given up on such things to run with the boys. He'd talked to her once before, in a moment they shouldn't have shared, and after that he

was always aware of her watching him, under the eye of a jealous sun and Ethan Sprat.

Then all hell broke loose; men died, tension mounted, and it had to be then, be then or Johnny's nerve would have gone forever. Red said no; he must have known it was madness, but Johnny pushed him. The plan had been made, the contact, all of it. It wasn't that though; it was something else, something that alluded me in the world of my imagination. There was a reason why Red had let him go, one that he'd nearly died for, one he'd killed for.

Ali had been disguised in army fatigues and Johnny had gone with him, to be disguised in turn in other men's clothes. How had they done it, the video, their cover? Johnny Rockwell shown to the camera, made to kneel, a bag thrust over his head and then? A blast of static across the screen, well, what could one expect from such basic equipment? Who'd notice that when a man leant in to shout at the camera, he also blocked the lens just long enough for the switch to be made? Not even that, just long enough to hit the pause button and stuff Johnny's clothes onto an already dead body to fake the beheading. Goat's blood over US army issue, and everyone seeing what they wanted to see, what they'd been dreading – just as Red had seen me in that locker when it had been Molly.

Over the hills then, Johnny Rockwell, with his dark eyes and his dark skin, tanned darker by months in the sun, learning enough words from his friend to get by.

'Forgive my brother, he is shy. Forgive him, he is a mute, but he is strong, yes? Forgive my brother.'

I walked with them for a while. I sat beside them in the busted-up Toyota Flatbed that took them through the hills, I was silent with them. There was treasure, not much, but enough to buy passage to Turkey with the other men who went that way with them, who could pay. Turkey, a heart's beat from Europe, then Germany, Johnny useful then because he could speak English, because he could repay his brother.

'Forgive him, he's real shy. He's strong though, I'll look out for him, I promise. Forgive my brother.'

They didn't travel alone. There were others, always others, and men to pay to take them, to find them work, to take their cut as they put them on a boat. When Ali left him, which he did after a while, once he was alone and it was just Johnny and I, I felt it, his mind slowly slipping away. Like a knot of hair caught at the back of his head, it was cut away one thread at a time, until he was sure he was dead after all. Well, he must have been, because nobody seemed to see him anymore, to talk to him, even to hear him coming. He walked as a shadow back into his homeland, a man among all the other ghosts that slip in under fences, and past patrols, and dogs, and men with guns, squinting into the light. No name, no rank, no number, back to his mother to live in limbo. I walked with him all the way home, and then I slept.

CHAPTER TWENTY-FIVE

WHEN RED CAME to see me, I'd been unhooked from everything. He still didn't bring me roses. The nurse had just finished, reporting that everything was healing nicely, and she really couldn't see why the doctor would have any problem letting me go home, oh, and my husband was hoping he could pop in at last, and she really couldn't see any reason to say no, so why didn't she just go ahead and give him the nod?

'Husband? Really ...' I said as he closed the door and gave his smirk full reign.

'Just easier that way,' he said. 'Makes me your next of kin, an' saves a whole lot of questions.'

'I doubt that,' I said. He'd even brought my case, freed from the trunk of Ralph's car and in remarkably good condition, which was more than could be said for the Audi. They'd found it half-sunk in a canal a little way off from where I'd been car-jacked, rear end up in the air and so preserving my luggage, which Red set on the chair by the door. He went to the window and tweaked back the blinds the nurse had drawn, so he could watch out to sea.

'I dare say Ethan's not so lucky with the view. Did they say? They had to get all manner of kit up there to cut him free. If it were me, I'd have let him bleed out. No sign of Molly an' the other one, gone to ground. Gone ... to ... ground.' He tweaked the cord and pulled up the blind.

'You did call them, those guys who came?'

Red tapped his finger on the glass. 'Now, you didn't really think I'd be so goddamn stupid as to go in without back-up, did you?'

'I had my doubts,' I said. I was dressed in hospital green, not a good color on anyone. The nurse had helped me get a shower, Red's insurance even stretching as far as an en-suite, but I felt that Red, in a clean grey t-shirt and jacket, had the advantage over me yet again.

'Rita ...' he said, his finger paused in its tapping. 'Or are you ...?'

'I'm me,' I said. 'I'm ... me.' He looked back to the window and the ghost of his reflection smiled.

'I guess I owe you an apology, yet again. Seems all I got to do these days, is feel sorry.'

'It doesn't suit you,' I said. 'I think I liked you better when you were an arrogant son of a bitch.'

'Oh, I never said I'd changed–' he glanced over at me. 'Just that I was sorry.'

'Scorpion and frog, Red?'

'Scorpion an' frog,' he agreed.

'You know,' I said, sitting on the edge of the bed, dangling my blue plastic splint. 'I never did ask. Why d'you never sign those papers Lisa sent you? You know, so you could get a divorce?'

He reached up and scratched the back of his neck, then turned to lean against the window before he spoke.

'Oh, that.' He looked at me until I felt his smile touch the corners of my mouth.

'You really are a son of a bitch, aren't you?'

He held up his hands. 'Well, what the hell else was I gonna do? I didn't exactly have your cell, now did I? I figured eventually she'd ask you to come find me.'

'That is if I was still speaking with her, after everything.'

Red frowned. 'Oh, hell no. You love her too much to do that, even after everything, you know you do. There's some people that just get like that, deeper than skin.'

'I hate it when you're right,' I said.

'Stopped clock, darlin'. Even I get to be right twice a day.' He stretched his arms up, then settled both hands behind his head, leaning on the glass. Against the winter blue of the sky, he looked rather as if he were flying. He closed his eyes, then opened them and asked me, 'You really seen him, Rock ... Johnny?'

'In a way,' I said. 'He really is in a shack on the opposite side of the road to his mother's diner, the one you went to. You think I could make up shit like that?' He let his hands drop and turned back to the window, leaning on the sill to look out again. I saw him as he'd been in the wreck of the fairground, his clothes muddy and soaked, his face running with water as he'd put Ethan's gun to his chest. The moment shivered over my skin and my heartbeat nagged behind my eyes.

'Would you really have let Ethan shoot you?' I asked, before I'd thought better of it. Red didn't reply. I wasn't sure that he'd heard me, until he said:

'Why didn't you run? Moment you got yourself free, why didn't you run?'

'I had my reasons,' I said.

'Well, damn, that was my answer. Word for word.'

'That's no answer.'

He breathed out a laugh and let his forehead rest against the window. 'I had my reasons, an' a hundred-thousand-dollar security firm at my back.'

'You really blame yourself for what happened to Johnny, what you thought happened? Enough to die?'

'Damn it!' He slapped the glass with the flat of his hand and pulled himself upright, as if his thoughts were a flight of birds startled from their roost. 'Who knows, who knows any goddamn thing when it comes to it, darlin'? Other than the price of eggs, an' which way's up, an' even that's debatable.' He flicked at the air with his hand. 'Sure you'll figure it out. What you fixin' on doin' next, anyhow?'

'Well ...' I bit my lip, the part of it that wasn't quite so swollen. 'I thought I might go back there, to the diner? Not sure what else. I spoke to work, and they've given me some time off. They were quite worried about me, which was nice. Jose started giving me all sorts of advice, an' asking what the police said, and if I needed anything. I asked him to tell Olaf about Ralph's car.' I picked at the edge of the sheet, a guilty smirk on my lips. 'Not sure what I'm gonna do about that yet ...'

'I think you should,' Red said. 'I mean, you should go see Johnny. I'd go myself, but–'

'You might freak him out,' I said. I saw him run his tongue over his teeth before he answered.

'Something like that,' he said. Then he sniffed, gathered himself and hooked his thumbs into his belt loops before loping toward me. 'I guess that means you won't be hanging around, then?'

'Well, the police know where to find me.' I looked up at him. 'Besides, I've got a few things I need to see to. Things I've been ... been putting off for a while.'

Red nodded. He unhooked his thumbs and came to lean against the bed beside me, his right hand by my left, the other in his jacket pocket.

'You fixin' on perhaps leavin' me your number this time?'

'Suppose I could,' I said. 'Seein' as the police have it, I guess you can too.'

'I kind of like you in that color. Hospital green suits you.'

  **BROKEN PONIES**

'Really?' I said. 'Goes with what seems to be my favourite shade of lipstick too, hit-in-the-face pink.'

'Well, I don't care so much for that,' he said. 'That's one look I don't want to see you with again.' He looked at me for a long time, in that way which made me feel he was seeing a little bit more than the rest of the world did.

'I better get dressed I suppose, seein' as you brought my case an' all. Nurse said I can go home today, soon as the doctor's signed me off ...' I slipped my hand over his. 'You know, this ain't exactly the hotel room I had in mind, but you're payin' and it's none too shabby.'

Red looked sideways at me. 'Thought you were heading off into the wilds?'

'An' you're my husband, come to say goodbye.'

'Why, Rita ...' he said. He straightened up, pulling his hand from mine. 'What do you take me for?'

It was quiet, all that way up in the sky, staring out across the ocean like a lighthouse, blinking on and off. I felt the sweep of imagined light behind me, then I was bathed in its shadow. Red shrugged off his jacket and dropped it on the chair where he'd put my case.

'Like I said, Red. You're a scorpion.'

'Scorpion, am I?' He pulled his foot from one sneaker, then the other as he stepped over to me. 'Well, I remember how that goes–' He reached behind me, face close enough to mine for him to whisper in my ear. 'I guess we're both gonna drown.' His lips grazed the skin at my throat. I felt his words chuckle against me as his fingers eased my hospital gown open at the back. 'That bein' the case, you best let me help you out of them wet things, now hadn't you?'

Afterwards, as we lay together in the confined space of the hospital bed, Red ran his fingers over my mermaid tattoo.

'I suppose there's a story behind this?' he said. 'Not altogether sure as I want to know.'

'Honestly, I just liked it, that's all. Saw it in a book at this tattoo place and thought, why the hell not? That, and I liked the way it hurt, getting it done. They say it's addictive, they're not wrong.'

Red smiled. 'I got to wonder about some of your hobbies, darlin'. Not all of them are what most would consider healthy for a nice girl.' He kissed the mermaid on her lips, then got up, stretching his arms above his head, back toward me. I watched his shoulder blades roll under his skin, pushing against the white tracery of scars across his back. I didn't ask.

'You're one to talk,' I said. 'Why did you put yourself in front of Ethan's gun like that? You know, he could have done it, killed you right in front of me?'

'Playing for time,' he said. He picked up his boxers and put them on, then reached for his pants. 'Don't let it worry you none.' I watched him dress from under the sanctuary of the hospital sheet, watched him fasten his fly and pull on his t-shirt, tucking it into his waist band before he buckled his belt. I'd seen it of course, looked for it; the smiling white scar on his thigh I'd left him, after I'd stuck him with a broken bottle back in the swamp. I didn't want to think about it, but I had, and it had made me feel good to know it was there, and ashamed.

'Rita, darlin',' he said. 'You spoken to the police yet? I mean, above a formality?'

'Oh, not yet.' I slipped from the bed, naked but for the sheet and the splint on my foot. 'Do you ever think I'll ever be able to wear heels? Not that I do much, but you know, it's nice to have the option.'

 **BROKEN PONIES**

'Rita–' he smiled, but not as if anything I'd said was funny. 'When you do come to sit down with them–' he waved his hand. 'When you do, you don't need mention anything about Rockwell not being dead.'

'Why not?' I drew the sheet around myself, feeling the chill of the air on my skin.

'Indulge me,' he said.

'Well, it's not all down to me, now is it?' Red bent to pick up his jacket. 'I mean, Ethan's gonna say what he can, isn't he? I can't imagine he's gonna spare any detail.'

'He'll say what his legal team advises,' Red said, brushing his lapels. 'If he's got any sense.'

'Sense?' Then I saw the way he was looking at me, as if he'd stepped back behind a line in the sand and was suddenly older again, older and in command. I slumped against the hospital bed. 'You're paying for them, aren't you? Ethan's lawyer or whatever?'

'World don't need to know 'bout Johnny,' he said.

'Oh, really?' I limped over to my case, ripped open its lid and, regardless that he was watching, threw off my sheet. 'Jesus, I know you're what you are, but seriously Red, you've got some fuckin' front.'

'What's got you all riled up?' he said. I pulled out clean underwear and forced them on over my foot split, cursing at how clumsy and awkward it made me in front of him.

'This doesn't have anything to do with Johnny, does it?' I said, turning on him, brassiere in hand.

'You gonna put something on?' he asked.

'Why, this make you uncomfortable?'

'No, but–'

'Fuck you, you're still hiding something, aren't you? Some shit from Iraq and what happened–' I jabbed my finger at him. 'You're still saving your sorry ass and buying your way out of this, aren't you?' He didn't answer. 'What, you worried it will come out, what you were up to? Or did you end up with whatever that stuff was after all? Safe full of illegal Iraqi gold, is that it, Red?'

'Put some clothes on,' Red said and turned away from me.

'Fuck you.' I yanked my brassiere on and snatched up a t-shirt from the bag.

'Well, darlin', that would be nice, but I'm gonna need a moment, and next time, I'd rather the place didn't smell of disinfectant–'

'Oh, no,' I rounded on him, sweatpants in hand. 'Is that what you thought? You think because you stick your cock in my mouth, I'm gonna shut up about what happened? Do what you want me to, out of what? Some sort of stupid–'

Red slammed his fist against the bedstead. 'Jesus, no. Once in your life, can't you do as I ask just because I ask you? This ain't nothing to do with anything, other than Johnny, an' I don't got to explain myself to you, or no one.' His shout echoed against the plate glass window and then died, and the silence that came after fell heavily between us. Red put his fingers to his forehead and smoothed his brow.

'What you gonna do if I don't, tan my hide for me? No thanks, Red, I already had one Daddy in my life, I don't need another.'

'Oh sure, it ain't like that–'

'Get the fuck out.' I turned back to my case and thrust my good foot, well, the one that was less fucked up, into my track pants. I heard him take a step closer to me.

'Rita ... I didn't–'

'Some fuckhead tries to kill me because of something you did, Red.' I got my splinted foot into the pants and had to lean against the bed to force it home. 'An' you're still not being honest with me, after all of it, after everything. You still can't trust me enough to

tell me what the fuck's going on.' I staggered when my foot finally came free, caught myself, winced because it hurt and grabbed at the chair. 'Goddamn this fucking foot!'

'Rita ...' Red looked at me and drew his fingers through his hair. Then he walked toward the door.

'Hey – you look at me! Some fuckin' asshole has a gun to my head, a gun to my head to kill me, because of you, because of something you've done, and then I'm supposed to forget about it? And, if I am, it's because of some shit you don't want coming out? Ethan gets to walk, because of that?'

'He's not gonna walk, for God's sake Rita!' He let go of the door and slapped the air with frustration. 'He's gonna do his time an' shut the fuck up. You want to go to court with this? Have some defense attorney full of righteous indignation go diggin' into just how come they thought you were my wife?'

'Now, you're just tryin' to–'

'Your ex-boyfriend, one Paris France–' Red jabbed his finger at me. 'Sitting on his thumbs down state, you think he wouldn't love to spend an hour flappin' his jaw 'bout you and I, if he thought someone wanted to listen?'

'Oh,' I said, and he saw the shock in me.

'What, didn't you know? Hell, you asked me to see to him, darlin'. Your partin' gift, as I remember.'

I laughed, not a laugh, not with any humor in it. 'That's all bullshit. No one's gonna care about him or us, or any of that. You're just tryin' to control everything, twistin' the truth to hide your lies.' My voice sounded ugly in that pristine room, a fly caught and buzzing in a bell jar.

'Maybe I am.' Red drew his shoulders back, hands on hips again. 'Maybe I need to. Better than doin' it with a gun to my head, which as you know, ain't a nice way to go about things, is it?'

'Oh, I know that. I seem to remember that you were once the one shooting at me.'

'We going there again, are we?'

'If you like, yes – you brought it up. So, what was all this, this thing with Ethan an' Molly? That your way of letting me see what a bad girl I was to you? The whole… walk a mile in my shoes shit? Is that what you were doin', you were teachin' me another lesson, Daddy?'

'What the hell you think?' he snapped. 'Of course I weren't doing that, you think I knew they were out there, what they intended?'

'You said–'

'Oh sure, I had an idea someone was sniffin' about the house, but not that it was them. Sweet Jesus, d'you really think I'd have put you through all that, if I'd known what they were gonna do?' He stalked away from me, hands in the air, then turned back to point at me. 'I came to give myself in exchange for you, an' I'd have done anything, anything, t' get you free.'

'Really?' I said, arms folded in response. 'But not call the FBI or the police, right? Because whatever shit it is you're hiding, might have come out if you had?'

'That was not–'

'I don't believe you.'

Red shook his head. 'Well, that don't surprise me. Seems to me you're pretty good at deciding which way the world is, against all evidence to the contrary. You know, God don't got no great plan he's reluctant to let us see, shit just happens. How the hell was I supposed to know you'd met Johnny Rockwell on the roadside? You think I'm behind that somehow, because you' giftin' me a whole lot of power I ain't got.' He slapped his hand against the foot of the bed. I went to speak, to tell him that there wasn't a damn thing I'd put past him, but he cut across me.

'You wanna know what's goin' on? Two generations ago, one maybe, he'd have been shot for what he did. Desertion is tantamount to treason, darlin', or don't you know that? He's a deserter an' worse, an' all I want is to stop some dickhead from Fort Worth comin' on down an' havin' him up on a charge. An' sure,' he swept his hands wide as if to encompass the world, 'I could go pay every lawyer I could lay my hands on to argue him insane, but you got any idea what that might do to him? You any idea how hard it is to get released, if they think you're crazy? Sure, Ethan can do his time, but crazy time don't ever end. I'm doin' this for him, an' if you think otherwise, you tell me now.'

'You know what I think? I think you're doing it to save your sorry hide.'

Red reached into his jacket and brought out a wad of paper. He slapped it onto the hospital bed.

'Them's the papers you wanted me to sign for your sister, an' which I was foolish enough not to do before. You know what, Rita? I've spent as long as you've been alive looking over my shoulder at something I did. I admit,' he jabbed his thumb at himself, 'I didn't know that part of what was following me, was you, an' hell, we all had a blast an' all with that one, but look – if you're gonna take one thing from me, one thing at all, let this shit go. You cannot live your life like I have. I'm not prepared to do it no more and neither should you.' He put his hand to his forehead for a moment. 'Jesus, I know you've had more to deal with in your young life than most, I appreciate that, Rita, but sometimes, you just got to walk away. That's what I'm doin' here.' He tapped the papers again.

'You walkin' away from me?' I said, hating how I sounded, how nasal and needy my voice became.

'Hardly. I love you, Rita, an' it's taken me my whole life to say that to someone and know it's true. But until you come to terms with the darkness inside o' you, that ain't never gonna be enough.'

'Oh, I'm so sorry,' I said, ignoring the echo of his words in my head. 'And there's me expecting you to sweep me off to your big fuckin' house, an' all your big fuckin' money, 'cause that was really part of my plan, here.'

'Well, I'm sorry too, because that was never part of mine. I told you I love you, and you can throw it back in my face hard as you like, an' I'm sure I deserve it, but the only thing I'm askin' you here, the only thing, is do not tell anybody else 'bout Johnny Rockwell bein' alive.'

'You're still lyin' to me–'

'I love you,' he yelled. 'Jesus, you want me go tattoo it on your fuckin' ass?'

'Not about that–' I caught my breath, horrified at my own arrogance. 'About what's behind all this.'

'Rita!'

'Tell me, you bastard!'

'Johnny's my son!'

CHAPTER TWENTY-SIX

I STARED AT RED, so he said it again. 'He's my son.' I put my hand to my mouth and I laughed, not quite, not a laugh, but a sob of astonishment.

'You're joking,' I said, because of course, that's what it would be – a huge, cosmic joke on his behalf. Only he wasn't. 'You and Martha, you and ... your son? That's not possible.'

The door clicked open, and the nurse looked in on us, with the kind of expression that takes years to perfect, and the kind of smile that indicated she'd been listening at the door.

'So, you folks all done here?'

Red, with consummate ease and an equal level of professionalism, stepped toward her and took hold of her elbow, as if recognizing an old friend across the lawn at a summer party.

'We're doin' just fine, darlin', but we're gonna need a little while longer. Not putting you to any trouble, now are we?'

And we weren't, and the two of them were laughing about something even before he'd seen her out, and was wishing her well, and complimenting her on the job she was doing. The door clicked shut over her smile.

'Johnny's your son,' I said. Red walked over to the chair, lifted off my case and thumped it onto the floor. 'D'you want me to tie you to it?' I suggested.

'If you got some rope handy, why not? Seein' as it worked last time.'

I stepped back toward the bed and leant against it. 'Why didn't you just tell me, if you wanted to keep him safe, why?'

'Because what does blood mean? It don't mean nothin', not really. He was a good man s'all, he don't need to be dragged through the courts for what he did. He fought for his country when there were many as wouldn't.'

'Blood matters to you, you said as much.'

'Sure, it matters, but I don't got no right to use it for my own ends. I wasn't his father, not what the word really means.' He shook his head, then smiled up at me. 'Besides, I promised his mother I wouldn't tell no one who or what I was.'

'Martha, you promised Martha.'

'I didn't know you were on first name terms, darlin'.'

'You and her?'

'I was eighteen,' he said. 'An' she was twenty-eight or so.' He looked at me, something sly about his eyes. 'Closer in age than you an' I, darlin'.'

'Thank you, I can do the math,' I said, feeling the tumble of figures roll through my mind, faster than a payout at the Savannah Heights. 'Your son, did you know in ... did he know who you were?'

Red shook his head. 'No.' He drummed his fingers on his knees. 'It behoves an officer to know who's serving under him. I read his file, an' ... well, I guess I did the math too.'

'Martha would have been listed as his next of kin?'

'An' his ... father, Johnny Rockwell senior. I knew him once, though we never exactly saw eye to eye.'

'I can imagine,' I said. 'How did you know them?'

'Way back when. Just a young man, running away. Martha was ... is a remarkable woman. They were living with others in what you might call a commune, of sorts.'

I smirked at him. 'You were a hippy, Red?'

'I ain't that old,' he said. 'An' they weren't hippies. They were ... convinced of the complexity of the political situation, I suppose. They thought it was just a matter of time before we all went up in a mushroom cloud.'

'But you didn't stay with them, you left?'

'Under something of a cloud,' he said, and for a moment I thought he was going to say something more, only he shivered and shook his head, his hand twitching up and coming to rest in his lap.

'You left Martha pregnant,' I said.

'She never said nothin', I swear, never told me. Not that I gave her much chance to.'

'So, what happened when you realized, you told Johnny who you were?'

'I did not. What was I to him, Rita?'

'But you got to know him, out there in Iraq?'

'Like I said, I've always worked with a team about me.' Oh and he had, Captain Levine, and what a team. Molly Pike and Ethan Sprat, and the man he knew to be his son, desperate to go home, his escape route all worked out, if only he could find his exit.

'And all that time, when you thought he'd been taken, when you thought he'd been killed?'

Red dropped his head into his hands, resting his elbows on his knees. I sensed it then, the creeping, inching realization of what he'd felt, of what he'd done. The son he'd found, the son he'd sent out into the night, that he'd seen taken, that he'd thought killed. The son who'd betrayed him, without even knowing he was his father.

'That's why you did it, why you ... you killed that other man, because you thought you'd killed your son?'

'I killed plenty of sons,' he said, but didn't look at me.

'When did you know about him, that he was alive?' I narrowed my eyes. 'You knew before the whole thing with Ethan and Molly, didn't you? I didn't tell you anything new, did I?'

'No.' He lifted his head from his hands and straightened up to face me. 'It was ... some-time after you took your leave. When the ... considerable dust had settled, found I needed to say sorry to Martha, for what had happened.' He smirked at himself. 'Called unannounced upon her.'

'Right, and how did that go down with Martha?'

'That ... did not go well.' I thought of him, going to Martha's diner for absolution and coffee, cap in hand.

'My god–' I put my hand to my mouth. 'Did Lisa know, did you tell her?' Red shook his head, eyes downcast. 'So, no one else knew?'

'Who was there to tell?' he said. 'Lisa–' and he swallowed after he'd said her name and exhaled. 'She was already gone, in a manner of speakin'.' He touched his hand to his eyes. 'Weren't no excuse, it weren't–'

'Then, when I first met you, all that time–' I cut across him, the flicker of too many memories setting my heart thudding. 'When we were together before, you thought you'd killed your son?'

'Well, not quite.' Red put both hands to his forehead, then let them drop back. 'I didn't let myself think like that. I didn't let myself think 'bout nothing much, just closed my mind to everything, so as I could put one foot before t'other.' He'd come home, he'd done what he'd done and so had I, both of us convinced he was a murderer.

He slapped his knee and got up. 'Look, darlin', I pretty much said everything I gotta say. Rest's up to you.'

'I don't know,' I said. My legs were aching, my feet, my face, all of me, as the last of the morphine faded from my body, along

with my anger. I didn't feel anything, as if all feeling had been used up, leaked out without my noticing, until nothing of it was left. 'I think I need ...' I met his gaze, felt it take in all of me, then I looked away. Something guilty crept across my skin, burning my cheeks. 'I think ... I need some time, Red.'

People walked past the room, utilitarian shoes yelping against the polished floor, the clatter of instruments on a trolley, a snatch of laughter. Red reached up to scratch the back of his neck, then didn't, and let the arm fall again.

'Sure thing ... darlin', he said, as if the words were splinters pulled from him.

'Red, I know you–'

'Like you said, darlin'. Time.' He came over to me, and I almost thought he meant to shake my hand goodbye. And I really meant to take hold of him, and tell him that I was wrong, that I didn't need time and it didn't matter, I really did. Or so I thought. But instead, I let him kiss me on the cheek and I didn't look at him, even when he lingered, his body close enough for me to feel the air warm between us.

'It's just–' I began, but he turned away and left the room without looking back, and without my stopping him.

CHAPTER TWENTY-SEVEN

MARTHA TOOK a cigarette from her pack and lit it. I had to wait for her to see to three other customers before she could join me at the table where we'd sat before. When I came in, Betty's devilish eyebrows raised as her golden eyes turned to regard me. Her tail thunked on the floor but she didn't get up. I felt suitably honored by the acknowledgment.

Johnny was inside his hut. I thought about going to speak with him first but decided against it. Since I'd left the hospital, I'd felt Margarita settle back inside me, and since I'd reentered Nevada, she'd been surprisingly quiet. I wasn't sure if I liked it better or not; I could see the appeal of the backseat from time to time. I felt sure she'd have something to say to Johnny and was sure I wasn't quite ready to listen to it just yet.

'Now, what have you been doin' to yourself?' Martha asked. She took a moment to look me over.

'That ... unfinished business we spoke about before. I guess I've been finishing it.'

'You girls today. Why, when I was your age, I'd never have ended up like that.' She grinned. 'I'd have put the other fellow down first.'

'Oh, this was mostly a girl,' I said.

'That explains it.'

I looked out at Johnny's shack again. He'd been doing up the place. A bandaged couch had been added to the back of the property, shaded by the ribs of a golfing umbrella strung with a plastic bag awning. I didn't know how to start and so I just did, putting my plate to one side with my knife and fork at twelve o'clock.

'Johnny's your son, isn't he? The one who's supposed to be MIA?' Martha exhaled a long stream of smoke through pursed lips, then ground the rest of her cigarette into the ash-tray.

'How do you know?' she asked.

'We have a mutual ... friend.' I saw her forehead crease, then relax as her eyes widened. A smile flickered over her lips, then cooled to sadness.

'If they were to find out,' she said.

'It's alright,' I said. 'Really, I do understand.'

'If they took him away, I'd never see him again.' She looked out of the window, it's reflection bright on her eyes. 'I put things out by the rocks for him, food, water, clothes, when I think he needs them. Some of the neighbors bring things too. No one minds him, not out here. What harm does he do?'

'But–' I couldn't help the edge of anger that slipped under my words. 'He let you think he was dead, he ... lied to you.'

Betty got to her feet and came over, her claws tip-tapping their way across the floor. She sat next to Martha and yawned at me, then clicked her muzzle in warning. Martha put her hand out and stroked the dog's ear.

'I'm sorry,' I said. 'That was ... that was rude of me.'

'I was angry,' she said. 'I stood on the roadside, demanded he speak with me, but what was I doin'? Yellin' at God because he'd answered my prayers and given me back my son?' I stared at my plate, an altogether more shameful blush creeping over me. 'Anger's like the sun, darlin'. Burns like hell if you stay in it for too long. Dead's the only place of no return, everything else?

Everything else, there's a chance. You ever wonder just how angry Mary was when they took her son an' nailed him to the cross? You think she didn't cuss him for his uppity ways, for making trouble for himself all that time?'

I couldn't help but smile at Martha's depiction of Christ as a disobedient teenager.

'Oh darlin', we all got to do it. We all got to watch the ones we love walk away, do us wrong even, but that don't mean we ever stop lovin' them, even if we hate what they do. I've hope, an' there's plenty as don't have that.'

I looked at her, at those dark black eyes in the map of her face. She reached out and put her hand over mine, and I saw she was crying, a tear building against her lashes. I felt the shiver of it run over my skin, felt her fear and what I could do to her if I wanted to, if I was angry enough. Which I wasn't.

'I had to tell him,' Martha said, her hand still on mine. A truck made the place shudder as it roared past, and the world outside the window blinked out of existence for a second. 'Red gave me his word, after he'd composed himself, that he'd tell no one about Johnny, that he'd do everything he could as so he'd be safe.' Like paying for a lawyer to advise Ethan Sprat to plead guilty, so there was no trial and no danger of my being called as a witness. Like being prepared to die so that no one would know. Like letting your daughters hate you, because you thought there was no other way of protecting them, and to stop them protecting you, after you'd made a deal.

'Wouldn't they show him mercy?' I said. 'After all this time, would they really take him away?' Martha didn't answer. Why would she risk it, her son come back from the dead? One miracle was more than anyone had a right to expect, why risk everything on a second?

Betty the dog lowered herself onto the floor and then stretched out on her side, muttering her jaws together.

'When you got kids, you'll understand,' Martha said.

'It's okay,' I said. 'I don't think I need them to understand.'

'Can I trust you?' she asked. 'I mean, what will you do?'

'Nothing,' I said and got up. 'It's not for me to say anything to anyone, is it? It's not my place.' I could have told her, all about Red and Ethan and Skeet and Molly, and the fairground, and before, even, but it didn't seem the time.

'May I go... say hello?' I asked. 'To Johnny? I know he won't see me, but ... well, I know what I mean.'

'Will you come back?' Martha said. 'I'd be sorry to think I'd never get to see you again, Rita.'

'Sure,' I said. 'The light's good here, after all.'

Johnny was on the busted-up couch at the back of his place. He didn't get up until I'd nearly limped all the way over to him and when he did, it wasn't at any great speed. I realized what it was about Johnny that had seemed so familiar months before. His color came from Martha, that and being baked under the Nevada sun, and his beard and long hair rendered all trace of Red's hollow cheeks and high forehead obscure; but looking at him then, I saw what I'd not seen before, when I'd seen only as deep as the color of his skin, without noticing the bones of the man.

I wasn't sure what I felt about standing in front of Red's son and finding him to be a man an inch taller than him. I decided it was not the time or place to think too deeply on it.

'You back,' Johnny said, looking six inches left of my face. 'You caught the sun.' He twitched, shook his head. Then I saw his eyes focus on me and he frowned and put his hand up to shade his brow. It disconcerted me for a moment, until I felt Margarita smile behind my lips.

'You know, it's gonna be okay,' we told him. 'No one's ever gonna tell them you're here. You can come back, back over the road. You're home now, Johnny, you don't got to run no more.'

He tilted his head to the side, looking more like Betty than any one. Then he shrugged himself back to the couch and crossed one leg over the other, his movements easier and more natural than I'd seen them before.

'You get off,' he said, not looking at either of us. 'Go on, you get off. I ain't minded to-go anywhere right now. I'm good here.'

'Yes,' I said. 'You are.'

The hire company who'd been crazy enough to rent a car to me, had even gone so far as to provide the charger I needed for my new cell. I climbed into the driver's seat and tilted the rear-view so I could see my eyes. I picked up the phone and pressed the button on the side. The little logo that was illuminated at my touch, informed me that my phone was full to bursting. I put it down again and looked past myself to the diner in the mirror.

Martha was sweeping up when the door chimed my entrance.

'Are you alright, Rita?' she asked. 'Is there something wrong?'

'Who helps you with this place?' I asked. 'I mean, you don't really look after everything here alone, do you?'

She folded her arms again and leant against her broom.

'I got people. Girl come an' cleans for me every day, an' there's fellows as I take on when I get busy.'

'What about security, you must need security?' I grinned. 'Some of these paintings must be worth, well, dollars. If you need a security guard, then I might know someone.' Martha raised her eyebrow.

'Don't you got somewhere better to be, somewhere you ought to be?'

'Yeah,' I said. 'I can think of a whole load of places I ought to be, better than this one, an' a whole load of things I need to do and say, an' all of that. But now, right now, I kind of feel like I need to be here.'

'World won't leave you alone for long,' Martha said. 'I figure it ain't nearly done with you yet.'

'I know.' I pulled my hair band free and dragged my fingers through my hair. 'I just need a place to be, until I'm ready for it. I've ... I've got some things I need to work out, in my head.'

'You and me both,' Margarita said. 'You and me both.'

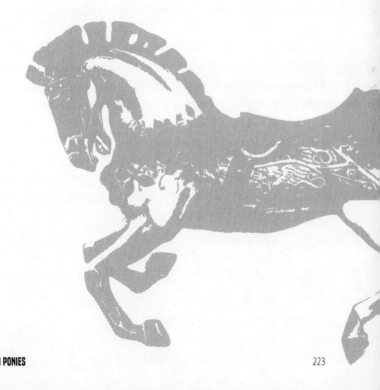

CHAPTER TWENTY-EIGHT

I'VE HEARD THAT when athletes want to train for a major event, they go to high up places where the air is thin, and train there. When they come back down for race day, the air at lower levels seems rich and generous, and they can squeeze just that little bit more out of the stopwatch. Martha's diner seemed plenty high above everywhere else, and I felt sure that if I could get used to being there, if I didn't think about anything, that when I came back down to earth, I'd be a whole lot better at working out just who the hell I was. Or something like that, anyway.

Margarita liked it pretty well, because there was so much to do, and so much of it was damn hard work. A lot of the place seemed to be held together with string and duct tape, and I made Martha let me work on it for her, and made her get some of the neighbors, who were always asking what they could do for her, to join in. We patched up the roof and fixed broken windows and dragged out beds to give them the once over and bought enough white paint to whitewash each tiny bedroom, until they gave the illusion of being clean and bright and comfortable.

'Trust you to paint everything white again,' Margarita said.

'Don't need no other colors,' I said. 'They're all outside.'

And while we worked we talked, and they told me stories about rattlesnakes and the artists who came by, and the doings around the local elections, and the trouble with the power company and

BROKEN PONIES

the water company. And I told them nothing at all, and they didn't seem to mind, as if that was just how I was, and there wasn't any need to ask why. They didn't even ask about my foot, which healed well enough for me to wear shoes again, and then until there was hardly any trace of a limp in my stride at all, while I carried groceries, swept floors, made beds and walked over to where Martha liked to sit out back at the end of the day. She even drew my picture, once or twice, both of us pretending I hadn't noticed she was doing it.

'Not as good as I once was,' she said. 'Some days I don't got the ... the grip no more. Matisse took to cutting shapes out of paper when he got old, maybe I should try it?' I didn't answer because I didn't like to think of her hands slowly shutting down, like clockwork toys running out of speed. Her drawings didn't exactly look like me, but they were familiar, like overhearing an uncomfortable truth.

I let Lisa have the address and she wrote to me, old school with pen and paper, and we spoke on the phone. Bob had forgiven me, she said, and I asked if Brandon had too, and she asked what did I mean?

Johnny talked to Margarita, at first as if each word were something he'd hoarded from the trash, but he did talk. He told her about the girl in the photograph, the one he'd sent Martha when he was in Germany, and sometimes about the pastor whose address she'd given him almost a year before he'd had a chance to use it. He seemed to think that she was going to come back to him, which was why he was making the place nice, so it would all be ready for when she came to visit, though over the weeks that faded. He started to look at her – me – when we talked, until I asked if I could bring someone next time, and he said it was okay, as long as they didn't mess up the place, seeing he'd got it just the way he wanted. That night, I brought Martha over to his couch and the three – or four – of us, sat in silence until the sky burned away into night, and the stars made that night almost milky white.

When I saw the truck pull up a month or so later, it was the end of the day and I was wiping down tables. I'd got most of them clear, and I'd just about put everything away that needed to be put away before the closed sign got flipped over. I frowned at it. 'Oh, snap, now who's that at this time, just when I'd–' then I saw who it was.

He got out, shades on, arms bare, and took a moment to stand by the truck after he'd closed its door. I went back behind the counter, an odd half-smiling, half-panicked expression on my face, as the blood surged in my ears. My hands shook worse than Martha's as I dumped the dust pail out of sight and remembered about the apron I'd got on. The doorbell chimed as I dropped it onto the floor and straightened up to meet his gaze.

He folded his shades away. 'You still open? I'm spittin' feathers. I'd kill for a cold one, darlin'.'

'There's no need to be dramatic,' I said. I reached down to the cooler, took out a beer and placed on the top of the counter.

'Care to join me?' he asked.

'I was just about to close up,' I said. He glanced around the room and took in the chairs stacked on the tables. Then he nodded toward the door.

'Fine evening. What say you join me on the veranda, if you'll forgive my forwardness?'

'Are you being forward?' I asked.

He smirked. 'Time was a woman be ruined should she be seen on the veranda alone, no chaperone. Meant she was lookin' out for someone she ought not to.'

'I'll bear that in mind,' I said.

'You do that.' Red turned on his heel and walked out.

'You don't have to go,' Margarita said. 'What's he gonna do if you lock the door on him an' slip out back?'

'That would be mean, seeing as he's come all this way.'

'Be funny, though?'

I drummed my fingers on the counter and made myself count every table in the room twice before I took a bottle from the cooler.

'Spoilsport,' Margarita said.

'Bitch,' I told her.

'Love you too, doll.' I smiled.

Red was sitting on the bottom step, Betty a few feet away from him on her side. As I came down, she stretched her head back so she could watch me. I drew level with him, then sat. He turned his head to glance at me, then looked away. I cracked the cap off against the edge of the step and drank. Red leaned in to chink his bottle against mine.

'You just passing through?' I asked.

'Sort of,' he said. 'Thought I'd see how you were doin',' he peered behind us, 'in your new career in the service industry.'

'I like it,' I said. 'It's probably safer I'm in a job where they don't let me hit people.' Three cars passed us, travelling as if in convoy and nervous of where they were headed. The sun was low in the sky, the shadow of the diner blackened the road ahead of us and stretched all the way to Johnny's place. Red's eyes fixed on the shack.

'How's he doin'?' he asked.

'Not too bad,' I said.

'Is he ...' Red shrugged. 'Martha said he wouldn't talk to no one, that changed any?'

'Yeah, about that ...' I smiled. 'Seems as if he's prepared to talk to

me. Well, sort of.' Red looked sideways at me. 'He started talking to Margarita.'

'Oh, really?' Red frowned.

'Yeah, they get on quite well, or so it seems. And yeah, I know how crazy that sounds.' I put the bottle to my lips again. Red went to speak, paused, then started laughing. 'What?'

'Nothin'.'

'No, come on.' I nudged his leg with my knee. 'You don't get to do that. Look, nothin' about us is in any way normal. You're my ex brother-in-law, and my alternate personality is best friends with your son. Not to mention that I'm living with your ex-girlfriend, his mother, oh, and you're old enough to be my father.' Red grimaced.

'That last one, the whole thing about me bein' old enough to be your daddy? Could we drop that? Seein' as what I'd like to do to you right now, it kind of turns my stomach.'

'Yeah, okay.' I tilted my bottle toward him again. 'What were you gonna say?'

'Oh, that.' He shook his head, then combed his hair with his fingers the way he did, as if he had to shake his thoughts free before he could say them. 'It just struck me as the most crazy-ass thing I'd ever thought.' He looked at me, one eyebrow raised. 'An' trust me, with my history, that's sayin' one hell of a thing.'

'Go on,' I said.

'Okay ... so,' he grinned at his shoes. 'Your alternate personality and my son, just how well they gettin' on? Anything I should know about?'

'You're right,' I said. 'That possibly is the most crazy-ass thing you've ever said in your life.'

'Darlin', I'm just thinkin' of the practicalities here. Besides, not sure I'd want any son of mine datin' a girl like that. She's trouble, that one.'

 **BROKEN PONIES**

'Stop it–' I pushed at him while he sniggered. 'Margarita an' Johnny are just friends. Fuck you, laughing at me, you weren't here.'

Red looked away from me then, past the colored rocks and along down the asphalt that ran like a blue vein under brown skin, and then I was sorry that I'd said it, about his not being here. I looked down at the bottle and where my thumbnail was picking at the label, where it was coming free.

'I don't know why,' I said, 'but he talked to her, slowly, you know? Then after a while, I guess he was just talking to me.'

'An' his mother,' Red said. 'Does he talk to her?'

I nodded toward the shack. 'She's over there now. He used to talk through me, you know, her standin' there next to me, an' me sayin' everything each of them said all over again. Then I just stopped it, slowly. Now she goes an' sees him every day. He ain't come over here yet, but he's gonna.'

The wind got up then and sent a scurry of sand across the dry earth in front of us. Betty muttered and let out a long sigh, as if we were a terrible burden to her.

'What 'bout you?' Red said. 'You talkin' to your mamma yet?'

I took a moment to drink before I spoke, feeling the burn of the bubbles against my teeth and gums, and letting the liquid warm to body temperature before I swallowed.

We'd met at Bob's house, Lisa and Bob's house. Before she came, I took myself off to the back yard, sadly devoid of all Christmas relics, and lurked at the bottom near the fence, smoking the cigarettes that I, a non-smoker, had slipped from Martha's prescription. Brandon came and found me there.

'Can I get one?' he asked as I stamped on the one I was halfway through.

'Good God, no. Why the hell you wanna to do that?' I said. He grinned at me.

'I've had one before.'

'Not like these you haven't, and that's a shitty idea, Brandon, they really do give you cancer you know?'

'Well, why you smoking them?' he asked, hands in pockets.

'Because I'm full of shitty ideas,' I told him.

Mom got up from Lisa's new Prussian blue sofa as I came in, turning at the sound of my foot catching on the top step, and the creak of the screen door as I opened it. It was only when she did not shout at me, or scream, or demand what I thought I'd been playing at, that I realised that this was what I'd been dreading.

'Rita,' she said and came to me and got hold of me, which was worse, in a way. She smelled of herself, of the perfume she always wore and the face cream and her skin, with its dapple of freckles. I held her and wished that I'd got her freckles, and the apricot tone of her skin and not just her smile, uncertain thing that it was.

'We've talked,' I said. 'It's been, you know. Hard.' I drank again, looking away from him, blinking into a wind that stung my face. 'Good though, I mean, it's been good.' It hadn't, but as Red had said once, it had been real. And that was better.

'So,' I said, when more time had passed between us than would be comfortable, if we were two other people. 'What you doin' here?'

'Like I said–' Red sniffed. 'Just passin' by.'

'Where to? There ain't nowhere here to pass to.'

'I've run away from home,' he said. 'Again.'

'Can you run away from home when you're forty-two?'

'Hell yeah–' He grinned at me. 'Seein' as I'm forty-four.' He nodded toward the truck. 'I liquidated my assets. Turns out, they didn't amount to all that much, 'specially as Daddy was more than a little pissed at the way I've been behavin' over the last few years.'

'An' you bought a truck.'

'I bought a truck,' he said. 'An' ...' He tapped his bottle against his foot. 'An' I don't know as I'll be comin' this way again.'

From the other side of the road the last inch of sunlight caught on the CDs that were hung at the door of Johnny's shack; they blazed, then winked out.

'Don't you want to know him?' I said. 'Don't you want him to know you?'

'I ain't his father,' Red said. 'An' he don't need me in his life.' He drank, and I heard the swill of the liquid in the bottle. 'I did what I could as his commanding officer, I don't think I'm qualified to call myself anything more.'

'You were going to die for him,' I said.

'Like I said, commanding officer.'

'An' what about me, would you have let Ethan shoot me to keep him safe?' Red hunched forward and pressed the beer bottle into the dirt, turning it so I could hear the squeak of stone against glass.

'Darlin', I swear, I never knew as he was gonna do that. If it had come to it, I'd have killed him first. You really think otherwise?' The bottle squeaked against grit and stone.

'No, I never did. You bein' an officer, an' all.'

'Well now, I notice that you did not append the word gentleman to that?' I smiled and drank my beer, turning to look at the truck he'd parked up at the side of the diner.

'That truck all you bought?'

Red smirked. 'Few other things, you know. Man's gotta live. Not quite ready to give up the–'

'Ask me,' I said.

'Ask you what?'

'For once in your life, Red, just come the fuck out with it. Ask me.'

'Fine,' he said, eyebrows raised, and his mouth pulled into an inverted 'U'. Then he straightened up and talked to the road ahead. 'What if you'd just met me for the very first time? If you was workin' here, payin' off your summer vacation or whatever, an' I come in, got myself a beer an' sat down. An', say you look out the window as your shift ends an' think to yourself, why, whoever is that handsome stranger–' I laughed. 'Humor me,' he said. 'That handsome stranger, why, I might just go find out? An' you come out an' sat wit' me, an' had a beer with me, an' I asked you to get in my truck and go away wit' me. What in the hell would you say?'

'I don't know,' I said. I turned to him, my hand up, shading my eyes. It was the first time I'd looked at him full in the face, at his eyes made pale by shadow and looking at me as if they could see deeper than skin. 'Which one of us you askin'?'

'You,' he said. 'I'm askin' you. Both of you, either of you, whichever one you want me to be asking.' He slumped forward and crunched the bottle against the stones again. 'Neither of you, someone else.'

'If I didn't know you, I'd tell you to go fuck yourself,' I said. 'But that's the problem, Red. I do know you, don't I?'

EPILOGUE

MARTHA BENDS DOWN behind the counter, the dustpan and brush in hand. She's dropped a muffin, the last one left, which she was thinking of having herself. When she took hold of its plate, her hands, which are not behaving, flinched and the plate jolted, and the muffin rolled off and hit the floor in an explosion of crumbs. It's such a waste, and she can't abide waste, but even she can't quite bring herself to eat the piece that's left, however good and moist it looks in the dustpan. When she stands up, Red's there.

She didn't hear him come in, because he caught the door and eased it past the bell as if he'd been prepared, and this is before Betty and the click-click of her claws on the tiled floor. Martha was only thinking about getting a dog the other day, but she doesn't know yet that she'll have one in a week's time.

She knows who he is without remembering him. She knows that there was something between them, that she's thought about him on and off for years, and that the years are as dust, as muffin crumbs in that moment. At first all she sees is the man he was when she last saw him, almost grown and all the way cocksure. Then she sees the time that has spun out between them, feels it blow back in around her and she has to put her hand on the top of the counter to steady herself, in the face of the man he now is.

'Hello, Martha,' he says. Finally she sees him much as you can see the pencil lines under a watercolor sketch. She wants to say that he hasn't changed, only he has, and seeing that he's changed makes her aware of how she has too. I've been pencil drawn since he last saw me, she thinks, in HB on white paper, all my colors drained.

'What the hell is you doin' here, Rooster Levine?' she says. He's in uniform, his hat tucked under his arm and the dot-dash of silks over his pocket. If she knew what they all meant, she feels that she could decipher him, read back the way he's come to be standing in her diner. Steeped in blood, she thinks, and wherever is that from?

'I heard the coffee's good,' he says, and he nearly smiles, and she nearly does too, only he can't meet her eyes. 'I knew your boy, Martha. I was his commanding officer in Iraq.' Then he looks at her. 'Our boy, Martha. I knew our boy.'

'You say somethin' to him?' she asks.

'Martha, I came because–'

'Did he know, Rooster? Did you tell him who you were?' She slams the dustpan down on the counter, her hand obeying her anger.

'No, Martha. I did not,' he says. She relents and goes to pour coffee, rather than him see the tremble building in her.

'Go sit down,' she says. 'I was about to close up, so you'll have to give me a moment.' Her hand shakes when she gets the milk from the refrigerator. There's an angel food cake there also, put away after the day's trading and already cut into slices. She puts one on a plate for him, lying it on its side so that it won't fall like the muffin.

She looks over at him as the coffee machine steams and hisses. He's taken a seat under the huge ochre and brown abstract, the one she's never liked and only hung there because there's one hell of a crack in the wall. God, who the hell was it that painted it, and insisted on leaving it with her? That fat German, with the wife who did nothing but moan about the heat, as if she was personally responsible for it. She's thinking about them to stop herself thinking

about Red, and that she hasn't seen him for over twenty years, and that he's Johnny's father, and whatever does that mean anyway?

No, she thinks, angry as the coffee swills dark into the mug. You don't get to do that, Mr Red, Mr Rooster Levine, rich boy running away – too young for me then, too old for me now – you don't get to walk in here and be the Daddy. She glances toward the window, but there isn't one in the kitchen and from where she is, she can't see Johnny in his shack. Does he know, has he seen? Christ, what if Rooster knows, what if he's seen him? Look at him all dressed up and official!

The memory of him burns in her eyes like sunlight from a photograph. Rich boy running away, with darkness snapping at his heels and the wolf in his eyes. Not your type, she reminds herself, never was; rich boy trying to get back at daddy, well, aren't they all? And look at him now, what a man he's become, the man he was always meant to be, and what was she? His walk on the wild side? Too young for me then, too old for me now.

She straightens up with the tray and forces herself not to limp, snarling internally at her leg, at the left side of her which is slowly, inexorably letting her down. She fixes her gaze on Red and holds her head up. She's going to speak with him, she knows it. She's going to sit with him, because she wants to know what he knows, what he's here for.

'That's mighty nice of you,' he says as she puts down the tray. She looks at the cake on its side, a pathetic offering. Whatever is she thinking, that he won't have her son arrested for desertion because she brought him cake? She fumbles the pack when she gets out her cigarettes, and the lighter won't spark the first time and she sits and tries again as he tries not to watch her.

'I have MS,' she says before he asks, when the cigarette's lit and she's drawn deeply on it. 'Right now, it's in remission, or whatever they say.'

'I'm sorry,' he says, putting down the fork he'd picked up.

'Nothing you got to be sorry about,' she says.

Red looks at his cake. It's a mistake, the uniform. It feels wrong on him, as if he were a snake that's crawled back into a cast-off skin.

'How did it happen?' Martha says, and he feels panic itch at the base of his spine until she says, 'That he was under your command?' and he realizes that she's not asking about how he died, their son. Her son.

'Ain't nothing I had a hand in,' he says, touching the handle of the coffee cup. 'We go where we're sent for the most part. I weren't sure at first, not until I saw your name.'

'An', what did you think of him, your son?' she asks. 'Once you got to know him.' Red turns his fork against the plate, pressing it into the cake as if he might hurt it.

'He was an excellent man,' he says. Martha kisses her teeth at him and gets up, her chair juddering against the floor. 'What do you want me to say, Martha? I know I ain't been nothin' to him, I couldn't be, you know that!'

'An' I never wanted you to be nothin' to him,' she says. 'He has a father, a father who loves him and was there for him, he never needed you. Hell, he never needed anything but me, but me an'–'

'Jesus, I'm so sorry,' Red says. He doesn't cry, he never cries, but a sound breaks from him, a sob. 'I was tryin', I swear, I never meant for this to happen, what happened.' He pulls at his collar to loosen it.

'Why didn't you come tell me that before?' Martha says, without an inch she's willing to give. 'Been over a year or more. You been busy?'

'I was too scared,' he says, telling her the truth before he's had time to think of a lie. 'I was too fuckin' ashamed.'

'Of what?' she demands.

Red stands up and his coffee goes over, spills onto the plate, and the cup rolls on its side, and falls to shatter on the floor.

 BROKEN PONIES

'Of what happened, Martha, of what ... of what I am, what I've done since ... please!' And he can't speak, and Martha doesn't move even when his hands flinch toward her. They hear the whirr of the air conditioning and the mutter of the refrigerator as it shudders and then falls silent. Red clears his throat.

'Forgive me, Martha,' he says. His feet crunch against the shards of the coffee cup as he returns to his chair. 'I can pretend as everything was just what I was asked to do, but that'd be a lie. I did what I was asked because ... because I was asked, an' there didn't seem to be no reason not to. After ...' and he waved his hand.

Martha raises her chin. 'So what changed your mind? Something has, Rooster Levine. Seein' as you here, after all this time.'

Red smirked despite everything, then reached up to scratch the back of his neck.

'Someone took the time to show me what I'd become.' He sits down, elbows on his knees, hands hanging limp. 'I thought if ... if he could–' he frowns. 'If he did good, then I might have been able to recommend him ... send him home early.'

'He asked to come home,' Martha says. She folds her arms across her chest to keep the tremble from building in her left hand. 'He wrote me from Germany, said they'd turned him down, said he had to go back.' She can feel him on the road outside, Johnny, as if he were something on fire. She wants Red to go now, go before he finds out, and yet she can't bear it, the pain in him.

'I watched him die, Martha, and there was nothing I could do–' and he is crying, he really is, tears running over the bones of his face. 'I could do nothing for your son, for our son – I killed for him, I killed for him, Martha, and–'

'Stop it,' Martha says, hand to the side of her head. 'Stop it, please. There's...something I gotta tell you.'

Sophie Jonas Hill lives next to the sea in Kent with her family.

She is an antenatal teacher, a steampunk adventuress and a writer.

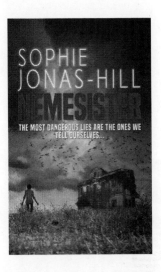

Have you read the first book in the Crooked Little Sisters series?

A page-turning thriller of deception and obsession!

A mysterious woman stumbles into a deserted shack with no memory but a gun in her hand. There she meets an apparent stranger, Red, and the two find themselves isolated and under attack from unseen assailants.

Barricaded inside for a sweltering night, cabin fever sets in and brings her flashes of insight which might be memory or vision as the swamp sighs and moans around her.

Exploring in the dark she finds hidden keys that seem to reveal her identity and that of her mysterious host, but which are the more dangerous - the lies he's told her, or the ones she's told herself?

Sophie Jonas-Hill's gripping and highly original debut will thrill fans of John Connolly, Holly Seddon and the Women's Murder Club thrillers.

URBANE

Urbane Publications is dedicated to
developing new author voices, and publishing
fiction and non-fiction that challenges, thrills and
fascinates.

From page-turning novels to innovative
reference books, our goal is to publish what
YOU want to read.

Find out more at
urbanepublications.com